Other Books by AJ Adaire

Friend Series

Awaiting My Assignment - Book 2

Sunset Island

by

AJ Adaire

Desert Palm Press

Sunset Island
Friends Series Book 1

Copyright © 2013 by AJ Adaire

ISBN-13 978-1494426071
ISBN-10 1494426072

This is a work of fiction - names, characters, places, and incidents are the product of the author's imagination or are used fictitiously. Any resemblance to actual person living or dead, business, events or locales is entirely coincidental. All rights reserved.

No part of this publication may be reproduced, distributed, or transmitted in any form or by any means, including photocopying, recording, or other electronic or mechanical methods, without the prior written permission of the publisher, except in the case of brief quotations embodied in critical reviews and certain other noncommercial uses permitted by copyright law.
 For permission requests, write to the publisher, addressed "Attention: Permissions Coordinator," at the address below.

Desert Palm Press
1961 Main Street, Suite 220
Watsonville, California 95076
www.desertpalmpress.com

Editor: Sue Hilliker
Editor: R. Lee Fitzsimmons
Cover Design: © Erin Lark: http://www.erinlark.com
Photo by: ©John Mansfield | Dreamstime.com

Printed in the United States of America
First Edition - September 2013

Dedication

    One would think that, because this is my first book, there wouldn't be too much for me to say. Quite to the contrary...I have a multitude of people to thank. First on the list is my partner, ICL, who has put up with weeks and months of my long silences as I write. When I'm heavy into writing and things are going well, I tend to work for very long hours. If things aren't going well, and I'm struggling with where the story is going, it seems I'm always preoccupied. When I apologize to her for my shortcomings as a companion, she contends that I shouldn't worry because she knows where I am. She credits my writing for 'keeping me off the streets.' I'm not exactly sure what that means, but I'm glad she isn't angry with me.

    Next on my list is Lee. She stuck with me through the five or six rewrites of Sunset Island, reading and then rereading it each time, suggesting, editing, and encouraging me through to the end, and finally taking a chance to publish me, a new and untested author. I've learned a great deal from her foremost being not to overpopulate my sentences with commas and to be judicious in the use of exclamation points! (Please forgive me that one, Lee...I just couldn't resist.)

    Along the way several other people have read my books and encouraged me, including my friend Pat S. who reads, then makes corrections and suggestions. As I finish each book she encourages me to get busy on the next one.

Kris, thanks for reading this one about four times and for all the helpful suggestions you've made over the last year for this book and the other two you worked on.

Martha, who was the first, followed by Andrea, Bee, Lin, and Pat G., all read and encouraged me not to give up. I'd like to extend special appreciation to the friend who read it after each edit (you know who you are), and to Frankie who read it twice. Lastly, thanks to Michelle who got recruited for a final read through at the last possible minute and who gave me positive feedback just when I needed it most. Thank you everyone.

I especially appreciated the appearance of Sue Hilliker in my life just when I'd exhausted everyone else. You supplied a fresh pair of eyes for corrections and some very supportive comments. Becoming a friend was an added bonus.

Lastly, thank you to my readers who have taken a chance by purchasing this book from a new author. I hope I won't disappoint you. If you like the book, please use the contact information at the end to drop me a note and tell me so. If you didn't like it, write to me anyway and I'll try to do better next time.

Sunset Island

Table of Contents

Chapter 1:   Look At Those Eyes 9
Chapter 2:   I Hear Michelangelo Is No Longer Available 17
Chapter 3:   Really, It's Me, Not You 29
Chapter 4:   Let's Pay Her A Toast 35
Chapter 5:   It Is The Right Thing To Do For Both Of Us 43
Chapter 6:   She Tells Me 47
Chapter 7:   Wonder Why She's Not Married 51
Chapter 8:   One Per Customer 61
Chapter 9:   I Wonder If You'd Pose for Me 67
Chapter 10: She Never Left Me Wondering For A Minute? 73
Chapter 11: How Much Of Our Story Do You Want To Hear? 79
Chapter 12: I Don't Want To Feel Like A Kept Woman 83
Chapter 13: I Think I Might Have Changed My Mind 89
Chapter 14: I Have Some Bad News 95
Chapter 15: She's A Keeper, You Know 99
Chapter 16: I've Finally Met Her 103
Chapter 17: I'm So Happy Sometimes It Scares Me 107
Chapter 18: How Many Sets Of Eyes Do You Think I Have? 119

Chapter 19: I Could Be Naked Too	127
Chapter 20: May I Ask You Something?	135
Chapter 21: Wonder If She Really Has That Tattoo?	143
Chapter 22: Where's My Sketch Pad When I Need One?	153
Chapter 23: I'm Watching You And You're Cheating	163
Chapter 24: You Are A Vision In Flannel And Wool, Miss Scarlet	169
Chapter 25: You Could Get Your Toaster Oven After All	175
Chapter 26: Someday She's Going To Learn She Can't Outsmart Me	183
Chapter 27: Those Two Left Feet Of Yours Are Stepping On My Toes	189
Chapter 28: Will You Tell Them I'm a Lesbian?	201
Chapter 29: What Do You Have On Our Agenda For Today?	211
Chapter 30: She's Trying To Make Ren Make The First Move	217
Chapter 31: For Now, Forever, And For Always	225
Chapter 32: Will This Do?	233
Chapter 33: I Took It Down--It's Time	239
Chapter 34: Come Here You Two And Give Us A Big Hug	243
Chapter 35: If It Bothers You, We Don't Have To Make Love Tonight	253
Chapter 36: I Still Think The Last Words Should Be...	257
About AJ Adaire	259
Awaiting My Assignment	261
Chapter 1	261
Chapter 2	269
Chapter 3	285

Sunset Island

Sunset Island

Chapter 1: Look At Those Eyes

September 2005

Ren Madison watched out of the office window of the marina she owned with her brother, Jack, as the door of the out-of-state car opened and a pair of feet clad in comfortable shoes hit the gravel of the parking lot. A grin slowly curled her lips as the rest of Dr. Lindy Caprini emerged from the sports car. The woman stood and stretched before she slowly pivoted to take in the scenery, finally stopping to enjoy the gorgeous view of the ocean.

The picture on the university's website certainly didn't do her justice. Look at those eyes. I'd love to paint her. Collaborating with the lovely Lindy to illustrate her book should prove to be extremely pleasant working conditions, indeed. Ren made a mental note to call her sister-in-law, Marie, to thank her again for referring her to the alluring Professor Caprini.

Lindy pushed her sunglasses to the top of her head and tilted her face upwards, eyes closed, soaking in the warmth of the sun. As if she felt Ren's eyes on her, she turned to glance at the window of the marina office where the dark haired woman sat watching. She smiled and tossed a jaunty wave before turning away to retrieve her coat from the back seat of the car.

Sad that her ability to ogle unobserved was no longer possible she closed up the file she was working on. Ren stood, quickly strode to the door, and went outside to welcome her visitor. She called over her shoulder as she locked the office door, "Lindy? I'm Ren. How was the trip up?"

"It was fun—long, though." As Ren neared the car, Lindy opened her arms, offering a welcoming hug. "I hope you feel we know each other well enough to hug hello."

Ren stepped into the quick embrace Lindy offered. She was pleased to find the woman as warm in person as she had been on the phone and through their written communication over the past months. Glancing at her watch, Ren said, "You must have either made good time, or you woke up the rooster when you left this morning."

"Probably a combination of both. I was eager to get on my way, so I left first thing." She made a melodic sound somewhere between a giggle and a laugh. "You can probably count on me falling face first into my cup of tea if I have to stay up much past nine tonight."

"You can make it an early night if you like. Are you starving? We can eat here if you like or, if you feel you can wait, we can get your stuff loaded into the boat, and make it back to the Inn before it gets dark."

"Let's do that, the latter I mean." She flashed a quick smile. "Wouldn't that be easier?"

"Yes, a bit. However, we can do either, honest."

"No. I'm eager to settle in. I did stop for a break this morning around eleven, so it's not like I haven't eaten for weeks. Fair warning however, when dinner arrives I'm going to eat like a truck driver."

There was that infectious laugh again. Ren liked hearing the sound of the woman's laughter. "Okay, let's get what you have packed in your car down to the boat. We'll eat when we get back to the Inn."

Using her cell phone, Ren made a quick call to Maggie, her housekeeper, to be sure that dinner was underway so that they could eat shortly after they arrived at the Inn. Ren expected that it would take them several trips to move the contents of

Lindy's car to her boat, and another twenty minutes or so to make the trip to Sunset Island and the Inn she and her brother Jack also owned. It was a surprise when she snapped the phone closed and looked up to find Lindy waiting for her with just her computer and one suitcase. "We can move your car closer to the dock. It'll be easier to get the rest of your things," said Ren.

"Nope, this is all of it. I sent you everything I thought I'd need. I stored all my suits, heels, fancy dresses, and any jewelry worth more than fifty dollars. I did keep out one black cocktail dress and a few things to go with it, just in case it's necessary for me to go somewhere I can't wear jeans, shorts, tees, sweatshirts, and fleece. Hope that's okay, because I'm on a much needed vacation from all that."

"Works for me," laughed Ren. "I think we're going to get along well together, at the least, we'll have the same wardrobes. If you're stuck, we're about the same size so, in a pinch, I can lend you something."

"Do you want me to move my car somewhere out of the way?"

"Yes," Ren said, gesturing to an empty spot next to her own vehicle. "Park down there next to the red SUV. I'll meet you at that red power boat over there."

Because it was a cool and windy day, Ren chose the boat with the enclosed cabin. The cabin wouldn't warm up until they were more than half way to the Inn. At least they'd be out of the September wind because even when the sun was warm, the breeze over the water could be chilling. Once the bags were stored and Lindy was onboard, Ren cast off and they began their first trip together to the island.

"It's certainly lovely here. Marie described everything, although I think she understated the charm." As they neared the island and the Inn came into view, Lindy uttered the almost imperceptible exclamation, "My God, it's absolutely beautiful!" Turning to Ren, she asked, "Is that where we'll be living?"

"Yes, think you'll like it?"

"Why wouldn't I? What's not to like?"

Ren returned Lindy's warm smile. "It is a great place with a long list of positives to recommend it." Ren slowed the boat as she neared the island so she could maneuver into the inlet. "If you need the things the city offers on a regular basis, like the shows, museums, and other cultural events, it'll be a long year for you."

"Do you miss all that?"

"Not really. Although I went to college in the city, I left there years ago and I'm not often drawn back. With my schedule, I'm free to travel there, off-season, when I need a culture fix. Anyway, I've always enjoyed the solitude this place offers, even as a kid." Ren looked at Lindy to gauge her response. "Think you'll miss the city?"

"I can't imagine that I'll have a problem. I'll keep you posted if I start to go stir crazy," replied Lindy, again flashing a quick smile. "My best friend describes me as having no life outside of my work. I tend to focus on my books, writing, and a few close friendships. So, I think this environment will suit my personality.

Ren slipped the boat smoothly into the dock at the base of the stairway leading to the Inn, cutting the engine before she grabbed a line to tie up to the piling. Without having to be asked, Lindy tossed the forward line to Ren to secure the boat to the dock.

"Thanks. Want to hand me the bags?"

Ren carried the suitcase and Lindy shouldered her laptop as they climbed up the stone steps to the entryway of the massive Inn sitting at the highest point on the island. "We're here, Maggie," Ren called as she turned to go straight down the expansive central corridor to the core of the living area. She turned down one of the side hallways and led Lindy to the first door on the left. Opening the door to what would be Lindy's bedroom for the duration of her stay she said, "This is your new home away from home until we finish the book." She smiled at Lindy. "Hope you'll be comfortable here."

Lindy glanced around the nicely appointed room furnished with a beautiful antique dresser, night table, and a queen-sized bed festooned with decorative pillows that matched the blue shades in the wallpaper. "Ren, this is fabulous. Blue is my favorite color, too. I couldn't be more pleased."

After dropping the bag she carried, Ren led Lindy through the doorway into the adjoining room. "This is your private bath and through here," she said as she swung open the door on the opposite wall, "is your sitting room slash office." Ren stepped aside to allow Lindy to enter.

Lindy glanced around, her broad smile and sparkling eyes indicating her pleasure with the accommodations.

Ren gestured at the neatly stacked boxes lining the one wall. "Obviously, I resisted all urges to unpack for you. I figured everyone should keep her stuff organized the way she wants it. There doesn't seem to be that much here. All the boxes were light...thanks for that." Ren flashed a quick grin. "If you need it, I can help you tomorrow."

"Sounds good. Thanks for everything. The pile looks imposing, but you're right, there's really not that much. I'm sure I'll manage." She smiled. "I just packed everything really, really well. I must have used fifty bags of those foam peanuts."

"I'm going to go check on the progress of our dinner. You can freshen up if you want. Then we can eat before I give you the tour if you feel up to it."

"Where do I meet you?"

"Just go out the door, and turn right. Keep going and you'll eventually come to the dining room."

Ten minutes later, Lindy showed up for dinner and Ren introduced her to Maggie. "It's a definite pleasure to meet you. Ren has been working hard on the illustrations for you. It's made her happier."

Lindy's raised eyebrows conveyed her puzzlement at Maggie's statement regarding Ren's happiness. In response, she settled for a noncommittal, "It's a pleasure to be here. I've been enjoying the work we've been doing together long distance and look forward to being able to do more now that I'm here. I'm glad that Ren and I will finally be working in the same place—no more mailing, e-mailing, and waiting."

The three women ate dinner, a simple meal of broiled chicken with roasted vegetables and a huge salad. When Lindy commented about how good the food was, Maggie accepted the compliment. "Can you cook?"

"I love to cook. Because I live alone I don't do it very often. Cooking for one is no fun. If I make a roast I have to eat it for a week. So I guess the answer is I can, but don't usually. Why?"

Ren interjected, "Maggie takes pity on me during the off season, when the Inn is closed. Left to my own devices, she thinks I'd starve to death. I think she worries about my limited diet of the few things I'm capable of making for myself."

"What are they?"

"Actually, I'm not a bad cook. I learned from one of the best." Ren glanced away for a minute and blinked several times, sadness clouding her eyes. "Like you, I don't. Besides soups, salads, hotdogs, and steak, peanut butter and jelly sandwiches are my staples. They are all quick and easy to make and there aren't usually any leftovers to deal with."

"Yes," Maggie agreed. "I cook for her because if I didn't, there wouldn't be a single vegetable pass through those lips of hers."

Ren laughed. "Guilty as charged."

"You won't have to worry, Maggie, I promise to ply her with vegetables."

They all laughed when Maggie looked towards the heavens, and folded her hands as if in prayer. "My prayers have been answered."

When dinner was over, Maggie took the dishes back to the kitchen to clean up while Ren gave Lindy the promised tour of the house.

"This place is huge," Lindy commented. "I may need to drop breadcrumbs for the first few days until I get the layout down pat. I'm sure the views are spectacular in the daytime. I can't wait to see the rest of the island, too."

"It's too dark to see the cabins tonight. Tomorrow should be nice so you can tour them in the morning." Ren told Lindy about the cabins generally rented to families with children after showing her the rooms in the other wing that were available for rent in season. She returned to the main living area to show her the library, porch, and sitting areas, ending the tour back at Lindy's bedroom door. Pointing down the hallway she said, "My studio is next to your sitting room, and my bedroom is next to that should you need anything during the night."

"I think once my head hits the pillow, that'll be it for me tonight."

"Okay, in that case, I'll wish you a good night. Don't forget, if you'd like some help unpacking tomorrow, I'd be glad to assist. When we don't have guests, Maggie and I usually fend for ourselves for breakfast and lunch. Off-season, we generally eat dinner together a few nights a week. You know, the vegetable thing." She was pleased when Lindy grinned. "I think she'll be glad you're here though, because it will free her up to spend more time with Bob, her fiancé. They're planning their wedding...the big day is in February. After that they're taking a couple of weeks off for their honeymoon. She doesn't know it yet, but my wedding present to them is two additional weeks in Tahiti. So we'll be on our own for over a month." Ren grinned. "I think she was relieved to hear you're capable of cooking because she's convinced herself that, left to my own devices, I'd starve to death if she wasn't here." Ren shrugged. "Sadly, there's probably some small degree of truth to her fears."

Lindy looked Ren up and down and smiled. "You don't seem to look like you've suffered any ill effects from your lack of vegetables. Besides, I know exactly what it's like to have to eat alone. I'm glad we'll be sharing meals together."

"Well I'd better let you get to bed. Goodnight."

Lindy put her hand on Ren's arm to stall her departure. "Oh, one more thing. About tomorrow...the first item on my agenda is to set up my office and unpack. Once that's done, I'll take a survey to see if I need anything that I've forgotten. After that, I have a little more to do on the analysis of the first series of fairy tales. I've been working on them at home and I only have a bit more to write before I pass them off to you so you can get started whenever you're ready. Snow White is our next series. With the work I need to do, I'd say I'd probably be out of your hair for about two days before I'll be ready to meet to discuss the next group of stories. Will that be acceptable to you?"

"Yes, absolutely. I'm still working on one of the other sketches from the information you sent me before, plus I have a couple of other jobs I'm finishing up. I'm sure that we'll get into a routine as we work together."

"No doubt. Will I disturb you if I use the computer late at night or early in the morning? I could type in my bedroom if it will."

"No, my studio is between your office and my bedroom. I'm sure you won't bother me." As Ren turned to go towards the library, she paused. "Lindy, this is your home now, so make yourself comfortable. There's brandy and wine in the library if you'd like a nightcap before you turn in. Please feel free to help yourself if I'm not around. I think I'll head down and have a sherry now. Sure you won't join me?"

Lindy shook her head. "Thanks anyway. After that long drive, I won't need that tonight. I'll see you in the morning." Lindy smiled and gave a little wave.

Ren tossed back a quick wave in response before heading down the hallway toward the library. She recognized that she was enjoying her time with Lindy and felt a bit disappointed that she would not be joining her for a drink. However, she fully appreciated that Lindy was tired after her long drive.

As Ren sat in the library sipping her grandfather's favorite sherry, her thoughts turned to the many evenings she, her grandfather, and her lover had sat together in the beautiful room. She wished that he and Brooke were there with her now. She had no problem admitting that she was lonely. During the season, having guests meant that there were people around. Regardless, it was completely possible for her to be lonely even with a group of people in the house. She was looking forward to having Lindy around for the long, dark winter months. From what she had seen since Lindy arrived, she was sure that the friendship they began on the phone and through e-mails, several months before, would deepen with time spent together. At least she sure hoped so. She allowed her mind to wander back to the spring when she'd had her first contact with the lovely Dr. Lindy Caprini.

Chapter 2: I Hear Michelangelo Is No Longer Available

March 2005

Ren Madison was lonely. Her phone calls several times a week with her old friend Mallory helped assuage her loneliness to the point that she was able to function, as did seeing her friends Joey and Ben, and Peg and Penny. Still, it had been a difficult few years and a long winter season at the Inn while it was closed. With some free time on her hands, it was still two months until the Inn reopened in late May. She decided to reorganize her workspace, store her excess paintings and photos she wasn't yet ready to part with, and display some of her work on the longest wall of her studio. She sorted through the plethora of pictures and paintings currently stacked in the corners of the studio and chose a selection of those she wanted to hang. She laid the body of her work on the floor so she could organize the different sized works into a display pleasing to her eye. Once she knew how she wanted them displayed, she got out the ladder and began to hang the frames on the wall. When finished, she stepped back to admire the display of her work from the earliest to her most current efforts.

For the centerpiece of the display she chose the nude she'd painted years ago, her largest painting. Brooke, her now deceased partner, stared back at her from the canvas. The piece had always held special significance for her and looking at the painting still evoked mixed feelings. When her lover was alive, it served to remind her of how much Brooke loved and wanted her. Now, especially when she was depressed, it sometimes reminded her of all that she'd lost. *As if I need an additional reminder*, she chided herself. After serious consideration, she concluded that the painting provided her with memories and feelings, most of them pleasant. In her heart, she knew that particular painting was her best work--a true labor of love. Regardless, she couldn't bring herself to part with it, so it went up on the wall with the rest of the artwork she was placing on display.

Mixed in with a large number of sketches she'd made of Brooke when they'd first met, were several pictures of her grandfather and grandmother who had raised her and her older brother Jack. Ren was only two when her parents died, leaving her and Jack orphans. As she shuffled through the pile her mind drifted back to her first date with Brooke. She recalled how nervous she was to meet the tall, willowy blonde for their first date, nearly twenty years ago, during the second semester of her freshman year in college. It was not only her first date with Brooke—it was also her first date with a woman. She smiled as she remembered how her heart pounded and her palms perspired while she waited in front of the restaurant where they'd agreed to meet. When the bus stopped and Brooke stepped off, she had greeted Ren with a quick kiss on the lips and a warm hug.

She shook her head and chuckled as she thought about how they had struggled to find a place to be alone during the first few months they'd dated. Brooke had multiple roommates, and Ren had a dorm mate they had dubbed 'the mole' since she never left the room except sporadically for a class. All seemed to conspire to keep the young couple from sharing any intimate time together. As a last resort, they had turned to meeting in the campus library for a quick kiss behind the shelves in a remote area of the stacks of dusty research tomes.

Ren shook herself from her reverie and forced herself to focus on her project. She selected several more paintings and put those aside to store. Those she was ready to part with she would wrap and send to her art dealer in New York. Some of the darker paintings of storms over the ocean that she completed after Brooke's death, along with many photos of the island, the ocean, local landmarks, and other sites of interest she had taken over the past few years, she would take to the local gallery. The ocean scenes sold better to the tourists who visited the local area than they did in the city. *Makes sense*, she thought.

Ren felt better now that her work area was more functionally organized and presented a much more welcoming environment. It was almost too coincidental when her sister-in-law, Marie, called the day after Ren finished cleaning and organizing her studio. Ren answered the phone when it rang. "Hello Marie. Welcome back. How was your week in the city?"

"Great. I really enjoyed it. Despite the fact that I missed Jack and Laura, of course, I have to admit that I had a nice time and learned a lot. Hey Ren, I gave out your phone number to a friend of mine," Marie said without further preamble. "Dr. Lindy Caprini is a woman I've known since college--one of my sorority sisters. I just spent the week with her at that conference I attended. We talked a lot about a big project she's been working on. She received a grant to write a book about fairy tales from around the world. Lindy told me that she needs an illustrator to work closely with her so, of course, I immediately thought of my favorite artist."

Ren, who loved to tease her sister-in-law, asked, "Really? And who would that be?"

"Well, I hear Michelangelo is no longer available--so I suggested you."

Ren could picture her sister-in-law's raised eyebrow just from the tone of her voice. Laughing together gave an additional boost to Ren's already positive mood. "Okay, I'll be happy to talk with her if she calls. Thank you."

"I think her project is right up your alley. Lindy has been teaching at the college level for quite a few years now and, in September, she's taking off a year to do some writing. Apparently the college encourages their professors to publish. From what she told me, she'd prefer to write her own fairy tales even though she's obligated to, as she put it, do something 'more scholarly.' So she's doing research now and plans to produce a textbook of some sort. Really, it'd be better if she tells you about it. She's a lovely woman. She speaks a gazillion languages and I think you'll enjoy her sense of humor. She's really fun."

"She sounds fascinating. It's impressive that she speaks all those languages. She'd be a great person to have as a travel companion." Changing the subject, Ren asked, "How's my older brother and my favorite niece?"

"What do you mean older brother, you nut?" Marie laughed. "Jack, your *only* brother, and Laura, your *only* niece, are both fine. Think you can join us for dinner later this week?"

"Sounds good. I'll give you a call when I figure out when I'll be on the mainland."

After a few more minutes of light banter, they completed their call and Ren returned to her work. Less than an hour after she concluded the conversation with her sister-in-law, Lindy Caprini called to speak to Ren about her project.

Following brief introductions and shared pleasantries, Lindy explained the reason for her call. "Marie suggested that I contact you. She seems to think you're quite talented."

"Well, she might be a bit prejudiced."

"I don't know, I've known Marie a long time. I think she's an honest person. How about I describe the project to you and then we can discuss if it's something you might be interested in doing. Is this a convenient time?"

Ren glanced around her work area disappointed that Lindy couldn't see the condition of her workspace, knowing it probably would never be this neat again. "Absolutely. I'm eager to hear about it."

Lindy took a deep breath. "I've been fortunate to land a grant to study something I have an interest in anyway. I've always found it intriguing that the fairy tales my mother and grandmother told me in Spanish are quite different from the fairy tales that kids in the States hear. I became intrigued enough that I began researching fairy tales throughout the world and am now in the process of writing up my findings. I'm planning to take a year off, after I do the summer session here at the college, to write and work with an illustrator on a book comparing fairy tales from around the world."

"You're lucky, at least that sounds like an interesting topic."

"Yes, it is," agreed Lindy. "When I began my research, I was amazed to learn that there are at least six or seven hundred versions of Cinderella alone."

"Really? I'd never have guessed that there are that many."

"It's true. In one of the Italian versions, Cinderella kills her stepmother. If I remember correctly, she ends up marrying a king instead of a prince. I'm not really sure what kind of moral that teaches." She laughed.

Ren noted that Lindy's melodic laugh was very nearly a giggle. She liked the sound. "At least you can read many of them in the original language. Marie tells me you speak a gazillion languages."

"Sadly, that's a slight exaggeration. I only know four and a half. I was lucky to grow up in a multi-lingual household. I speak my father's native language, Italian, and my mother's, which is Spanish. There is English, obviously, and I took French in college with Marie."

Ren's brow furrowed. "Tell me about the half of a language."

Lindy giggled. "Well, my half-language is Latin. I can read it; however, Latin is not really spoken anymore except, on rare occasions, in church––ergo, half a language."

Ren chuckled. "Oh, I see. Now it makes sense."

"Anyway, I can't write while I'm working full time, so I've been doing most of my research after teaching hours. I find it difficult because just when I find something of interest it's time to stop, and I lose momentum. It makes for slow progress. I need time to lock myself away so I can really concentrate uninterrupted by the real world. I find that I'm not all that disciplined at home, so I need to be somewhere other than here where I'm tempted to do anything and everything other than what I should be doing. Without distractions, I can be pretty disciplined. In addition, I need to work closely with the illustrator, probably almost on a daily basis. When I find someone to work with, I'll probably rent a place nearby wherever the artist I hire lives. Although I want the drawings to be a collaboration, I do have some specific ideas I want incorporated into the style of the illustrations."

"Marie told me that she'd mentioned you might stay here if we agree to work together."

"Yes. After she raved about your artistic talents, she mentioned that you and Jack have an apartment over your marina's office. The availability of possible accommodations, either with or near you, was one of the supporting reasons I decided to give you a call."

"Tell me a little more about the project."

"I'm happy to see I haven't bored you to death yet. I love to talk about it, so stop me if I go on too much." Lindy inhaled another deep breath. "My intention is to concentrate on fairy tales from the countries whose languages I speak, in addition to the stories from Germany and China. I already have someone working on the German and Chinese translations of the stories I plan to focus on in the book, so as soon as that's finished I'll be prepared with information for the text. What I want to do is to select several of the tales, such as Cinderella, then tell each story by country. Your role would be to provide an original illustration for each country's version that visually conveys the major variants for each of the tales. Following each of the translations, I plan to summarize and compare the differences and similarities of the stories. Marie told me that in addition to your painting and photography work, you've done some illustration work for a local author. Do you think this project is something you'd enjoy doing?"

Lindy's animated and enthusiastic detailing of the project intrigued Ren, her mind already thinking of how she might bring visual life to Lindy's words with her art. "I have to admit that you make it sound like a great adventure so yes, I'd be interested. Besides the mediums Marie mentioned, I also have some experience with generating graphics on the computer. It may be an avenue we can explore for this project, depending on what you have in mind. I'm sure before we go any further, you'll want to see some samples of my work. I have a website that shows some of my drawings and photographs, although none of it will relate directly to what you indicate you want for the book. It won't hurt for you to take a look at the work there anyway just to see the quality of the work I do. Why don't you send me a story you want to illustrate, give me an idea of what you want me to highlight in the drawing, and I'll whip up a couple of sample illustrations. That should at least give you an idea of whether you like my work and if we'll be able to communicate along the same wave length."

"Perfect! I love your willingness to send me samples of your drawing style and being open to collaborate to create exactly what I want in the illustrations." Lindy's smile was evident in her tone. "That sounds great...very good suggestion. The fact that I know Marie and through her I have heard a bit about you and your brother—well, it will be nice to work with someone I feel I almost know rather than with a total stranger."

After they exchanged e-mail addresses Ren asked, "What's your timeline on this project?"

Lindy flipped her calendar to month view. "I'll be able to send you the first story in, hopefully, two weeks."

"That fits perfectly with my schedule. I have off hours even while the Inn is open."

"Now for the hard part. I'm excited about our working together. I'm almost afraid to ask what your fees will be for this project."

"Let's wait to discuss fees until after we're sure you like my work and want me to do the illustrations," suggested Ren.

"What happens if I can't afford you?"

"Trust me. If you like my work I can assure you we can arrange something agreeable. I promise." Ren didn't tell Lindy that she felt interested enough by the proposal that she would almost pay her to do the job. The idea itself intrigued her and she loved the excitement that Lindy demonstrated when she talked about her plans.

True to her word, within the specified time, a copy of the different versions of Cinderella showed up as an attachment in Ren's e-mail. Along with the stories, Lindy sent a separate sheet indicating what she had in mind for the illustrations. Ren was relieved that the instructions were clear and gave her a good idea of what the woman would like to see. At the same time, they also left her a great deal of flexibility to explore her imagination and create a work of art that would please the artist in her. The illustration work she'd done in the past definitely didn't offer her this degree of artistic freedom. She wanted to do this job badly so, although Lindy expected that she would do less, she made three different detailed drawings in three different styles. Ren enclosed a note along with her illustrations that explained her thinking on each sketch. In conclusion, she added that she had a favorite among the three, but she wasn't saying which and requested that Lindy call her when she finished reviewing the submissions. She was so excited to get the illustrations into the mail that she made a special trip to the mainland post office to send them using overnight delivery.

While she waited for the call from Lindy, Ren continued to work on the sketches, playing with texture and light to refine her original illustrations. Seeing Lindy's name on the caller ID when the phone rang elicited a sharp intake of breath from Ren. Her pounding heart, and the fluttering butterflies in her stomach, confirmed that she was nervous.

Lindy didn't waste any time on pleasantries. After a simple, "Hello," she said, "Okay, bottom line, I love the sketches. They are fantastic, amazing, in fact. Now, let's talk about the details."

"Okay, let's," said Ren, excitement evident in her tone.

"I liked all three styles of sketches you sent very much. Personally, I identify with the second sketch you sent the most, so I guess I'd say that was my favorite. However, I was wondering if we should consider using a different style for each country? What do you think?"

"That would be an interesting approach. It's something we could try to see how it works. For me, it would certainly be more interesting. I have the three stories you sent me that I can play around with for now." Ren laughed, "I take it I got the job?"

"Oh, I'm sorry. I was so excited when I got your drawings, that there was no other option in my mind. Yes, will you work with me?"

"I can't wait to get started on the rest of the illustrations."

"Well, we have until September to play around and decide what approach we want to take. I won't be starting my full time work on the book until after I finish up my obligations here. I've collected the majority of my data, however, I'm still working with the Chinese translators on some of the stories. I'll need to finish my analysis and comparisons once I've had the chance to review the text they provide me. Can you hang on a minute till I get my calendar?"

"Sure." Ren could hear papers shuffling as Lindy got her calendar open and could hear her thinking aloud as she calculated when she could have some preliminary material to Ren.

"I think in a month or so I can finish the text for the introduction and complete the analysis for the first fable within a couple of months, say by June. Will that work for you?"

"I start to get busy here at the Inn from early June through Labor Day when we close for the season. Still, even when we have guests, I should have enough time to work during the down times each day and evenings after dinner. I'll definitely be able to pick up the pace in September after the Inn closes, which seems to mesh well with your schedule."

"All we have left to do now is work out how much you'll charge for your illustration services and find me a place to stay."

"If it's all right with you, I'd prefer to charge you a flat fee for my work. I like to be able to tinker with my drawings so that they please me. If I don't charge a flat fee per illustration, I end up feeling rushed because I don't want to spend more of my client's money than I have to."

"That sounds very fair."

"Good. So, we're agreed. I feel very excited about your book and am eager to work with you on it. I think it'll be a fun venture." Ren paused, the artist in her hating this part of the negotiation process. "I'll send you an e-mail with a list of some additional information I'll need from you and once you respond, I'll give you a price. I'll enclose a contract for you, too. It's my standard contract, and although it's reasonably straightforward, I still suggest you have your lawyer review it."

"Yes, I will. Thank you."

"We've begun limiting our months of operation, so from mid-September until May I rattle around here in the house, essentially by myself. Although the apartment at the marina is an option, my preference would be for you to stay here on the island with me. Especially for the winter when there are times that making the commute to the mainland can be difficult. It would just be more convenient for me to have you here while we're working together...I won't have to travel to you or you to me."

"That's a very generous offer."

"I don't view it that way. This is a project that has really excited me, and there's certainly ample space here for both of us. I think it's a perfect solution."

"I can see your logic regarding being easily accessible while I'm working on the book with you," Lindy agreed. "I'll need to be there nearly a year, so I insist you let me pay for my board and that, at the least, when you are in season you charge me as a guest. My grant covers living expenses for me, so I have a budget for it."

"Okay, done. We'll give you the special 'friends and family long term rate.' I'll put rates, contracts, and information about the Inn in writing and e-mail it to you in a day or two. If you agree to everything, let me know and I'll send you notarized copies in the mail."

"Ren, I can't tell you how much I appreciate everything you're doing for me. I've been excited about writing this book since I started talking to my publisher about it. Finally being able to begin seriously planning a strategy and making final arrangements has just stoked my enthusiasm. I'm very optimistic that we'll make a good team."

"Yes, me too. So, tell me more about what you envision for the illustrations." With the business out of the way, the two women talked for another half hour discussing their project and relating how they got interested in their fields.

By the time they hung up, Ren had to stop herself from skipping down the hall. She went into her studio and began another sketch for the Italian version of Cinderella's story. As she reread the tale, the thought crossed her mind—*this is certainly more macabre than the American version.*

As Ren started her sketch, she began to wonder what Lindy would be like. She knew from the sample stories that she was a talented writer. Marie had told her "Lindy is a very sweet and caring person with a good sense of humor, an easy laugh, and an infectious giggle. She's probably about the same height, maybe a little taller than you. She's shorter than my 5'7". She has dark hair like yours, although hers is straight and yours is wavy. You wear yours short, while hers is shoulder length, and she has dark brown eyes instead of your dark blue ones."

Ren enjoyed and looked forward to her phone conversations with Lindy and to listening to her voice with its pleasing, slightly husky, timbre. The thought of Lindy's voice piqued her curiosity. Taking a break from her drawing, she looked Lindy up on the web and found her picture in the staff section on the university's website.

"Good God, she's gorgeous. She could pass for that famous movie star's sister." Her right eyebrow rose of its own accord and she uttered softly, "Next year is certainly looking up."

***

Over the rest of that summer Lindy sent information to Ren who was spending nearly all of her free time working on the sketches. Until the time when they would begin working together at the Inn, they spoke frequently, collaborating on the phone and sending drawings back and forth over the Internet. Together they developed a look and feel for the style of the pictures for each country that satisfied both of them. Lindy was so impressed with the pictures Ren sent that she asked that there be one full-page sized illustration as a lead in to the story, and two or three additional smaller drawings inserted within the text for each tale. Ren was more than happy to agree to do the extra work, especially since she was enjoying the collaboration between them and their chats about the creation of the drawings. By August, Lindy and Ren were eager to get started working seriously on the project every day. As the two women worked to plan the layout, look and feel of the book, they began to appreciate their extremely positive working relationship and quickly deepening friendship. They often called each other just to chat about their days, sometimes not even mentioning the book during their conversations.

In August, becoming more excited by the day, Ren began to make plans for Lindy's arrival. She decided to put Lindy in a suite of rooms next to her studio. The two bedrooms, joined by a private bath between them would make a comfortable and private suite area where Lindy could live and work. Ren had the bed and dressers removed from the larger of the two bedrooms, before setting it up as a sitting room and office for Lindy. Two comfortable chairs, one on each side of the window with a table separating them, would make for a comfortable reading area. Opposite, on the shorter wall next to the door, she placed the desk and a bookshelf. As the neatly labeled boxes that Lindy shipped to her began to arrive, Ren stacked them carefully in the office/sitting room or bedroom, depending on the neatly written list of contents on the side of each box. Although tempted to stack the books on the bookshelf, she restrained her curiosity and refrained from doing so. In town one day running errands, Ren stopped at the office supply store and bought all the necessary supplies for the new office. She even picked up a new, faster router so they would be able to share access to the Internet and printer. Ren hoped Lindy would be pleased with the work area and the living arrangement.

Chapter 3: Really, It's Me, Not You

"Ready to go?" Jim yelled as he bounded up the steps to Lindy's apartment? "I've got the picnic supplies packed in the car. All I need is you. You might want to toss in a sweater. I know it's July, but the air seems a bit damp...hope it doesn't rain. By the time they set off the fireworks tonight, it could get really chilly."

"Thanks. Yes, I'm ready." They were attending the 'Concert and Picnic In The Park' fundraising event the local orchestra presented annually. It was an event that was usually well attended, and the spots on the grass near the bandstand filled up quickly. Local garage-type bands performed first, followed by the small local professional orchestra. The evening concluded with a fireworks display. Lindy looked forward to the event every year. She hurried to grab a jacket and joined Jim for the short ride to the park.

"Look. There's a perfect parking spot near the fence. I can hand everything to you and we won't have to carry it all the way to the gate and back up here. Here's your ticket. Go inside and meet me back here."

Lindy did as instructed. She walked to the gate, produced her ticket, entered the park, and made her way back to where Jim was standing on the other side of the plastic fence strung around the perimeter of the field. He handed the cooler and blanket over the fence to her. "Careful, the wine's in this. I'll just lock up the car. Now where's my ticket?" He patted his pockets. He flashed a grin as he held up his ticket. "Looks like there's a line at the gate now. I'll see you in a couple of minutes."

Lindy nodded, her fondness for him showing on her face. "Okay."

As he darted off, she spread the blanket and began to organize their belongings. So far the rain was holding off even though the threatening sky promised a downpour any minute.

"Hope it doesn't rain until after the fireworks," Jim said as he joined Lindy on the blanket.

By the time they finished their picnic lunch, the concert was ready to begin. The crowd that had chatted and had their meals as the local rock bands played quieted when the orchestra began to play a selection of patriotic music. Everyone was clapping along to some of the marches they played just before the finale of the 1812 Overture, which signaled the beginning of the fireworks display. The colors burst in the sky in time with the music. The rain arrived with the final massive crescendo of fireworks. Rain poured down as the crowd scattered as leaves would if blown by gusting winds. People tugged the orange plastic fence from the support posts and ran for their vehicles as the first bolts of lightening flashed.

Jim and Lindy were soaked by the time they made it into the car. "Wow! What a cloudburst," Jim said as he wiped the rain from his glasses. We're lucky we were parked so close."

Lindy wiped her face with her sleeve. "I know. Look, those people are soaked through. I'm glad we got to see the whole concert before the heavens opened up, though."

"Yes, me too. It was fun."

It was amazing how quickly they made it home. The traffic leaving the park was orderly and they made it back to Lindy's place in just a few minutes.

"Thanks, Jim. I had a wonderful time."

"Shall I come in?"

"Do you mind if I beg off tonight? I'm kind of tired and want to get an early start tomorrow morning with the last of my chores."

"I understand. Can't say I'm not disappointed though."

"I know. I'll see you later in the week, once I have things more organized."

He gave her a gentle kiss before leaving.

Lindy Caprini Journal

July 6th already. Had a nice holiday. It's less than two months until I leave. I've been so busy that I've been even worse than normal in recording life events here. I'm notoriously bad about writing in my journal, but this time I've been especially remiss, even for me, who is not all that diligent about keeping up with my writing under the best of conditions. I've come to a conclusion, and I dread the conversation I need to have with Jim. It's been over a year now that I've been dating him. There isn't a man on the face of the earth better suited to me in so many ways. Jim is intelligent, tall, good looking, well built, affectionate, witty, and a wonderfully entertaining companion. He's my mental equal, adept at arguing his point without anger or sarcasm, and someone who can admit defeat with humor and grace when I best him in a discussion. Perhaps his most admirable trait is that he doesn't gloat when he wins. Overall, Jim is the perfect man, someone I'm happy with in every way except one and the fault there is mine, not his.

I fully accept the blame for the fact that we don't mesh sexually. He really has been very patient with me, and is gentle and considerate as a lover. Even though, in bed, he spends a sufficient amount of time on foreplay before attempting intercourse with me, he just has never been able to bring me to orgasm. It is a point of issue for us. I'm reticent to continue this relationship with him for this reason alone. Both of us feel a failure, and neither of us should have to settle for this. Eventually, I think it will tell on our relationship even though I've told him repeatedly it's not his fault. I've even gone so far as to confess to him that the two previous lovers I was intimate with faced the same challenge with me, with considerably less aplomb. The first gave up after a month of unsuccessful attempts at sexual intimacy. Bill, the second man, was much less gracious, calling me 'a frigid bitch' before he stormed out, slamming the door behind him.

When I told Jim the story he held me and told me, for the first time, that he'd fallen in love with me. He told me it was his desire to please me sexually, as well as in all other aspects of our relationship. So, at his suggestion we agreed to try sex without condoms, using birth control pills instead, to avoid pregnancy. After we both got tested and waited the requisite couple of months, we went away for a weekend.

I was hopeful. I felt optimistic. I knew I loved him. Still, I continued to wonder why I didn't get excited, wet, and breathless like the heroines in the paperback novels did when the rugged men of their dreams kissed them, making their blood boil, their pulse race and fireworks explode. After all, I view Jim as everything any woman could ask for. He should be perfect for me, and he is…except for the racing, boiling, sparks flying and fireworks thing.

He took me away for a romantic weekend in the mountains. After dinner, we took a walk through the garden where he kissed me in the moonlight and told me he loved me. Later, in bed, he was tender and spent an extended amount of time touching and kissing me before he entered me. We were both disappointed that the results were just not earth shattering. I have to admit that, to some extent, the act was better without a condom, and I did eventually have an orgasm. Sadly, the earth barely trembled for me. What's the expression something about not with a bang but a whimper? In my case, it definitely hadn't moved and no fireworks either. He swears we'll be okay and things will improve. Yet, in my heart, I know this is just not going to happen for me. Maybe I am a frigid bitch.

If I'm honest, the sex act itself is a bit distasteful to me, especially now that I have to deal with the aftermath that intercourse without the condom leaves. I hate to disappoint him. I feel I owe him honesty and an opportunity to find someone who would be a better sexual partner for him than I'm able to be. All that remains is for me to tell him, a task I dread.

Seven weeks from now I'll be leaving here for a year to work on my book with Ren Madison. This is probably a convenient way for us to separate without having to run into each other at work, day after day. I dread the conversation with him and having to hurt him. I need to tell him that I don't want him to wait for me. I sincerely want him to find someone who can offer him everything I can't. I feel this decision is fair to both of us. Although I'll miss his friendship, in my mind, our love affair is already over.

Chapter 4: Let's Pay Her A Toast

September 5th – One Week Until Lindy's Arrival in Maine

The Inn closed after Labor Day. Ren had no demands on her time until Lindy's arrival. Free from any daily responsibility, with nothing else pending that couldn't wait, she decided to take a vacation and visit her New York City friends. Carol and Nancy, the couple who were with Brooke the first time Ren met her, were now two of her oldest friends. She and Brooke had remained friends with them, even after moving to Maine to live on the island and care for Ren's grandfather. Although they saw them infrequently they continued to enjoy a strong friendship thanks to e-mail and phone conversations. This would be her first visit with them since Brooke passed away nearly four years ago.

The heaviness of how much she missed Brooke draped over Ren like a heavy coat. She hid her feelings the best she could as she sat having dinner and talking with Carol and Nancy. "I can't believe you two have lived together for nearly eighteen years." Everyone at the table was aware of Brooke's absence, and none of them wanted to be the first to mention it.

"Okay," said Carol as she raised her wine glass. "Enough. We're all sitting here missing Brooke, so let's pay her a toast and acknowledge that she's very much missed and remembered."

Carol's bravery in addressing Brooke's absence broke the tension everyone was feeling, Carol laughed. "Remember when we all met at the dance? You were so nervous. When you went to the restroom, Brooke warned us not to tease you because she already knew she wanted to ask you out. You two were just like magnets. I don't think anything could have kept you apart."

"Yeah." Ren exhaled a short humph. "I remember that my palms were sweating so badly that they were still damp even after I'd wiped them on my jeans."

Now free to speak, conversation came easily, and the three friends had a wonderful time telling stories about the woman who was gone but certainly not forgotten.

Ren stayed with Carol and Nancy for five days. During that time, she went to see Brooke's parents. Although they had spoken on the phone, she hadn't seen them since the funeral, and they expressed how appreciative they were that she'd stopped in to visit.

The trip was cathartic, somehow calming and healing for Ren. She was feeling stronger and if not completely happy, was at least more content. All the good memories she'd shared with her friends coalesced to help push away the sadness she'd been feeling when she arrived for the visit. Ren still longed for Brooke's presence, and was sad to acknowledge that her lover was gone. At least it no longer hurt in the same way now when she thought of her.

While Carol and Nancy were at work, Ren went to a couple of art museums. She enjoyed the opportunity to remember the good times she and her hosts had shared together with Brooke. Now, after spending several days with them, the constant reminders of her life with Brooke were beginning to weigh on her. Although for the most part she'd enjoyed her visit, when the time came for her to go home she was ready to make her escape. She hoped that the next time they got together they would also have made a transition and would be able to view her as a single friend instead of the surviving member of a couple.

"I hope you'll come up to visit me on the island. This has been great. I've really enjoyed my time here in the city and with you two. I have a big job I'm looking forward to when I get back home. If all goes according to plan, I should have that under control after a couple of months. So, open invitation, any time after the holidays but before we open toward the end of May. See when you can get off from work to make the trip up."

"Thanks for the invitation. It would be a nice trip for us. We'll look into it." Nancy said as she gave Ren a goodbye hug.

Carol and Nancy waved goodbye as Ren drove away. She flipped on the radio to her favorite oldies station and smiled when she realized she was humming along to the tune they were playing. She laughed out loud. *What the hell are you guys saying anyway and what does that phrase mean...makes no sense.* Regardless, she was bobbing her head in time to the beat and realized she felt really good. Inspired by her conversations with Carol and Nancy, she allowed her mind to wander back in time. As Ren drove she thought about her life with Brooke recalling the first time they were able to make love after weeks of not having anywhere to be alone.

As a surprise, Ren rented a hotel room so they could be alone for their first time together. Brooke complained all the way to the room that it would cost too much money and it wasn't fair that Ren pay. As they exited the elevator, they continued to bicker as they went down the hallway and opened the door to their room. "It's not that I don't want to be with you, but I'm paying half," Brooke protested. "I'll take some extra shifts at work. No argument. Please."

"No argument tonight. I promise we'll talk about this eventually, okay? I don't want to fight tonight. I came here for something other than fighting with you." Once in the room, Ren locked the door and drew Brooke into an embrace. With each desiring the long-denied skin-to-skin contact, as they kissed, their rapidly shed clothing marked their path across the room. They found themselves breathless, standing at the edge of the bed in just their slacks. Somehow, they'd divested coats, hats, blouses, and bras as they crossed the room, lips locked together in long unfulfilled desire.

Ren, arms still around Brooke, leaned away. "Can we take this a little slower? I want to remember every minute of this.

First, I want to see you then I want to feel your skin next to mine." She turned down the bed. *The kisses were slower, gentler, and no less exciting as they savored the taste of each other's mouths. Slowly, Brooke stepped away from Ren and slipped her slacks and panties down her long legs. Ren stood entranced, as Brooke stepped out of them and stood naked before her. Ren felt the heat emanating from Brooke's body and smelled the now familiar aroma of her perfume mixed with the scent of her arousal.*

Ren duplicated Brooke's actions, shed her remaining clothes, and simply extended her hand. Brooke took it, using it to pull her closer before she slowly and gently lowered Ren to the bed. The wonder of Ren's first sexual experience unfolded under Brooke's gentle caresses. Passionate kisses, tongues, lips, and inquisitive fingers all combined to make the new lovers murmur phrases of love to each other and moan in discovery of passion never previously experienced by either of them.

They couldn't stop touching each other and spent the night wrapped in each other's arms, alternately sleeping and waking to make love yet again. Late the next morning they showered and dressed. Over Brooke's protests, Ren ordered breakfast from room service. Brooke was a bit angry with Ren about the additional expense, although she mellowed as soon as she tasted the stuffed French toast Ren had ordered.

They hung the 'Do Not Disturb" sign on the doorknob and returned to bed to enjoy the physical intimacies and explorations typical of new lovers. "It's never been like this for me," Brooke told Ren.

Later that afternoon they dressed and left the hotel to go for a walk. They enjoyed hamburgers for dinner, purchased from a tiny restaurant nestled unobtrusively amongst the stores. When Brooke insisted on paying for the hamburgers commenting that at least she could afford to pay for them, Ren knew she had her work cut out for her when they finally discussed finances. Aware that Brooke struggled financially, paying for most of her education on her own, Ren was worried what Brooke's reaction to Ren's financial abundance would be. However, she also trusted that Brooke did love her and that together they'd work out the money issues regarding the disparity in their net worth and available funds. She realized that her family's assets allowed her the capability to enjoy more of the finer things in life than Brooke was accustomed to. However, because Ren took comfort in knowing that she wasn't used to living an extravagant lifestyle, she remained confident that they would be okay.

By the time the two women returned to the hotel with their shopping bags in hand, they were laughing together again about the fact that the only change of clothes they had were the new underwear they'd just bought.

"Don't worry about it, Brooke. In total, we've worn the clothes we've had on less than six hours. Besides, when we get back to the room, the clock will stop ticking again, because I plan to get your clothes off of you as quickly as I possibly can."

The two lovers enjoyed another evening talking and planning their future together. Later, cuddled together in bed, Brooke rested her chin on the top of Ren's head. "This has been wonderful." She kissed Ren's forehead. "I know that, initially, I was angry about spending so much money. After this weekend together, I've changed my mind. This will be something we'll always remember. It's really been special. Thank you for not allowing me to be too sensible."

"Yes, I agree. It's been amazing for me, too."

"So tell me, how often do you think we can afford to get a hotel room...maybe a less expensive hotel next time. I'm sure we can pinch a few pennies if it means we can be together like this again. Now that we've made love like this, we're not going to be content if we can't be together physically."

Ren's response was a smile and a kiss. "Maybe we should get an apartment together? Both of us are already paying rent. If we're not too extravagant with our choice of living arrangements, you can continue to pay what you're paying where you're living now, and I'm reasonably sure I'll be able to arrange to pay for the rest. After being with you here, whatever the amount, it would cost less than our renting a hotel room so we can be together every chance we get."

"Living with you would be a wondrous thing. Do you think it would even be possible? I don't know if I'll be able to afford my half of the rent. We'd have to find a cheap place somewhere."

"Let me talk with my brother. He knows I don't like living in the dorm. It's almost impossible to paint in my dorm room, and it is a real pain to have to put all the supplies away when I'm finished working on a painting. Maybe I can convince him to help me out with a little extra money in my monthly allowance so we can find a cheap place together. I'll call him later."

"Much later, I hope," Brooke replied, pulling Ren to her.

That evening, while Brooke was in the shower, Ren rolled over and reached for the telephone to lay the groundwork for getting her brother to agree to give her enough money to rent an apartment with her lover. She dialed the number and waited for Jack to answer.

"Hey sis, I wondered when you'd call. You missed our usual time."

"Yeah, I was busy this morning." She choked back a nervous giggle. "I'm here now. How are you and how is Grandpop?"

Jack brought her up to date with all the news from home. She told him almost all of her news about the past week. She had a close relationship with her brother and knew she could share anything with him. She'd even confessed her crush on her best friend to him when she was in high school. Pretending she was finished the conversation, she closed with her standard goodbye. "So have you met her yet?" It was a private joke between them that they were both still unattached because neither of them had met the right girl yet.

Ren could picture her brother smiling at her on the other end of the phone.

"No, have you?"

"Yes, I think I have. Her name is Brooke. I love her, Jack," she said simply.

There was a long pause. "When do I get to meet her?"

"How about I bring her home for a long weekend in a couple of weeks. I want to talk to you about something anyway."

"You're not quitting school are you?"

Ren laughed. "I'm fine, really, and no, I have no intention of quitting school. I need to talk about my living arrangements. I want to get an apartment next year instead of staying in the dorm."

"With Brooke?"

"Yep."

"Isn't it a little sudden?"

"Maybe, but not if you consider that 'she's the one.' Straight up, Jack, I love her."

"I understand. Let me think about it. And, Ren," Jack cautioned, "don't hound me. No decision until after I meet her."

"You don't trust my judgment?" She was happy that he couldn't see her expression.

"You know I do. It's just that I trust mine more."

Despite herself, she joined her brother in laughter. "Okay. I understand. How long are you going to make me wait?"

"I'll tell you before your visit home is over."

The siblings dropped the subject of money and discussed the upcoming visit before they hung up. When Brooke joined her lover in bed after her shower, they talked logistics regarding their visit to Ren's home.

"I talked with my brother about an apartment while you were in the shower."

Brooke waited for Ren to continue and when she didn't, she prodded. "And?"

"He said we would talk when I come home."

"Is that good news or bad?"

"I can't see him denying me, so I would say they're good. He may attach some strings. He knows that I rarely, if ever, ask him for extra money for anything. He gives me a budget and I live within it. I don't think he'll outright say no. He'll probably wait until after he meets you to give me the green light."

"Now I'll have to be nervous when I meet him."

"Nah, don't worry about it. He'll love you as much as I do."

Brooke slid into bed. They talked, laughed, and made love until time required them to return to the real world. When they left on Monday morning, they shared their final kiss goodbye.

Ren breathed in Brook's scent, imprinting it on her memory. "I can't wait for our trip so we can be alone again,"

"Me too." Brooke pulled Ren to her and whispered for probably the twentieth time that weekend, "I love you."

"Ditto," Ren replied, lightening the mood, making them both laugh.

Ren shook her head. Although today's memories had been happy ones, she didn't want to think any more about the past because she didn't want to risk experiencing again any of the feelings she'd struggled with after Brooke's death. It was too painful to think of all they'd had that was now gone. Earlier it felt okay to do that, maybe because she just spent the week with Carol and Nancy and the memory of Brooke, witnessing their loss. Or maybe it was because she'd visited Brooke's family and shared more of her grief with them. Whatever the reason, she felt like she'd crossed some invisible boundary she'd not previously been able to pass through since Brooke's death. She still felt an enormous sadness about her loss, except now there was a perceptible difference in her feelings somehow.

When Ren negotiated the last turn off the main highway that would lead her home, she shifted her focus from the past to navigating the last few miles of her trip home. The week away had been nice, and she felt like she had reached a degree of closure on that chapter of her life. Inhaling the familiar scents of the sea and the forest she felt strangely renewed. She was looking forward to the arrival of her new client, the prospect of being busy on a new project and, being honest with herself, relieved that she'd have company for the lonely winter months.

Chapter 5: It Is The Right Thing To Do For Both Of Us

LINDY CAPRINI JOURNAL

With summer session finally over, I finished up in my office for what will be the last time for a year. As I tossed my briefcase on the desk before I sagged into the chair and slipped off my heels, it was hard for me to believe that the time for me to leave for Maine has nearly arrived. My leave of absence is set to begin on the day after Labor Day. I made quick work of the two final papers I had to evaluate, recorded the final grades for the summer session, emptied my office, and turned in my key cards to the office and the building's main entrance. I quickly completed the remaining chores and was ready to head for home within a little over two hours after arriving at my office. Yes! This girl's still got it. The building was essentially empty by the time I headed for the parking lot. Even though I'd been anticipating this time for months, somehow it was hard to assimilate that I won't be returning here to teach the fall semester.

I've spent the remaining couple of weeks of August packing up my apartment and storing my files and boxes as well as many of my personal belongings in the tiny storage *unit I've rented. When I first started on the list of chores to accomplish before I leave for Sunset Island, it felt like there were a million things to do and fewer than a million days to accomplish them all. However, being a very organized person helps, and before long everything was well in hand. This afternoon I filled out my change of address notice at the post office, cancelled my phone, stuffed the last of the boxes I won't need into the storage unit, and completed the rest of the items on my list of things to do. My thoughts are churning as I ponder the risks and rewards of leaving the university for a year. I succeeded in negotiating a leave of absence without pay when the college denied my request for a sabbatical.*

It's been my desire all my adult life to write a children's book that might inspire another generation to love books and literature as much as I did as a kid, and continue to do as an adult. Because the university encourages their professors to publish texts of a more scholarly nature, I've reluctantly put aside my first love, 'Flint's Folly,' the children's story I've been working on. I have begun to focus on the book about fairy tales from around the world that I'm collaborating on with Ren Madison. Working with her and talking with her on the phone has made putting aside the children's book a bit easier. The grant I landed, combined with the money I recently inherited from my aunt, will give me the financial cushion I'll need to survive a full year without my salary. My dream is that I'll be able to finish the fairy tale project and eventually have enough time remaining to work on 'Flint's Folly.' The analytical portion of the fairy tale book is geared to adults. I know it's too analytical for children to read independently. However, I hope that parents might be able to use it as a resource for themselves and read just the stories to their children, which is why I want to have it beautifully illustrated.

I've spent the Labor Day weekend and a few days following it with my folks. It was fun to see them, and I cried when I kissed them goodbye. I'll probably not see them until I finish my work on the book. I'll miss them.

Tomorrow, my last day here before I leave for Maine, I will see Jim and deliver the news I hate to tell him. I don't want to hurt him, but it is a decision that I'm comfortable that I've made, and I am even more convinced it is the right thing to do for both of us.

More to come...

***

Lindy felt the pressure to hurry, because she was running a little late for her date with Jim. As she rushed to finish and neared her apartment, her thoughts turned to Jim and the unpleasant task that faced her.

Terry, her landlady, greeted her as she entered the building. "Jim's in here," she called to Lindy when she started up the stairs. "He apparently arrived early; I found him sitting on the stairs when I got home, so I had him come in."

Lindy retraced her steps and greeted Terry with a warm hug. Terry was not only her landlady...she was also a close friend. She generously agreed to allow Lindy to sublet the apartment for the next year. As a favor she was allowing her to use her attic to store extra boxes filled with some of her more treasured belongings that she didn't want to put into public storage while she was away.

After dinner, Jim and Lindy sat on the sofa. She inhaled a deep breath, exhaling a long sigh as she dreaded the impending conversation. "Jim, I'm leaving tomorrow. I think both of us will admit that although our sexual encounters are very loving, they're not what they should be. We've tried everything. I think that while I'm away, we should...It's just that I think we shouldn't continue our romantic relationship. I'm so sorry, Jim. I hope we'll stay friends."

The conversation was difficult for both of them but in the end, Jim agreed with her. "I'll always love you, Lindy. I completely understand why you feel it's best for us not to pursue this any longer. As much as I hate to admit it, I have to agree with you. It will be less hurtful for both of us to end our affair now, while we're on good terms." Jim gave her a hug and a kiss goodbye before he left, promising that he would write while she was away, something that never would happen.

When Jim was gone, Lindy retrieved a bottle of her best wine and went downstairs to ring Terry's doorbell. Terry welcomed her friend with a hug and quickly asked, "So how'd it go?"

"As well as could be expected, I guess. I care so much for him, I hated to hurt him." Lindy had sought Terry's advice before she made her decision to end her relationship with Jim, so her friend was familiar with the issue. "I know that if we continued our relationship it would be unfair to both of us, especially him. I know it hurt him every time we made love unsuccessfully, and I know that a lot of women fake it. I care too much for him to do that. It wouldn't be fair to either of us."

Terry handed Lindy a glass filled with wine. "Well, come on, let's have a drink and we'll enjoy our last evening together before you leave."

Together, the two women drank two bottles of wine and ended up falling asleep on the oversized sofa together. When Lindy woke up, she realized Terry was propped up against the pillows at the end of the sofa and Lindy was snuggled against her friend using Terry's breast as a pillow while her left hand had somehow tucked itself between Terry's thighs. As she came more fully awake, she felt an unexpected rush clear to her core and she abruptly snatched her hand away and sat up. She negated the unexpected response to the situation as just being surprised to find the two of them in such an intimate position. Somewhat disquieted by the experience, she made a hurried departure explaining that she still had some final packing to do before she left.

The next morning, eager to get on the road, Lindy gave Terry a hurried hug and kiss before she got into her car. She returned Terry's wave as she pulled away. Lindy was able to travel light for the trip. She carried her one suitcase and her computer gear in the car with her. Everything else she'd already sent to Maine. Lindy was so excited she could hardly contain her enthusiasm as she dropped the gearshift lever to 'D' and began her journey to Ren's island.

Chapter 6: She Tells Me

Lindy Caprini Journal

Wow, am I tired after my long drive up to Sunset Island today. I want to record some of my impressions while they're still fresh in my memory. I arrived late this afternoon and met Ren Madison at the marina she owns with her brother. Ren is an amazing woman—funny, personable, rich, and gorgeous. At first blush, one would say she has it all. She has all that and yet she is alone, rattling around in this massive Inn. No doubt it is magnificent, fabulous really. Even so, she's by herself here—except for a skeleton staff, a young couple who help take care of the place during the off-season. It's probably odd to feel sorry for someone who seemingly has so much, yet there's an aura of loneliness that adheres to her like a heavily scented perfume.

As we approached the island, those deep blue eyes of hers watched me as I saw the Inn for the first time. Ren pointed to the ridge along the top of the cliff where the Inn, an imposing structure, sits silhouetted against the blue grey sky. The Inn and the surrounding cottages cling to the top of the island along with several giant evergreen trees that have remained steadfast and impervious to all the elements that Mother Nature has thrown at them during the harsh Maine winters. Pine forests decorated the tops of the cliffs that dropped dramatically to the rugged coastline of the island. When I told Ren it was impressive, she responded that she loves viewing it through the fresh eyes of other people who are seeing it for the first time.

My room is in the wing of the main house that contains the private living quarters for the family. The wing on the opposite side of the house contains a large number of suites available for rent by those not requiring the amount of space provided by the cabins that radiate out around the main building. The central area, between the two wings, provides eating facilities and communal areas. The place is massive. Today, knowing I'm tired, Ren took pity on me and didn't show me the lower level where the gym and laundry facilities are, promising me she'd show me some other time.

In the center of the main part of the house are the common areas for the guests, meeting rooms, and a large library. There is also a lovely wraparound porch, most of which is glass enclosed, for guests to gather when the wind, weather, and mosquitoes are too intense for the faint of heart to sit outside. Each end of the porch has open areas that include rockers where guests can sit and absorb the ocean views, and when the wind comes in just the right direction, inhale the air scented by the sea and the balsam and other evergreen trees which Ren described as nature's perfume.

Ren told me that her grandfather, Maynard, and her grandmother, Sally, took one look at the island and were overcome with the desire to build the Inn on the island. They wanted to raise Jack and Ren here after their parents died. Ren was only two, so she doesn't remember any other home than here. It makes me sad for her to think she lost so much so early in life. I can't imagine...

I asked her if she was lonely growing up here. She denied ever feeling that way because often the guests brought children that she and her brother were able to play with. Plus she and Jack were very close despite their age difference, so they had each other for company. She told me that she and Jack had the benefit of meeting a constant rotation of guests from all over the globe, and because she *was exposed to so many different people, she rarely feels uncomfortable in any social situation. It's wonderful that she has that confidence.*

Ren reveres her grandparents, especially her grandfather, and adores her brother, Jack, and his family, Marie and Laura. Apparently her grandfather was some sort of a genius businessman who made his fortune in shipping before he came here to build this place. He passed on his skills to his grandchildren. Jack owns the marina in partnership with Ren. He bought it after his grandmother died, and Ren runs this place that they inherited after their grandfather died.

I'm looking forward to getting to know Ren better and anxious to start working on our project. Enough for tonight—I'm tuckered out. Yet, at the same time, I feel so excited about this opportunity.

Chapter 7: Wonder Why She's Not Married

The following morning Ren was in the kitchen heating water for tea when Lindy came shuffling out in sweats and her bedroom slippers. "Good morning," she very nearly sang.

Ren smiled. "You really are a morning person, aren't you?"

"Yup. Too cheery?" Lindy smiled despite herself. "Morning and bedtime are the hardest times for people to be compatible, I think."

"No, not too cheery. It's nice to have someone greet the day as a happy event. I'm usually upbeat in the morning, too." In a conspiratorial whisper, she said, "And then there's Maggie." They both laughed enjoying the sense of camaraderie. "Tea or coffee?"

"What are you having?"

"Tea for me this morning and a bagel."

"That's perfect. Point me to where everything is kept."

"Watch and learn, grasshopper," teased Ren. With the bagels toasted and the tea poured, Ren said, "Follow me."

They settled on the porch. The sun streaming in the windows was warm and the two women sat watching the ocean, sipping their tea and eating their bagels as they enjoyed a comfortable silence. "It is very peaceful here," commented Lindy. "And look at the view…it's breathtaking."

After they finished breakfast, Lindy excused herself to go unpack the boxes in her bedroom and office. Ren went to her studio to finish the brochure she'd been working on the past week for the bed and breakfast on Main Street.

Around one o'clock, Ren realized that she was hungry. On her way to the kitchen to grab a sandwich, she passed Lindy's open office door and stuck her head in as she tapped lightly on the jamb.

"Come in, please," Lindy called, welcoming the interruption.

The room already had a lived in look. Books and a few other personal items had found their way onto the bookcase, neatly stacked folders decorated the desktop, and the computer was on with the screensaver flashing pictures every few seconds. As Ren examined the area, she noticed a picture that was on the table between the two chairs. Approaching the picture of a very handsome and happy looking couple Ren asked, "Your parents?"

"Yes."

"They're a very attractive couple. I can see where you get your good looks from."

Lindy blushed, turned, and brushed her collar length hair back. She reached for a rubber band and used it to pull her hair back into a ponytail. "Well, thank you. Since my dad is from Italy and my mom is from Spain, I had virtually no chance in the world to be a blue eyed blonde."

Ren laughed at the unexpected response.

"Our house was always filled with people. Both sets of grandparents lived with us. Dinnertime was like a United Nations meeting with English being the common language. My mom's parents always spoke to each other in Spanish and my father's parents always spoke Italian. Therefore, every conversation we had occurred at least twice. The telling of a story was a little like whispering down the lane."

"Do you have siblings?"

"No." Lindy shook her head. "Tell me about growing up on the island." Lindy met Ren's eyes when she looked up.

"What do you want to know?"

"Is what you told me before true...that you don't remember your parents at all?"

"Yes. I only have memories of them through Jack, my grandparents, and some pictures. The Inn is the only home I can remember. What I know of my parents comes from the photos my grandparents kept in the family album and the stories they and my brother told. I think I've mentioned that Jack was twelve when our parents died, so he had clear and vivid memories of them and would sometimes tell me stories about them. Still, no matter how hard I've tried I can't claim a memory of my own of how it felt to be held by my mother. I know, although I can't recall on my own, the scent of her perfume or that Dad's jacket always smelled like the pipe tobacco he smoked. They are all Jack's memories that he generously shared with me as I grew up. I'm grateful to have that much and, at the same time, I feel sad that they're vicarious memories, not ones of my own."

"I'm sorry." Lindy felt her eyes fill and she blinked back the tears. "That's very sad."

"No, not really. It just is." She smiled. "It's all I've ever known, so it's my normal. I've been lucky to be so loved by my family. I'm used to being an orphan, so it doesn't bother me. I've been very fortunate, really. I've been loved all my life, despite so many people having left me behind before I was ready to say goodbye. So don't feel sorry for me."

"Okay, I'll try. So you and your brother moved to the island to be with your grandparents right after your parents died?"

"Well, when my folks died, my grandfather retired right away and bought the island. He and his partner were already in negotiations to sell the business, so my parents' death expedited his decision. It took him a couple of years to get the Inn finished. While they were building the main building, we lived in one of the cabins until the Inn was ready. I don't really remember, as a kid, living anywhere other than on the island, and later, when Jack returned from college to settle here, in the apartment above the marina office."

"So you've owned the marina a long time?"

"Yes. Grandmother died just as Jack finished college. He returned home to help Grandpop take care of me and bought the marina after her estate was settled. Jack wanted to expand the facility, so when I got access to my trust fund, I bought in as a partner. I keep the books for him. That's about all the involvement I have in the marina. The place was very rundown when he bought it. You should see it now. I'm proud of him and what he's achieved."

"It's nice that you're close to your brother."

"Very. I don't think we've ever exchanged an angry word." Ren smiled before she continued. "And, of course, I love my sister-in-law, and my niece. He couldn't have chosen a better partner. I'll have them over once we've settled in so you can meet their daughter Laura. She's an expert on fairy tales, too."

Lindy made a humorous gesture, placing her pointer finger in her dimple, "Yes, but only in English."

"Okay, you've got me there." Laughing she grabbed Lindy by the hand and pulled her towards the door. "Come on. Time to leave the salt mines so we can eat."

In the huge kitchen, working together to make sandwiches, they discovered that they were both peanut butter and jelly on white bread aficionados, each with differing theories of how to make the sandwich. The teacher in Lindy emerged when she took it upon herself to tell Ren the 'best' way to make the sandwich. "Take it from me," she said, "if you spread a thin layer of peanut butter on each piece of bread and put the jelly in the middle, you won't get jelly bleed through. Truthfully, I like jam better than jelly--more texture."

"Spoken like the voice of experience by someone who probably had to carry her lunch to work." Pointing at her chest with her thumb, Ren replied emphasizing the I. "I, on the other hand, have enjoyed the luxury of walking in here to make my sandwich and consume it within thirty-seconds...never any bleed." Ren took a big bite of her sandwich then licked her lips. "It is one of the biggest perks of being self-employed and working at home."

"I'm sure," replied Lindy who giggled. She took an equally big bite of her own sandwich. She wiped her hands on her napkin and reached over to rub her thumb across the corner of Ren's mouth removing a smear of jelly. Eyes bright she said, "Missed some." Lindy started to brush Ren's cheek with her palm, but pulled back.

They worked together to clean the kitchen. Ren, after she finished washing the plates, leaned casually against the center island, resting her weight on her elbows as she watched Lindy dry the dishes. "I'm thinking about taking a run over to town tomorrow afternoon, if you want to come. I have to drop off a brochure I finished for one of the local businesses."

"I'm eager to get started working on the stories. I guess it probably wouldn't hurt to go get a library card. I'll also check today to see if I need any supplies. You really have thought of pretty much everything, though. Thank you."

"I'm glad you think so." Ren looked out the window before turning her focus back to Lindy. "It's a nice day today, no wind. Would you like to explore some of the island? We should probably seize the opportunity to see as much of it as we can while the weather cooperates. Once it turns really cold, we won't be able to spend as much time outdoors."

"Do you run?"

Ren replied, "I used to, however I haven't for a while. Why?"

"Well, I thought maybe we could cover more ground if we ran rather than walked. My job is so sedentary, when I have time I like to do some exercise. Running is a favorite."

"You may have to take pity on me, since I haven't done it lately."

"You have nothing to fear."

***

Grabbing Ren's arm and giving her a tug to get her moving, Lindy headed for her bedroom. She called back over her shoulder, "Let's give the sandwiches a chance to settle. I'll change into my running gear and meet you back here in an hour."

Lindy and Ren met as arranged and after stretching set off at an easy pace on the trail that followed the rocky coastline. The trail climbed gradually to the highest point on the island. It was a natural stopping point. The bench overlooking the ocean was a welcome sight to Ren who found she was working hard to catch her breath. She always used to enjoy running this path with Brooke, and she wondered to herself why she had given up running it regularly when Brooke died. *She was the one who dragged me out.* "I only run half as often as I should," she mumbled, rubbing her hand over her mouth as she said it, to hide the guilt of her white lie.

"Yeah, right. Half as often?"

"Okay...maybe a quarter as often as I should." Once Ren was able to breathe at a more normal rate, she began pointing out spots of interest to Lindy.

When both were ready, they traveled down the hill to the far end of the island and up the other, more protected side, heading back towards the house. They approached an especially lovely spot at the end of a gradual decline in the path, where flat rocks provided a perfect resting place to watch the waves crash against the rugged coastline below. Nestled nearby was a bench surrounded by pine scented trees, a perfect spot to relax and observe the ocean. Ren asked Lindy, "May I have a minute here?"

"Sure. I could use a rest, too." Lindy sat on the bench overlooking the rocks where Ren used to sit to watch the ocean with Brooke.

Ren went to the rocks and stood for a moment staring out at the ocean, lips moving in a silent prayer. She quickly brushed her hand over her eyes, before turning to join Lindy on the bench.

"This is a beautiful location, Ren."

Ren nodded her agreement. Not trusting her voice, she didn't speak.

Lindy, puzzled by the sudden change in Ren's demeanor, didn't want to probe for the cause. She preferred Ren to want to share, rather than feeling obligated to respond to Lindy's questioning purely out of curiosity.

After several minutes of silence, Ren smiled at Lindy and said, "Sorry, this spot has special significance to me and sometimes it makes me a little sad. I'm ready whenever you are."

They both stood up. "Come on, I'll race you back to the house." Lindy stood and faced the direction they were running in before they stopped to rest, feeling ready to continue on that path. It took a moment until she noticed that Ren was tiptoeing up the path waiting for Lindy to notice her.

Ren waited until Lindy made eye contact with her. "You're on!" She took off at full speed on the shortcut path back to the house. In honesty, she didn't think she would make it for the full run to the other end of the island and all the way back again to the house. She was very familiar with this path though, which gave her an advantage over Lindy who had to slow down when she was unsure of her footing. As she entered the groomed lawns surrounding the Inn, Ren could hear Lindy gaining on her. She knew if she ran all the way to the door, she would lose. Making a quick decision she stopped where she was and turned, yelling, "I win!"

Lindy pounded to a halt next to her. Smacking her on the arm and laughing, she said, "Yes, and you cheat, too."

Laughing as best she could, while breathing in large gulps of air, Ren replied, "What's the saying? Age and treachery will triumph over youth and skill any day."

"That was fun," said Lindy. "I had a great time, thanks."

"Yes, me too, thank you for suggesting the run." Her reply came automatically. She realized after she said it that she had really enjoyed herself. Not that there hadn't been times when she'd had pleasant times, over the past few years; however, they felt like a more mature, adult kind of fun. Today had been different. She'd had fun down to her bones, body and soul--kid fun. A sudden realization dawned, that she was having a different kind of fun than she'd become accustomed to.

"That was great. I'm ready to go to work as soon as I finish getting my bedroom organized—to get started on my writing. Now tell me, don't you feel better, more invigorated?"

"Yes, I do, actually." Ren smiled. "Come on, I'll show you the gym in case you want to run again this week. I can tell already that I'll need some time to recover." When the look on Lindy's face indicated her doubt about whether she was serious or not, Ren realized she'd better be clear. "I'm kidding, of course. Let me show it to you anyway, just in case you want to use it during your stay. Entering through the basement door in the back of the house, she took Lindy to the well-equipped gym.

"Look at this." Lindy took a quick tour around the facility. "You have everything here."

"Yes, there's more in there, including a sauna. It's for the guests too, although few really use it regularly with the outdoor activities available. When we used to be open for a longer season, during the period when the weather wasn't cooperative, it got used more frequently."

Turning to head down the hallway, Ren asked, "Got your breadcrumbs? It's a relatively circuitous route up to our rooms. I'm sure you'll get the hang of it eventually. If you don't show up for dinner one night, I'll send out a search party." Ren led the way through the basement and up through the guest wing, through the dining area, and down the hallway to their rooms.

"I know the library is around here somewhere. Where would that be?"

Ren pointed back toward the dining room. "Just head down the short hallway next to the dining room and you can't miss it."

"Ren, this is a beautiful house, without a doubt. I don't think I'd enjoy it here alone. Don't you get lonely here all by yourself month after month?"

Just for an instant, before she blinked them away, tears welled in Ren's eyes. She worked to gain control of the tears and keep them from sliding down her face. "Yes, it is lonely, at times. It didn't use to be, but things change. Because my illustration business has grown, I got Jack to agree to shorten the season for the Inn. It's been a both a blessing and a curse. The advantage is that I now have all the time I need or want to work on my art and on my illustrating." She shrugged. "The disadvantage is that there are no people around. It's one of the reasons I wanted to work with you on your manuscript." Gesturing with open palm in Lindy's direction, Ren confessed,

"It'll be a treat to have such pleasant company around over these lonely winter months when the Inn is closed."

"I'm going to go clean up and do some work." Ren started down the hallway towards her bedroom before turning back toward Lindy. "By the way, I'm cooking dinner tonight. If you're willing, I could use an assistant skilled at peeling, chopping, and dicing. Anyone want to volunteer?"

A broad grin on her face, Lindy raised her hand as if volunteering in class. "What about Maggie, won't we hurt her feelings?

"Cooking dinner for me is not really one of her responsibilities. She sort of watches out for me and keeps me company when she can. Right now, she has other things on her mind and someone she'd rather be with, so I told her we could fend for ourselves in the kitchen."

"Oh, fine, I'm sure we can too. If all else fails, there's always PB & J."

"Good. Let's get started on dinner around five. I'm making a beef stew, if that's okay with you. Maybe over dinner, we can figure out our menus for the next few weeks so I can order in supplies for what we need. We can take turns cooking if that works for you. Or, if you prefer, we can do it together."

"I think I'd like to do it together, if possible. It'll be another opportunity for us to talk about our project. If it's not convenient for one or the other of us, we can work out what seems best."

"Okay. Sounds like a plan. See you later in the kitchen." She paused at the doorway. "Thanks, Lindy, I had fun."

LINDY CAPRINI JOURNAL

This will be short, I'm tired and we've had a full day today, both work and play. I feel blessed that we're working so well together and am enjoying the growing closeness of our friendship. I like her very much.

This morning she told me a bit about her parents. Sadly, she remembers nothing about them. The saddest thing she said was that she has no memories of her own of her parents, only shared memories of her grandparents and brother who generously shared them with her. I found myself tearing up, while she seems to have just accepted the facts of her life. A strange thing happened few minutes later. We were playfully arguing about PB&J sandwiches. Ren took a bite of her sandwich leaving a smudge of jelly on her cheek. As I reached over to rub it from the corner of her lips I don't know what came over me. I started to reach out to cup her cheek with my palm but pulled back before I made a complete ass of myself. I don't think she noticed, and I've pretty much rationalized my behavior away to still being emotional about the feelings she expressed regarding her parents.

After lunch we took a run, stopping by the flat rocks that she told me have special significance for her. She grew so sad. Sometimes I wonder about what is tormenting her. She and her brother own the island, the Inn, and the marina. On the surface she has so much, yet there are times she has such an aura of melancholy that I can't help but to feel a little sorry for her. Ren is a lovely person, gorgeous, bright, and witty. She's a hard worker with a wicked sense of humor. She loves to tease and I not only enjoy our working together, I especially enjoy our casual times. With so much to offer I can't help but wonder why she's not married.

Chapter 8: One Per Customer

At breakfast the next morning the two women agreed that it should be work before pleasure. Their planning for the day included that they work until around one o'clock then go to the mainland for errands and shopping. "I think I will have thought enough by the time we leave and I know I'll be ready for a break," Lindy laughed and stood to gather the plates.

"I feel sorry for you. Your job is definitely harder than mine."

Lindy frowned. "Why?"

"Because writing all those deep thoughts is hard work. I'm just drawing pictures, something I would do for fun anyway. You're working harder than I am, I think."

"Well, in that case, this hard working girl deserves a treat. It's only fair that I buy you dinner tonight."

"Gee, one night of cooking for ourselves and we're already resorting to eating out." Ren flashed a quick smile. "How spoiled are we?"

Shrugging her shoulders, her tone playful, Lindy said, "Well, if you really feel that way, we don't have to...."

Ren interrupted before Lindy could finish. "No, no, I'm not complaining. I agree, dinner out it is--your treat."

They each retired to their individual spaces to work separately until they took a break for lunch at noon. After their quick meal, they cast off and were underway a little after one. When they arrived at the marina, Lindy gracefully jumped onto the dock as Ren pulled into the slip. Ren tossed the lines to her to loop over the dock cleats. Ren adjusted the lines on the boat and tidied everything up before she too leaped to the dock. "Thanks. You're a quick learner. Come on," said Ren, gesturing toward her SUV, "I'll give you the fifty-cent tour of the town."

Ren drove through the main shopping area, pointing out landmarks and indicating her favorite stores. She directed Lindy to try the hardware store for any office supplies she might need. "If you want anything other than paper clips and paper, we can hit the office supply store in the mall about half an hour up the road."

"Where do Marie and Jack live? If I have time, I'd like to stop in just to say hello."

Ren took Lindy back to the center of town to get her bearings before she drove past Jack and Marie's house. "Had I thought about it, we could have asked Jack and Marie to join us tonight, although they'd probably have a hard time getting a baby sitter at such short notice. They aren't very regular customers because I usually sit for them."

"Why can't we bring Laura with us? We'll go to a family style restaurant and they can bring her along."

"Great idea! I'll come in with you to see if they can join us."

Ren knocked on the door before opening it and sticking her head in. A scream of delight greeted them.

"Auntie Ren," cried Laura as she raced across the living room and threw herself into Ren's outstretched arms. Marie gave Ren an equally warm greeting, albeit without the screaming and running. When Marie finished hugging Ren, she turned and greeted Lindy with a warm hug as well.

"Come in, come in. What an unexpected and pleasant surprise."

"Laura, I want you to meet my friend, Lindy. You can call her Aunt Lindy, okay?"

Laura stuck out her pudgy hand, which Lindy grasped and shook solemnly. "Hi, Laura. That's a very beautiful name."

"Thank you, Aunt Lindy." As only children can do, she turned to Ren and asked, "Is Aunt Lindy my daddy's sister, too?"

Ren answered quickly, reaching down to hoist the little girl into her arms. "Nope! It's just a polite way for you to use her first name when you talk to her. You know, Laura, Aunt Lindy can tell you some wonderful stories. I bet if she thinks really hard, she can tell you a story you've never heard before."

Laura's eyes grew wide, "Really? When?"

"How about now?" Lindy replied holding her arms out to the little girl in Ren's arms.

Laura abandoned Ren without even a look back. Lindy raised her eyebrows and shot Ren a smug look before softening it with a wink.

Ren grinned and shrugged in return. "Humph. Abandoned like a cold slice of pizza."

"Oh stop! Come with us, and you may hear a story you've never heard before either." Lindy sat on the sofa and balanced Laura on her knees.

As Marie and Ren sat down to listen to the story, Marie wondered to herself if Ren and Lindy were flirting. Whatever it was, they were certainly playful with each other. She hadn't seen Ren this happy or relaxed since Brooke was alive. *Interesting. I always assumed that Lindy was straight.* She watched Ren watch Lindy tell the story. *There was definitely a spark between them—friendship at the very least, maybe more?* She smiled to herself as she considered the pair before her. *This could be a very interesting winter.*

"Tell me another," begged Laura, when Lindy finished the story.

"Nope! Can't. One per customer...next time, okay? I need to talk with your Mom and your Aunt." She softened the denial with a warm smile and a hug.

Although not happy about not getting another story from Lindy, Laura remembered her manners. "Thank you, Aunt Lindy. You won't forget about next time, will you?"

"Never."

Handing her daughter a drawing tablet and some crayons Marie said, "Sweetie, why don't you go draw Aunt Lindy a picture. Maybe you can draw the fish from the story she just told you."

Laura took the drawing materials, stretched out on the floor near the grownups, and began to draw quietly.

"So, to what do I owe the pleasure of your surprise visit?"

Ren answered. "We're going to do some shopping before we have dinner. We wondered if you and Jack and the munchkin could join us."

"Why don't you come here? I've got a roast ready to go into the oven." Looking this time towards Lindy, "I'd love for you to meet Jack. It'll be easier for us to talk if we eat here." With the last comment, she subtly tipped her head toward the budding artist.

Ren and Lindy glanced towards each other and both shrugged. "Why not?" Lindy answered for both of them.

"Okay." Ren said, "We'd better get going if we're to make it back in time for some of Marie's famous cooking." As she stood up, she unconsciously extended her hand to Lindy who smiled at Ren as she grasped it to pull herself off the sofa. She dropped Ren's hand as she bent to say goodbye to Laura. "We need to be back around what, six-thirty?"

Marie nodded to Ren and walked the two women to the door. She couldn't wait to talk to Jack about the easy relationship she'd witnessed between his sister and Lindy after only two days at the Inn together.

※※※

Having agreed to where they would meet up later, Ren dropped Lindy off before delivering the brochure and returning to the marina to work. Having a hard time concentrating on the bills she was paying she idly began to doodle on the tablet next to the phone. She was surprised to recognize that the eyes that appeared on the page were those of Lindy. She's a beautiful woman, someone I'd love to sketch. I wonder if she'll pose for me. Ren made a mental note to approach her about the possibility, and got busy.

✳✳✳

Lindy enjoyed poking through the shops in the quaint tourist town. She really didn't need much of anything for herself, although she wanted to get something special for Ren for going out of her way to make her feel welcome. She couldn't believe her good fortune at finding someone like Ren to illustrate her book. As she passed the window of the art gallery, she saw a photo of a location she recognized. The photo was of a lonely bench that sat deserted, overlooking an angry sea. She was sure that it was the bench where she and Ren stopped to rest when they ran to the high point on the trail. The shop owner greeted her as she entered. "Hello there. I'm John. How can I help you?"

"Hi John, I wonder if you can tell me who took that photo?"

"It is one of a group of photos taken by one of our local artists, Ren Madison. Would you like to see the others?"

Lindy nodded affirmatively and he led her to a file of photos. "These are unframed originals. I also have some of them framed, too. I'll show you. I also have a frame that will hold four of the smaller photos over here." He pointed to a smaller box on the shelf above the larger photos. "If you want to select four of the smaller photos, I can put them into the frame while you wait."

"Thank you. Yes, let me see what you have. If I find four I like, I might just do that." Lindy found six shots she loved and had a hard time narrowing them down to just four. Finally happy with her choices, she handed the four photos to the man. "If it's okay, I'll look around a bit while you frame those."

The store was an interesting place. The back area held art supplies like drawing tablets, pens, paints, and the like. Along the side of the store, opposite the photographs and paintings, was a small display case that caught her eye. Contained in the case was the most interesting assortment of collectible prisms and kaleidoscopes. She was still leaning over the case examining the colorful display when the store clerk returned with her photo arrangement. He showed her the framed photo arrangement, and while she was admiring them he wisely unlocked the display cabinet.

"These are very unique," Lindy commented pointing to the kaleidoscopes.

"I agree that they are beautiful to look at. However, to really appreciate their uniqueness you need to look inside." He picked his favorite and handed it to her. "Hold it towards the light and turn the bottom."

"Ooooh," she exclaimed. "Lovely." *This would be perfect for Ren,* she thought, *just what I was looking for, something beautiful and unique, just like Ren.* She checked the price and was surprised to find it relatively affordable. "Okay, could you please box and wrap this for me. I love it." Checking her watch, she realized she would have to hurry to make it on time to meet Ren. She thanked John as she gathered her bags and hurried out the door. She saw Ren pull up to the corner as she jogged across the street and jumped into the front seat breathless from her rush to be on time.

Chapter 9: I Wonder If You'd Pose for Me

Ren looked at the bags Lindy shoved into the back seat and smiled. "Did you clean out the store?"

"No, but I'm pleased with what I got."

"Can I see?"

"Sure, I'll show you later."

Dinner at Jack and Marie's was fun. Laura greeted their arrival with a reminder to Lindy of her promise to tell her another story next time they got together.

Laura's mother suggested, "Maybe Aunt Lindy will tell you the story before you go to bed."

"I'd be happy to."

Everyone enjoyed the meal. Marie and Lindy told stories about college and Jack teased Ren about finally being able to walk barefoot in the grass without crying. Motivated by Lindy's puzzled expression, Jack told the story of how he contained Ren on the blanket when she was little by taking off her shoes and socks. "She wouldn't leave the blanket because she hated to have her bare feet touch grass." Lindy laughed so hard she had tears in her eyes by the time Jack and Ren stopped teasing each other.

At the end of the meal, Marie gratefully accepted Ren and Lindy's offer to clean up while Marie bathed Laura and prepared her for bed. Fresh from her bath and eager for her story, Laura crawled up onto Lindy's lap. Everyone was as mesmerized as Laura while Lindy told a tale about fairies and flowers none of them had ever heard before. Soon Laura's eyes began to droop and her father took the sleepy little girl from Lindy and carried her to bed.

"I've never heard that story before," said Marie.

Lindy laughed. "Neither have I. I just made it up."

"Really? That's incredible," remarked Ren truly in awe of Lindy's creativity.

When Jack returned, the adults continued to enjoy their time together. Conversation was easy and light. Everyone was disappointed when the clock struck ten and Ren said, "We'd better get back, or Maggie will begin to worry in another half hour. I told her I'd be home before eleven."

The trip back to the island in the boat was uneventful. Ren walked into the Inn, pushed the intercom button and Maggie answered immediately. "We're back," she said.

"Did you have fun?"

"Yes, we did, Maggie. It was a great day. We saw Jack and Marie. They said to say hello." Ren finished telling Maggie about the day before the women exchanged good nights.

Ren turned to Lindy. "Want anything to drink before you show me your purchases?"

"Just water, I think."

"I'll get it. Meet me in the library."

Ren joined Lindy with two glasses of water. "Okay, let's see the big secret purchase you made."

Lindy took her purchase from the bag, removed the wrapping, and turned it around to show Ren.

"Oh, I don't believe you bought them. I'd have given you copies if I knew you wanted them."

"I saw them in the gallery and couldn't resist. Look, they are all the places we stopped on our run."

"A sentimentalist?"

"Guilty as charged. I'm a romantic, too. Flowers and romantic cards, candlelit dinners, and let's not forget chocolates. I'm a real pushover." Rummaging in the bottom of the bag, she said, "I bought one more thing that reminded me of you." She handed the gift box to Ren.

Puzzled, Ren asked, "What's this for?"

"Open the card."

Ren slipped the small card out from under the brightly colored ribbon. She opened it and read, 'Just because...' A smile remained on Ren's lips as she shredded the striped paper, opened the box, and removed the beautiful kaleidoscope from its nest of tissue paper.

"Hold it to the light and turn it," Lindy instructed.

Ren did as directed. "This is exquisite," she remarked. "I'm not even going to complain that you shouldn't have bought this for me, it's too beautiful. I do love it. Thank you." She crossed the short distance between them and gave Lindy a quick hug and a kiss on the cheek.

"Thank you very much. I can't tell you the last time someone gave me something this special."

"You're very welcome. I'm so pleased you like it."

Lindy gathered the wrappings and the bag and took them to the kitchen for disposal. She returned to the library carrying a book she'd been reading that she'd retrieved from her room. Ren had a fire burning in the stove.

"Will it bother you if I turn on this light or perhaps you'd prefer just the light from the fire? I can go to my room to read if the lamp over here in the corner will bother you."

"No, that'll be fine."

The two women withdrew to their own areas of the room, Ren in front of the fire and Lindy reading on the opposite side of the room. She didn't notice that Ren was studying her, mentally recording every detail of her bone structure and the way she twirled her hair around her finger absent-mindedly as she read.

"Lindy, I wonder if I can ask a favor of you."

"Sure, anything."

"I wonder if you'd pose for me. I'd love to do some sketches of you and maybe a painting."

"Of me?"

Ren nodded and smiled. "Yes, of you. I'd love to paint you just as you are right now, reading. The soft light, the fire...they create such interesting textures of light and shadow."

"I'm really flattered. Okay, when do you want to do this?"

"I don't know, some afternoon, when we take a break like we did today. Instead of taking you to town so you can spend your money, I'll have you pose for me."

Ren stood, stretched, and picked up the kaleidoscope from the table where she'd carefully placed it. She knew just what she would give Lindy for Christmas. It should be an interesting project and she was eager to begin it. "I'll see you in the morning," she said cheerfully. "Thank you for a wonderful afternoon. I had a really nice time."

"Me too. I think I'll turn in too." Lindy waved her farewell before she retired to her office to make her journal entry.

LINDY CAPRINI JOURNAL

What a great day we had. Work this morning, and a break this afternoon. I love Ren's niece—what an adorable little girl. She has Ren's eyes. Meeting Ren's brother, seeing Marie today, and spending time with them as a family, was wonderful.

Ren seemed genuinely touched by my gift of the kaleidoscope. It gives me such satisfaction to bring a smile to her face. I don't ever remember feeling such pleasure at making someone else happy. I mean I like it when I can make anybody happy, who doesn't? I take particular pleasure at pleasing Ren. She was so relaxed and happy today spending time with her niece who obviously adores her. I want to do what I can to see her happy. I'm not sure yet what has caused this deep and abiding sadness that sneaks up on her, sometimes quite suddenly. She's fine one moment and an instant later, there's such a transformation. She's lucky to have Jack. She's very close to him and to his family, as well. There's no doubt she's loved, yet somehow it doesn't seem enough to sustain her.

Chapter 10: She Never Left Me Wondering For A Minute?

The two women quickly settled into a routine. They were enjoying a positive work relationship and were developing a deeper personal friendship. Breakfast every morning provided an opportunity for them to talk about their project. Once Ren had recovered from their first run together, they began to exercise regularly, frequently taking a quick run mid-morning before parting again to go to their separate work areas. If both their doors were open, Ren could hear the tapping of Lindy's fingers on the keyboard, a sound she found comforting. She enjoyed the companionship that Lindy's presence in the house provided. Even though they were working in different rooms, it was comforting to have someone else in the house. The fact that they worked well together was not a surprise, since they'd shared a positive collaboration for so many months over the phone and through e-mails. Despite that, initially, when she agreed to have Lindy stay for the year, she had worried if the constant presence of another person in the house would be intrusive. However, she was pleased to find that Lindy was anything but, and found herself looking forward to the times they spent together working on the book, chatting as they prepared and ate their meals, and especially their quiet times together in the evenings when they retired to the library to read or talk.

Ren started bringing her sketchpad to the library in the evenings. She did want Lindy to pose for her, but first she wanted to do a study of her eyes. It was her belief that it was the eyes in a portrait that captured the essence of the being. Capturing a specific expression was, in her opinion, what gave life to the picture and made a portrait different from a painting of an inanimate object. It was through the expression of the eyes that the observer could gain insight into what the person was thinking or feeling and, to Ren, also how the difference between a good portrait and a great portrait could be determined.

Ren liked to make sketches of her subject's eyes as they did various activities--casual things, such as now, with Lindy reading. Often she'd have the person just sit opposite her and talk to her about different subjects, so she could capture on paper the nuances of expression, as her subject told her various stories that conveyed a variety of emotions. Only after Ren felt that she'd captured the way the person's expressions revealed their different moods, was she ready to begin to work on the rest of the sketches and eventually the painting.

Lindy glanced up from the book she was reading, meeting Ren's eyes. "Is everything okay, Ren?"

"Why do you ask?"

"I don't know. You're very quiet tonight. I just wondered if there was something wrong."

"No, maybe just feeling a little tired tonight and maybe a little blue. I can assure you it's nothing that talking about would help." Ren paused a moment as she realized that Lindy might be concerned that she had done something to cause Ren's mood. "And everything between us is fine." She smiled. "Really, it's just that I'm feeling a little sad. I think I'll turn in. See you tomorrow."

As Ren passed by Lindy's chair, she touched her shoulder. "Don't worry. Everything will be okay."

"You know where to find me, if I can help."

When she finished the chapter she was reading, Lindy turned off the lights in the library. On her way to her bedroom she noticed that there was a light still on in Ren's studio. She considered stopping in, although it seemed that Ren wanted to deal with whatever was influencing her mood on her own.

The next morning, armed with a feeling for their work routine and pace, Lindy opened her calendar so she could begin to plan timelines and deadlines for herself. She was amazed that the time since she arrived had passed so quickly, noting that only a few days remained in September. Ren didn't have breakfast with her, a departure from their normal routine. She saw her come up the path from the sheltered side of the island and head directly to her studio instead of coming into the kitchen. When Ren didn't come out for lunch Lindy decided to check in on her. Armed with the information she'd compiled that morning she knocked at Ren's studio door.

"Yes?" Ren called from inside. "Come in."

Lindy entered Ren's studio for the first time and found Ren seated at her drawing table in the corner near the window. Opposite her was a wall covered with paintings, sketches, and photographs. Her eyes immediately traveled to the largest painting on the wall. It took a minute to recognize that the subject was nude because the woman's eyes captured her focus so completely.

"Hi. I have some timelines I'd like you to look over for me to see if they seem reasonable to you. I don't know if you have travel plans that might conflict or other jobs that you've accepted that might need your time. I can adjust anything you think is unrealistic." She crossed the room to hand the calendar to Ren.

As Ren looked over the plans, Lindy walked towards the wall of artwork to examine the display more closely. She found herself studying the picture of the lovely blonde woman. It was a powerful piece of art. She was beautiful, without doubt. However it was not beauty, specifically, that the painting conveyed--it was love. *Love and something more,* she thought. *Desire. Yes, it was pure desire. This woman was looking at the artist, at Ren, leaving no doubt about what was on her mind.* Lindy turned towards Ren to find that Ren was watching her as she studied the painting.

Lindy approached the drawing table, "Who is she?"

"Her name was Brooke. She was my friend, my partner," and after a brief a pause added, "my lover. Today is the anniversary of her death." Ren's eyes filled with tears as Lindy quickly came around the desk. She wanted to comfort Ren, even though she was not sure what she needed or would accept from her.

Lindy took Ren's hand in hers and led her to the loveseat. "Tell me about her," she said simply.

"I can't, not right now, not today." Huge tears tracked their way down Ren's face. "I just wasn't prepared for her to leave me."

Lindy put her arm around Ren and pulled her against her shoulder. Ren rested her head there accepting the comfort that Lindy offered. Together they looked up at the painting of Brooke.

"She was beautiful and she obviously loved you very much. You can see it in her expression."

"Yes," replied Ren as she sat up. She heaved a long sigh. Almost objectively, she stared up at the portrait of her lover. "She did that. She never left me wondering for a minute if she loved me." Ren turned her attention to Lindy, seeking her eyes. "Today is a particularly hard day for me. Thank you for listening to me and for holding me. Talking about her helped."

"Is she buried here, on the island?"

"Not exactly, her ashes were spread at sea."

Putting the now obvious clues together––Ren's return up the path alone this morning from the spot they'd stopped on their run the first day, the melancholy that had shrouded her when they stopped there––she knew even before Ren replied. "She surrounds me everywhere here on the island. When I feel the need to be closer to her I visit her down at the flat rocks."

"Come on," Lindy said, "let's go say hello. It'll do you good to get out of here for a little while and I could stand to take a break."

Together they walked the path to the spot where Ren felt closest to Brooke, and sat on the bench. Neither spoke after they settled there. When Lindy heard Ren expel several deep sighs she put her hand on her shoulder, hoping it would be a comfort.

Ren finally said, "Okay. Thank you, Lindy. I'm better now. Shall we go back?"

Returning to the house, they went to the kitchen for a drink. Maggie was just leaving after having placed a vase of fresh flowers on the table. Following a brief exchange of greetings, Maggie said, "Jack called. He, Marie, and Laura are coming over later for a visit. Joey called and said to tell you he was thinking about you. Oh, and Mallory called. She said not to bother you because she was at work and she wouldn't be available again until after five. She said to give her a call later tonight if you can."

"Thanks Maggie. I'll get in touch with Mallory before I go to bed."

As she left the room, Maggie gave Lindy's shoulder a brief squeeze. As Lindy looked up, she recognized the nod that Maggie gave her as approval and appreciation.

Everyone enjoyed themselves during the visit from Ren's family. Jack and Marie were amazed to find Ren relaxed and in a surprisingly good mood on what was usually a very somber day for her. Laura begged another story from Lindy who was more than happy to honor the request. Neither Jack nor Marie missed the hand Lindy placed on Ren's shoulder when Ren said, "Laura, go over there and get the book for Aunt Lindy that Aunt Brooke and I gave you when you were a little girl."

After the story, the group watched the video of Snow White. It wasn't until they were safely home and had tucked Laura into bed that Jack and Marie discussed Ren.

"I'm amazed to find her so relaxed."

"Yes. True," Marie concurred.

"Think she's finally coming back?"

"I think Lindy has a lot to do with it."

"I don't know if it's Lindy specifically, but I think it's good that she's not alone out there. Regardless, they seem to get along so well after such a short time," Jack observed.

"Don't forget," Marie reminded him, "they were in contact over the phone for a substantial part of a year before Lindy came here. I do agree however, that they seem very at ease with each other."

"I know. Still, I haven't seen Ren this comfortable with anyone since Brooke. Isn't this woman straight? I don't want to see Ren hurt again."

"Yes, from all I know of her, I think she is. Jack, we can't wrap Ren up and keep her away from people. Hopefully, she knows what she's doing and they'll both be okay."

Lindy Caprini Journal

Today I saw Ren's studio for the first time. She has a wall opposite her worktable that displays some selected works in a chronology of sorts. I didn't have a sufficient amount of time to really absorb to my satisfaction and to study her work. I did see enough to determine that she is even a more talented artist than I even expected. There is this one painting that's the largest on the wall. It is a portrait of her lover—a woman. Her name is Brooke, or more correctly, I should say was. Talking about her was difficult for Ren. Today was the anniversary of Brooke's death, normally a difficult day for Ren, she tells me. I hope that I was able to help a bit. I went with her to where she'd spread Brooke's ashes. We sat quietly there for a brief time. It seemed to comfort her. I'm glad I was here and could help. From the painting, it appears that Brooke loved Ren deeply and, obviously, Ren still suffers because of Brooke's death.

Chapter 11: How Much Of Our Story Do You Want To Hear?

After Jack and his family left, Ren and Lindy settled in the library. Ren poured a glass of sherry for Lindy and one for herself. After handing the drink to Lindy, Ren settled into the chair opposite her, in front of the fire.

After a brief pause Ren said, "I'm sorry I couldn't tell you about Brooke earlier. I think I can get through it now. How much of our story do you want to hear?"

"All of it...whatever you're willing or able to share."

"Ok." Ren paused, to collect her thoughts before she spoke. It was a pattern she'd follow throughout the evening. There would be pauses in their dialogue while Ren relived her memories, followed by a brief summary of the details she was ready to share. "We met at a dance when I was a freshman in college. Shortly thereafter we had our first dinner date, and I was probably already in love with her by the time we split dessert. We agreed to meet for our second date in front of my favorite museum the following Wednesday. I can remember that I stood at the top of the stairs enjoying watching Brooke climb up to meet me. I swear my heart nearly beat its way out of my chest when she looked up and smiled at me. She hugged me and gave me a kiss on the cheek. My entire insides did a happy dance." Ren, a smile on her face, reached her hand up, and touched her cheek, recalling how her cheek had tingled when Brooke kissed her there. "I linked my arm through hers and led her through the display as I pointed out features of the paintings we passed, shared information about the style, and some history about the period of time in which each was painted.

Ren smiled. "She told me she was impressed with how much I knew about art and the history associated with it and wondered how I'd learned so much. I told her art had been my love since I was a little girl. My grandfather realized, when I was still tiny, my artistic gift and paid for an excellent teacher to tutor me. He not only nurtured my artistic ability, he also encouraged me to experiment with different styles until I developed my own. I grew to love art history early on and have always read a lot on my own. Art is truly a passion for me, I'd guess like her cooking was for her, and your teaching and writing are for you."

Lindy nodded, not wanting to interrupt the story.

"We stayed late in the museum, until just before they closed the doors for the evening. It was misting as we strolled down the street towards the bus stop, where we huddled in a doorway together to share our first real kiss that left us equally breathless. We'd already arranged the where and when for our next date. Over the next couple of months we met whenever there was time in our schedules even if only to take a walk or to get together for a quick cup of tea or chocolate. Sometimes we'd double date with my friends, Piper and Mallory, or her friends, Carol and Nancy. Our relationship deepened with each time we were together and we phoned each other as often as we could, although the phone also offered little privacy. At the end of our dates, we were constrained to a few quick kisses in the library stairwell or in a doorway as we separated to return to our respective rooms we both shared with others. Frustrated by being unable to be alone together, one evening we were standing in a remote corner of the college library, far back in the stacks where we had relative privacy. As was often the case, Brooke was lamenting, in whispered tones due to our location, that she'd had more private time with her first girlfriend when she lived at home with her parents."

Lindy nodded in understanding. "Being young and in love isn't always easy. We've all been there."

Ren considered the next part of the story, before she pushed on. "Money was an issue for Brooke. She was working her way through school, paying for most of her education herself. When I suggested that maybe we could go somewhere for a weekend together, she told me that it wasn't that she didn't want to...she just didn't have the money to do that."

"She didn't know you could afford it?"

"No. She knew I grew up in an inn. Only I'd kind of failed to mention my family owned the Inn and, for that matter, the island it sits on." Ren shrugged. "Money had never been an issue for us until we had no place to be together. Often, when we got together we would do free things, just go to the park, take a walk—you know all the things kids do."

"So what happened? Did you finally tell her you could afford it?"

"Eventually, just not quite yet. I called Brooke the following week and asked if she could swap her schedule around to get a weekend free. When Brooke confirmed that she could, I told her I had a surprise in mind for her. Brooke finally gave up trying to get me to reveal my plans after begging, coaxing, trickery, and every other method she could think of failed to get me to spill what I had up my sleeve for the weekend. When Friday finally arrived, I took Brook to dinner and we enjoyed a wonderful meal."

"So, you still hadn't told her about your plans for the weekend yet?"

Ren chuckled, "No. I suppose at some point she gave up trying to guess. Finally at dinner, she asked me again. I told her all would become clear very soon." Ren's eyes twinkled with mirth. "I took her across the street into the hotel lobby, where we sat down on chairs opposite each other. Once settled in, after some small talk, I pulled an envelope from my pocket and slid it across the table towards Brooke. I asked if she was ready for dessert? Brooke opened the envelope and withdrew a hotel room key. When she then asked what the key was for, I told her it was dessert. When she asked me what kind of dessert required a key, I told her, 'me.' We argued all the way up to the room about how we couldn't afford the hotel until I begged her to pretend for a little while that, just this once, it wasn't too expensive and that I could afford it. Once I got her in the room, it was considerably easier to convince her I'd made a good decision, if you get my drift."

Ren looked away as her mind drifted back to that night. After a moment, lost in memories of the first time they made love, Ren mentally shook herself, drawing her mind back to the library and Lindy. "Sorry."

"Pleasant thoughts?"

"Yes, very. She was amazing, and I was so in love with her."

Ren realized that Lindy was waiting for her to continue her story. She didn't share the details but gave her a brief summary of her memories. "After our first weekend together, I still had to deal with telling her about my family. Financially, getting through school was difficult for Brooke. Her parents helped her all they could. Even with their assistance, she still had to work to help pay her way. Every penny was critical to her while I, obviously, was far from having to scrimp to make ends meet."

"So what happened? How did you tell her? Did you really expect she'd be upset?"

Chapter 12: I Don't Want To Feel Like A Kept Woman

"I suspected that the large disparity in our financial situation would be difficult for Brooke to accept. She was a proud woman." Ren's mind flashed to the past, reliving in an instant, the day she told her lover about her family...

A few days after their weekend in the hotel, Ren and Brooke met for a quick meal at a fast food restaurant. They were enjoying reminiscing about the weekend they'd spent together. Ren began the conversation she had avoided for months. "Did you mean it when you told me that you were in love with me?"

Somberly, Brooke nodded. "Of course. I meant it when I said it before and I still mean it now. However, you have to promise me not to spend that much money again without us agreeing on it first. It's not fair you pay for everything for our weekend. As much as I enjoyed our time together, it'll be difficult for us to pay for all of the expense of our first weekend together."

"Brooke, there is something I've been wanting to tell you, but I've never found the right time before. Because we're going home so you can meet my family, I have to tell you."

Ren's serious tone focused Brooke's attention. "You're scaring me. What is it?"

"Don't be worried. It's nothing bad, honest. In fact, some people would think of it as a positive." Ren shrugged a shoulder and kind of grimaced. Taking a deep breath, she moved the discussion quickly forward. "You remember that night at the hotel, when you suggested to me that the room was too expensive and I shouldn't have gotten it for us because I couldn't afford it?"

Brooke nodded, her expression expectant as she waited for Ren to continue.

Unsure of how Brooke was going to react, Ren's heart raced as she prepared to make her confession. "Well, you see, I really can."

"What do you mean?"

Ren put the palm of her right hand over her heart in an effort to keep it from beating out of her chest. "Well, technically, I can't yet, but my family certainly can. Eventually, I'll be able to as well. I told you that my parents died when I was two. I didn't mention that because of their accident, they left me very financially secure. They left both my brother and me trust funds. He got his when he turned twenty-five. For now, my brother manages my trust for me until I come of age five years from now, when I'm twenty-five." Ren paused to allow Brooke time to process the information. "That's not all. Remember when I told you before that I grew up in my grandparent's Inn?"

Brooke nodded.

"Well, the Inn is on an island."

Brooke's hand flew to her mouth. "What?" She shook her head trying to help the information to settle into her brain.

"My grandfather owns an island off the coast of Maine that they bought when I was still a little girl. I hope it won't be for a long time, but my brother and I are his heirs, so we'll eventually inherit the island and the Inn, along with his other sizable assets."

Brooke's mouth literally dropped open. Overwhelmed by this new bit of information about the woman she loved, Brooke said flatly, "I don't believe this. You will eventually own an island?" Brooke repeated the statement a second time under her breath,

Ren suspected, in an effort to make it more real in her mind. "Really?"

"Yes, I'm afraid so." Ren's nervous giggle, followed by a shrug with palms turned upward indicated there was nothing that she could do about it. "When my grandfather sold his company, my grandparents built the house, some cottages and opened an Inn on the island. I think that perhaps it was a good thing that he had money, because the Inn doesn't turn that much profit--still it pays all the expenses of owning the island and supporting the property, so he lives there rent free, so to speak. Regardless of the financial aspect, more importantly, my grandparents fell in love with it. Plus they felt it was a good environment for them to raise my brother and me."

Ren stopped when she saw the expression on Brooke's face. "I'm sorry that I didn't tell you before. It's just that that you and I were doing okay without money. It simply wasn't that important to me until we just had no place to be together."

"Ren, you know, I think that money is rarely important to those who have it. For me, who has minimal amounts of it, it can be very important. I won't ever be able to keep up with you financially. I don't want to feel like a kept woman or a charity case." She shook her head. "I can't see how I won't feel that way."

"Until I get access to my trust in a few more years, I'm essentially on a fixed budget too—just like you are. I will concede that my budget may be more generous than yours, yet I'm sure we can work out some sort of sliding scale where we each pay proportional amounts based on our individual financial resources. Honestly, I've never lived an extravagant lifestyle even though my family is very well off. Think about it. Whenever I treated you to dinner, I took us to places that were reasonably priced and offered good food. If I were trying to impress you with my money, I'd have taken you to ritzier places, wouldn't I?"

Brooke thought about that statement for a moment, shrugged, and nodded her agreement. "I guess so."

"What, now you just think I'm cheap?" Ren's eyes twinkled as she teased her lover, who rolled her eyes in response.

Encouraged, Ren continued. "Although I grew up with family wealth, I'm not your typical spoiled rich kid. I've always worked and have helped at the Inn and at the marina since I was a kid. I know how to work. Really, Brooke, please give me a chance to prove to you that money isn't what's important to me. My grandparents raised me to know that a good work ethic and treating others with respect is much more important than how much money one has."

Brooke rolled her eyes and shook her head in disbelief.

"No, really, you should see the modest apartment where my brother and I live most of the time. It's a very simple, small two-bedroom place above his marina office. He could certainly afford a much more lavish apartment, but we like where we live. It's cozy and we're both happy there. Yes, my grandfather is wealthy and I'll be first to admit that his home is jaw-droppingly fabulous. After my grandparents built it, they continued to work even though, technically, they really didn't have to ever work again after Grandpop sold his business. When you come home with me, you'll see for yourself."

Brooke's expression and her less rigid body posture told Ren that she was making progress. With Brooke relaxing, Ren thought it safe to tease her again. "Please promise me that since I've finally found you, and now that you've had your way with me I might add, you aren't going to dump me just because I have a little money." Ren reached across the table to touch her lover's hand, a little smile tugging at the corners of her mouth. She could see Brooke's mental wheels turning as she examined the potential impact of the bombshell Ren just dropped on their relationship.

Brooke shook her head, mumbling, "Yeah, right...a little money." She couldn't completely squelch the smile that begged to spread across her face. "It's a good thing that I'm crazy about you, because money can cause considerable problems in a relationship."

"Really? I always thought that not having money was something that caused problems. Who would ever imagine that having a lot of money would be a curse?"

Brooke shook her head as she uttered, "This is going to be impossible." This time, she said it with a smile. "Okay, I surrender. I guess there could be worse things than falling in love with someone with money. Just for the record, remember that I fell in love with you before I knew."

Sitting on the chair opposite Ren as she summarized the events of her conversation with Brooke, her chin resting on her palm, Lindy smiled as Ren paused in her story. "So sounds like she had a good sense of humor."

"Yes. She was usually pretty serious, although she had a dry sense of humor and made me laugh at the most unexpected times."

"So what happened after that, did you move in together?"

Chapter 13: I Think I Might Have Changed My Mind

"When I brought Brooke home to meet my family, there were a couple of rough moments when she saw the grandeur of the Inn. Once here, she fell completely in love with my family, especially with my grandfather." Ren stood up and refilled their sherry glasses. "Come on, I want to show you a drawing I did of him. It's one of my favorites."

Sherry in hand, they made their way to Ren's studio. She led Lindy to the wall where she'd displayed her work. "My grandfather," she said simply as she pointed to one of the paintings of an elderly gentleman with twinkling eyes and a warm smile. "He just thought the sun rose and set on Brooke's head."

Ren settled on the loveseat to gather her thoughts while Lindy studied the photos and drawings displayed on that section of the wall.

The lovers were again separated for the summer after Ren's freshman year because Ren had to return to the island to help at the Inn. With Jack's blessing and only a week remaining until her sophomore year of college began, Ren returned to New York so she and Brooke could hunt for a place to share. The rental that Brooke found proved to be a lovely, although tiny, apartment that was within their budget. Despite the tight living space, the one big plus the apartment offered was a small five by five room off the kitchen that the property owner described as a pantry. Ren quickly labeled it her studio, declaring that the space would be just large enough for her easel and painting supplies. "This will be perfect, Brooke. I won't have to put my painting supplies away every time I use them."

Her smile told Ren that Brooke was kidding when she said, "Well, you have a lot of nerve claiming the pantry for yourself. You are talking to a chef, you know. What's it worth to you to get me to give up custody of the pantry?"

Ren pulled Brooke close nuzzling her ear. She whispered, her voice seductive. "I'll make it worth your while, I promise." Stepping back, she placed a quick kiss on Brooke's lips and turned back to their task. "You have to admit that the kitchen isn't a bad size, there are ample closets, and the appliances are pretty new. Deal?"

"I guess. Anything to be with you all the time."

"I like it. I'm sold. Let's take this one."

Once settled into their new apartment, the two were indescribably happy. Ren's passion became recording Brooke's life artistically. She photographed her as she worked in the kitchen, as she studied, and as she slept. She painted portraits of her in different stages of dress. Her nude paintings conveyed Ren's love of her subject, and the expressions on Brooke's face illustrated in the paintings were often ones of more than love-- one especially conveying pure desire. Although Ren did paint and photograph other subjects, she recognized that the drawings and paintings of Brooke were her best work. Their life moved forward more quickly now that they had the luxury of being together. Ren's sophomore year flew by. Ren couldn't believe spring was around the corner, which meant a resurfacing of what was to become an annual argument about which of Ren's works she would display in the art show.

For the show at the end of her junior year, Ren persuaded Brooke to allow her to show some of her less explicit paintings of her, as well as some of the black and white photographic studies of Brooke at work. The pair struggled with a decision about which of Ren's more modest paintings of Brooke as well as which photographs of her at work in the kitchen she should select for display.

"You do realize, of course, that anyone looking at those paintings would have to be blind not to know that we're romantically involved," commented Brooke.

"I know. I was just a little nervous at first about being involved with a woman. Since I met you, I don't really care what anyone thinks. I love you. You're so beautiful, inside and out. I want everyone to see the beauty I see every time I look at you."

Ren received several show awards recognizing her work. At the end of the day, an art dealer approached Ren to ask if she'd be willing to hang some of her work at his gallery. Ren agreed, promising to pick several pieces to give him for display.

"I'm surprised that you agreed to sell any of them." Brooke wrapped her arms around her lover.

"Well, dear, I think it's a necessary evil. We'll keep the special ones. Come on help me. I promise to split any profit I make on any picture I sell for which you were the model.

"Deal!" Together they picked their least favorites of the paintings. "This is awful, Ren. It's like trying to select our least favorite child. Funny, I have less attachment for the photographs somehow."

"Me too, although I think that might have something to do with the fact that you have your clothes on in all the photos." Ren picked up one of the larger paintings. "We can't let this one go. I'll never part with it. Remember that rainy day you started posing for this one?"

Brooke wiggled her eyebrows and chuckled. "How could I forget that? Probably the best sex we ever had."

"Look at that expression on your face. Pure lust."

"I was just mirroring your expression. You tortured me with your paintbrush! It took me weeks to get all the paint off my stomach."

They laughed at the very special memory they shared. "Come on Brooke. Let's finish this so we can get to bed. All this talk is making me want to make love to you."

When they finished selecting the paintings Ren was willing to part with, Brooke stood behind Ren, wrapping her in an embrace. She nuzzled her neck, inhaling the warmth and familiar scent specific to her lover.

"Umm, I'll give you the rest of the day to stop that." Ren turned and moved into Brooke's embrace. The picture selection process was put on hold for the rest of the afternoon.

The next morning, Brooke said, "Come on, I'll help you load the children we're selling into the cab."

Ren laughed, before she replied. "It really does feel that way, doesn't it?" Ren's feelings were somewhat assuaged when she received a check for a tidy amount when the first painting, one of the larger ones, sold—enough to pay a decent portion of the rent. Later in the month, she received another check when the series of photos showing Brooke baking a tart sold to a local restaurant. Soon the dealer was asking for more of Ren's work. She promised to do some additional paintings over the summer and take more photographs, so she would be able to offer him more of her work in September when she returned to school.

The pair faced another dreaded summer separation. At night, in bed, they often talked about what would happen when Ren finished college at the end of the second year. They had yet to resolve the dilemma of where they would settle.

"I need to be in the city to advance my career and realize my goal of owning my own restaurant someday."

"I know," Ren replied. "I feel an obligation to Grandpop and Jack to return and help at the Inn."

"I can understand that. I don't think there's a solution other than to keep doing what we've been doing. You can paint anywhere. So, stay here with me for most of the year and return to help during the season when they need you the most."

At the end of Ren's junior year of college, Brooke took her two-week vacation and spent it on the island with Ren's family. She often volunteered to work in the kitchen to help the cook prepare the meals for the family and guests. No one told the cook that everyone looked forward to the nights that Brooke prepared the food. Except for their two weeks together on the island, their summer separation was difficult. Although they had become accustomed to the forced separation every summer, Ren did take a long weekend off to visit her lover in the city, which made their time apart a little less daunting. Piper and Mallory came up for the day to visit with them, and Ren felt renewed as she returned to Maine.

In September of Ren's senior year, Brooke struggled with a decision about changing her job. "I've heard about a position at the new Baltic Restaurant. It's a really trendy, up and coming place. I'd get a promotion, and more money. That's a big advantage. Plus, it's closer to the apartment. I can probably walk there."

"What's making you uneasy about taking the new job if they offer it?"

"Well, I've built some seniority where I am. I'm not the last hired anymore. I really like the people I work with there. In the new place, I'd be low man again. Plus, I hear their turnover rate is pretty high at the Baltic. The chef there has a well-earned reputation for being a real SOB. I'm hoping that because I'm a hard worker, I'll be okay."

Despite her concerns, Brooke decided to take the risk with the new restaurant and began work in November. The job proved to be more difficult than it really had to be because of the negative and critical attitude of her new boss. After a particularly difficult day, Brooke complained to Ren when she came home. "I mean this guy's a real bastard. He fired Mimi flat out without offering her an opportunity to explain what happened when she accidentally dropped the measuring cup from the shelf. It really wasn't her fault. The dishwasher had stacked things so precariously, the cup dropped on its own when she took down a plate. She wasn't really even near the cup that fell. When it hit Chef's favorite frying pan, it did put a big gouge in it and it shattered into a million shards of glass. My God, you would have thought she killed his cat. I've never seen anyone lose his temper like that, ever. I mean if he really felt someone should be fired, he should have fired the dishwasher. If there's any fault to be had, it should be his. Still, accidents happen, and the situation presented a prime opportunity for a teaching moment instead of a rant that resulted in him firing one of us. He's definitely not hinged properly."

"I hate it that you have to work in conditions like that. Why don't you try to get your old job back?"

"No. I checked. There's not even one job that I want in the list of positions available, and the ones I want require more experience than I have right now. I think I made a mistake changing jobs. Still, I'm going to try to stick it out. The place is getting great reviews, and my working there will be a feather in my cap, if I can survive for a while."

Lindy turned towards Ren who was staring off into space. She waited, knowing Ren was remembering.

Finally Ren looked up and smiled. "I was just..."

"I know. You're sharing about fifteen years of your life with me, and you need to recall it and organize your thoughts before you tell me. It's okay, really. Take your time." Lindy's eyes reflected kindness and understanding.

Ren smiled to acknowledge Lindy's patience. "Brooke thought she had Grandpop wrapped around her finger. The truth was, it was a mutual wrapping. Brooke would have done anything for him. Ren pointed. "See those next three photos on the top row?" When Lindy nodded, Ren continued. "Those were taken in our little apartment. We lived there for my sophomore, junior, and senior year."

Lindy studied the photos before returning to the loveseat. She drew her foot under her and turned towards Ren to wait for her to continue. When Ren didn't start, Lindy asked, "So you stayed in New York through college?"

With a nod, Ren began again. "Yes. We were still trying to figure out where we would live when I finished college. I was feeling very conflicted about leaving the Inn and leaving Jack to help Grandpop with the Inn. You can see how I was feeling there." Ren pointed to a painting depicting her obvious struggle. Her face peered out at them from the canvas, brows furrowed. Floating in the background behind her face were scenes of the Inn, her grandfather, her brother, Brooke, New York, and the island. "It was just before the end of my senior year. Brooke and I were discussing various options available to us when the call from Jack came in. With little preamble he said, 'I have some bad news, sis. Grandpop is in the hospital. He had a stroke. It's serious. The good news is that he's alive.' When I asked Jack if he was going to be okay, he told me the doctors thought so, but that I should come home. He'd made arrangements for a car."

Chapter 14: I Have Some Bad News

Ren called Brooke as soon as she hung up with Jack. Stress was evident in her voice and she was breathing heavily as she repeated the news her brother had given her only moments earlier. "Oh, God, I'm so afraid I'm going to lose him."

Brooke answered without missing a beat. "I want to go home with you, Ren. I belong with you, your brother, and the rest of the family. I'll go see Attila, my boss, and ask for a week off. How can he deny me, if I offer to take it without pay?"

Brooke's boss was unsympathetic. "Your first responsibility is to this restaurant, missy," he shouted, his face already red. "This old guy with the stroke has no relationship to you at all. What do you care if he's sick? Anyway, you're a cook, not a surgeon. Your presence there won't make one bit of difference in if he survives or not." He slammed his hand down on the counter causing a pot with a lid to fall to the floor in a cacophony of sound, making more than one observer of the argument jump in response.

Brooke's face turned red as she held in her anger. She opened her mouth to tell her boss to take his job and shove it, but regained control. Having never been rash in her whole life, she bit her tongue. Brooke had told Ren that she knew she couldn't afford to quit on the spot since she and Ren depended on her income to help pay expenses. Instead, she resorted to outright begging.

"Look, I do understand my responsibilities to the restaurant. However, Ren's grandfather is my family too, even if you don't recognize him as such. I need to make this happen. I'll take the time without pay, and Julie and Pam have offered to help cover my time off." Julie and Pam were two of her best friends who worked the earlier shift. "How can you deny me if my hours are covered? I'm not leaving you hanging."

Three other coworkers standing and listening to the heated exchange stepped forward volunteering to help cover her hours for the week she'd be gone. Brooke's boss, outmaneuvered by Brooke's friends on the staff, reluctantly agreed to allow her to take leave for a week. Brooke turned to tidy her work area, quickly explaining where she was in the prep to her friends.

Her boss started on another harangue. "Consider this your warning. Take even one more day off this year and I'm going to fire your ass. He made a gesture at the rest of the staff. And don't any of you think you're immune."

Brooke's friends hurried her out the door. "Go...don't worry about him, we'll take care of everything. Just go."

Brooke ran to the bus stop, calling Ren from the pay phone as she waited the few minutes for the bus to come. "I'm on my way home. I've got the week off—be there in a few minutes," she said, still out of breath. "Throw something I can wear into a bag for me, please."

✳✳✳

Ren sighed a deep breath. "Grandpop's stroke turned out to be a blessing in disguise in the end because it helped Brooke and me decide what our future together would be. When I got the call from Jack, it wasn't without difficulty that Brooke got time off from work for the week so she could go with me to see Grandpop. Her boss said some horrible things and she told me later that as she sat waiting for the bus to take her home to our apartment, she'd made the decision to actively seek another job when she got back. She said that one thing that became solidified for her after her argument with her boss, was that family should be the first priority in life."

"As we rode in the limo Jack hired for our trip back to the island, we talked quietly about Brooke's work situation. She had been so focused on telling me about the horrible experience with her boss that she hadn't even looked at the car. During a pause in the conversation, Brooke looked around at the fancy leather seats, mini bar, and tinted window separating us from the driver and said to me, 'Ren, look at this car. It's really nice. Remember when we went to the hotel to spend our first weekend together and I told you I didn't want to be a kept woman? I think I might have changed my mind.' She gestured around the limo and added, 'I could definitely get used to this.' I knew by the smile on her face that she was joking and was trying to lighten the mood."

"We arrived at the hospital a few minutes before visiting hours ended. Jack met us in the waiting room where we learned that they had moved Grandpop out of critical care into a step down unit, and that he was doing much better."

Ren looked up at the picture of her grandfather. The nurse told us we could visit but cautioned us not to stay too long. When we entered the room, I kissed my grandfather on the cheek and said, 'Look, I brought Brooke with me.'"

"He responded, 'Thank goodness, someone who can cook. At least they won't be able to starve me to death in here.' Brooke promised to bring him something nourishing if he'd not give the nurses a hard time."

"All too soon, the week passed and we had to return to the city. I told Jack I'd be home in a few weeks, after graduation, to help out at least for the summer. Jack knew that Brooke and I were struggling with our plans for the future. He assured me that we had many options. We could sell the Inn, close it temporarily, or keep it open with an Innkeeper. Many different choices, none of which required me to return to the Inn. I appreciated that he gave me options. As much as he hoped I would make the decision to come home, he wanted me to know it was okay if I decided not to return to the island to live. He didn't want me to come because I felt an obligation, only if I really wanted to be there."

"In the car on the way home I confessed my struggle about what to do. Brooke told me that despite the fuss she made about not wanting to be a 'kept woman' when we first got together, she would be willing to quit her job and come home with me for the summer to help with Grandpop. We agreed to that plan deciding that, over the summer, we would come to a conclusion about what we wanted to do in the future, either stay on the island or return to the city. We knew that the one thing we were sure about was that being together was the most important thing, no matter where it was."

Lindy interjected, "Interesting. So, Brooke gave up her career in the city to come home with you?"

"Technically, yes. However, the way it all turned out, everything worked out in her favor. We agreed that Brooke would be hired as chef for the Inn, and that the current cook would be engaged solely to be a companion for Grandpop. So she ended up running her own kitchen sooner than she'd expected by making the sacrifice to move out of the city and agreeing to come home for at least the summer. She was happy with her decision. She told me that her priorities had changed over the past three years. She said that she finally understood what was truly important in life—that no doubt, work was important, but only as a means to an end. She told me that her first priority would be me, then and always, and that as long as we were together, nothing else was important."

"So what happed next? I assume you both ended up here at the Inn?

Chapter 15: She's A Keeper, You Know

Ren shifted in her seat, took the final swig of her sherry and turned to face Lindy more directly. "I still had a few weeks of college, and they passed quickly. Brooke gave her notice, left work, and packed up our apartment while I finished my final requirements for graduation. Grandpop was still in rehab and was unable to attend my graduation ceremony. Risking being away for a day, Jack chartered a private plane and flew down to New York for the ceremony. Before we flew home, Brooke and I loaded the things we needed more immediately onto the plane. We'd already arranged to have the items we couldn't transport with us shipped back to the Inn."

"It took almost no time for everything to fall into place. The cook, who was getting along in years, actually welcomed the change in her assignment to helping Grandpop saying 'It's like being paid to have fun," She and my grandfather got along famously together as they passed the days playing cards and games, or talking with the guests at the Inn."

"So did you tell your grandfather about your relationship with Brooke?"

Ren felt a blush color her face and smiled at the recollection.

At first, Brooke and Ren were concerned they wouldn't be able to sleep together. Having Brooke in the room adjoining Ren's bedroom allowed them to be together overnight. After the first few nights of worrying about being discovered in bed together they finally relaxed. Because Brooke had to get up before everyone else anyway, the two lovers figured that they'd never be caught in bed together by anyone.

By the time Halloween arrived, Grandpop was doing much better and was once again functioning independently, although a bit more slowly than he had before the stroke. The former cook, now Grandpop's personal assistant, informed the family that she wanted to retire so she could spend some time with her sister who was having severe health issues of her own. With her hand on Grandpop's shoulder she added, "If he was honest, he'd admit he doesn't need me any more."

"I'm not sure about that," he replied, eyes twinkling in jest. "Who am I going to beat at gin?"

Ren and Brooke began to discuss what they wanted to do over the winter when there would be fewer guests. They agreed that Grandpop should not be alone and that they were the logical ones to stay with him.

A few days later, on the porch with her grandfather, Ren was making a sketch of Brooke who was standing on the beach below looking out at the ocean. Grandpop stood up and came closer to where Ren was working to admire her work. He put his hand on her shoulder adding a tender squeeze. "She's a keeper, you know, and she loves you very much."

Ren looked up from her drawing to see her grandfather smiling down at her with a look of love on his face. Not sure what to say, her eyes welled with tears and she settled for, "I know. I love her, too."

He bent and kissed her on the forehead. "I love you both, honey."

"Thank you, Grandpop," she replied simply. "We both love you too, very much."'

He said a few more words to her then simply squeezed her shoulder. "I think I'm going to go have a little sherry. I'll see you later, dear." He turned and left Ren with her mouth still open.

The second that Ren could get Brooke alone she whispered, "He knows."

"Knows what?"

Ren shrugged, "You know, about us."

"What are you talking about?"

Ren quickly told her lover about her conversation with her grandfather. "He says you're a keeper. I'm afraid I have to agree with him."

"So, that's it?"

"I guess so."

"Wow! You've been worried all your life about what he would think. Then he figures it out on his own, tells you he knows and that's it...'I guess so.' I mean what happened after that."

"I don't know. I mean my stomach dropped to my toes and I guess I must have looked a bit weak in the knees or something. He put his hand on my shoulder and gave me a squeeze after he kissed me on my forehead. Oh yeah, he said something about being happy is so important in this life. I couldn't even say anything. My mouth was so dry I thought someone must have glued my tongue to the roof of my mouth with some sort of epoxy. All I could manage to do by way of a response was to nod my head."

"So that was it?"

Ren nodded her head

Brooke moaned. "Good. I'm not at all sure I can stand to hear too much more." She looked at her partner. "There is more, isn't there?"

Ren turned bright red. "Oh yeah, there's more. He told me it wasn't what he would choose for me because..."

Brooke's hand went to her chest as though she could keep her heart from pounding its way out by applying pressure there.

Ren finished her statement, not sure if she should laugh. "...Because he always wanted me to give him great-grandchildren."

"Oh God." Brooke rolled her eyes heavenward a quiet moan escaping clenched lips. "What did you say?"

"Well, I was ready to get out of there, before I hyperventilated or something. I told him I'd mention that to you. Then he said he needed some sherry and he'd catch up with me later."

"You know, I've never been ashamed of being a lesbian, even though I've never been one to shout it from the rooftops. Still, I'm afraid to see Grandpop now for fear that I'll die of embarrassment."

"I know. Trust me, just the first time will be the worst. Actually, I'm relieved that he figured out our relationship for himself and appeared to be supportive of it." She was sure it helped that he loved Brooke, too. Still, it amazed her that someone from his generation would understand.

While they were standing there, Grandpop came around the corner and with twinkling eyes he asked, "So, you two finished talking about me yet?" Without acknowledging their bright red faces in any way he continued, "If you are, Brooke, I need to talk to you about a booking we just got in. One of these folks has an allergy to garlic. I told her that we'd call her back. Are you available now?"

Ren summarized what happened for Lindy. "I can't help myself. I still blush whenever I think about that day."

Lindy replied. "I can imagine. If I'd been in your shoes, I think I'd want a hole to open up and swallow me. Still, you were lucky, weren't you, that he and your brother were so accepting of you and Brooke?"

"Yes, I think so. So many gays' and lesbians' families reject them. I was lucky because my experience was different. Everyone loved Brooke."

Chapter 16: I've Finally Met Her

"Brooke fit in so perfectly here at the Inn. Time passed without our even recognizing it. At the end of each season when the Inn closed to customers, Brooke made improvements to the kitchen. Look there," Ren pointed. "That's a picture of the kitchen when she first came to the island."

"Amazing. It's so different from what's here now."

"Yes, she enjoyed creating a functional workspace for herself and her assistant. Brooke loved the freedom that running the kitchen on her own provided her. She was proud that under her guidance, the expansion of the dining options to include locals from off island who were not guests at the Inn increased our profit. She felt successful."

"Although Jack was still involved in the business of the Inn, he began taking more of an advisory role rather than an active role in the day-to-day management. We were able to handle everything without his help, so he gladly stepped back to allow us to take over. To Brooke and me, the change occurred gradually. At first, we began to notice that Jack was less available in general and was rarely attending the weekend dinners. When we asked him what was going on with him, he replied simply, 'I've finally met her.' His ear-to-ear grin told me that Jack had fallen in love at last."

Lindy stood to look at Jack and Marie's wedding photo. "Obviously, that's their wedding picture, there. Ren, there's a picture of a group of people next to it. Who are they?"

Tears welled in Ren's eyes. She blinked them away and continued her story. "In the spring of 1993, Grandpop had a fatal stroke. It seemed like half the town turned out for the service. Ren stood and pointed to the people as she named them in the photo. Our friends, Mallory, Piper, Carol, and Nancy made the trip up to attend. Our local friends Joey, Ben, Penny, and Peg also supported us through the difficult time."

They returned to the loveseat and Ren continued. "Over that next year, my trust fund reverted to my control. We expanded the restaurant and I bought in as a silent partner in Jack's marina. We opened the restaurant to the public, on a limited basis, and were lucky in that it was well received. The restaurant flourished."

In January 1994, Marie and Jack were busy with plans for their wedding. They arranged to have a small marriage ceremony at the Inn on February first. Brooke and I were thrilled for Jack and Marie, still we couldn't help but feel sad that we couldn't get married."

"Hmm. I never thought about that before. I mean, of course marriage for gay couples is in the news, even though I never knew anyone it impacted before. Couldn't you have had a commitment ceremony?"

"We could have. But it isn't marriage. It's different. Still, I'm sorry in a way we never did that. Brooke was willing. We just never seemed to get around to doing it because we were so busy. She said, 'It's never too late to celebrate us as a couple. I'm thankful every day I'm alive that you didn't let me get away,' and then she kissed me."

Ren and Lindy laughed together. "I love her sense of humor," Lindy said, a smile still tugging her lips.

"Yes. She was serious about work and any number of other things, but she had a way about her that made me laugh, often at the most inappropriate times."

"You going to tell me about that?"

"I don't think so. It's not G-rated." Ren stood up. "I could use a cup of cocoa, how about you?"

"Okay. I'll make it. I'll meet you in the library in a few minutes."

Ren was glad for the break. The next part of her story would be the hardest for her. She headed for the library, her mind racing.

Chapter 17: I'm So Happy Sometimes It Scares Me

When Lindy returned to the library with the cocoa, Ren told her the whole story, holding back nothing. In some parts they laughed together, and in others they cried as evidenced by the piles of tissues on the table next to each of them. Several times, during the most difficult part, Lindy reached across and held Ren's hand to encourage her to push through.

In April 1998, just before the Inn was scheduled to open for the season, Brooke and Ren were reviewing the restaurant reservations for the weekend. "We're fully booked and even have a waiting list. I'm having to turn people away, especially when the Inn is open."

The Inn and restaurant together were turning a healthy profit thanks in large part to Brooke's growing reputation as a chef.

Ren painted in her spare time. She took some classes through the local college and began experimenting with different techniques, even learning to draw and illustrate using the computer. When the Chamber of Commerce decided to put out a brochure to increase tourism, Ren volunteered to do the illustrations for them utilizing her newly acquired computer skills.

"We're really lucky, you know? It wasn't the path I expected, although I've realized my dream of running my own restaurant long before I ever anticipated I would."

"I know. Could we have it any better? We get to live here on the island. My artwork is doing well in the New York gallery as well as here, in the local galleries. Jack's marina, is doing great. Can you imagine one thing that would make us happier?"

The 'one thing' occurred in October, when Jack and Marie happily announced that they were expecting. In the spring of 2000, late in April, Marie gave birth to a little girl they named Laura. When they asked Brooke and Ren to be godmothers, their joy could hardly be contained. The women doted on Laura, babysitting every chance they got.

It was after one of their visits from Laura and her parents, the summer after Laura's birth, that Brooke and Ren began talking about whether they wanted a child of their own. In bed, curled against each other, talking about the joy Laura brought to their lives, neither was completely sure if they had room in their lives for a baby just then. "We're so busy right now," Ren said. "Children take up a lot of time. I guess we could always hire more help. The question is…do we want what we have now to change?"

"I'm not sure," said Brooke, "Although, if we are going to do it, we need to make a decision soon. I'm already thirty-five and you're thirty-three. Our window of opportunity is shrinking. Tick tock."

"We have time, at least two or three years. Let's enjoy Laura for now, and both think about having our own. It's a big decision and we need to be sure." She paused, and with a devilish wink she said, "The easiest thing for us would be to persuade my brother and sister-in-law to have another one."

Brooke laughed aloud. Still smiling, Brooke shook her head at Ren's outrageous comment. "You are too funny. I love you so very much."

Ren nodded, reached out to run her hand up Brooke's side, across her breast, and up to her cheek. "I love you, too. You are my life. You know that, right?"

"Yes, and you are mine," responded Brooke as she leaned in to kiss Ren. "I'm so happy, sometimes it scares me."

"Don't even think that." Their bodies melded together. Ren kissed her way down Brooke's body stopping along the way to nibble here or gently bite there, eventually centering herself between Brooke's legs. She never grew tired of making love to Brooke, treasuring how responsive Brooke was to her every touch.

"Oh, God, yes, that's it. Don't stop." Brooke arched her body harder against her lover's mouth, and a few seconds later, gasping for air, she fell back onto the bed.

When Brooke moaned her release, Ren slid up her lover's body to place a kiss on her lips.

"Umm." Brooke murmured, slowly recovering from her orgasm. "My turn." She kissed and gently bit Ren's neck, stopping long enough to inhale the scent of the woman she loved before she teased Ren's ear with her tongue and worked her way down Ren's neck and chest to stimulate her nipple into erection. A slow path of kisses followed the course of her hand down Ren's body, as she touched and kissed sensitive areas and raised goose bumps along the way. She teased the damp curls between Ren's legs then explored the swollen pink lips of her center with her tongue before entering her with her fingers. It didn't take long for Ren's movements to become frantic as Brooke stroked inside while she stimulated her lover's clitoris. Ren, inhaled shuddering breaths of air, tightened around Brooke's fingers, rising to meet each stroke until she collapsed in surrender to Brooke's loving. The touch of Ren's hand on Brooke's stilled her. She remained inside her lover until she felt the spasms stop. As was her habit, Ren pulled Brooke's hand up and tucked it around her waist indicating she was ready to cuddle.

"That was nice." Brooke was on her back with Ren wrapped in her arms. They snuggled together, a mixture of arms and legs. "You always know what I need."

Ren leaned back to smile at her partner. "You taught me well."

"True." Brooke laughed. "No, seriously. It amazes me that after all these years together, making love with you is still as exciting and satisfying as it was in the beginning. I couldn't love you more even if I tried."

"Yes, we're so blessed. Our lives are perfect. I can't think of one thing that I would change given the opportunity. We have each other, loving families, everything we ever could need or want. It scares me sometimes. What would I ever do without you?" Ren pulled Brooke tighter.

"I know what you mean...it's a scary thought. Let's not worry about that, because there's no chance of getting rid of me now. You're stuck with me."

Ren kissed her lover awakening renewed excitement. They made love again to fend off the frightening thoughts.

***

During the height of their busy season in July 2001, Brooke was finishing the desserts she was serving that evening for dinner. Ren entered the kitchen, having just returned from a trip to the marina for the mail. She placed the sack on the counter and began sorting through it.

"You've got to move that stuff, hon. I need that counter."

"Okay. Hey, looks like you got a wedding invitation, or an invitation to something. Look." Ren waved the envelope in Brooke's general direction.

"Open it. Who's it from?"

Ren slit the envelope with her finger, knowing Brooke would throttle her if she used one of her precious knives. "Julie. It says they're getting married near her parents' home in Pennsylvania. You haven't seen your friends in...I don't know, forever. You should go."

"Nah. Not without you, and we can't both be away while the Inn is open."

"I can stay here. You should take a trip down to see your parents on the way, and attend the wedding. You'll have fun. I can hold the fort here."

Although Brooke protested, Ren was able to assure, then reassure, Brooke that they had sufficient time to plan for her absence. "If you'll feel more comfortable, we'll hire extra help for the kitchen. Honest, Hon, we won't starve to death without you here for a few days. Besides, you have a great team in the kitchen and if I know my honey, you will have everything planned down to the last crumb while you're away."

Brooke's friend, Pam, called a few days later to say that she planned to attend the wedding and she hoped Brooke would come too. "Come on Brooke, I haven't seen you in ages. It'll be fun." Pam's enthusiasm was contagious and eventually Brooke surrendered to the pressure and agreed to go. Pam, Julie, and Brooke had worked together for the boss Brooke had nicknamed Attila, after Attila the Hun the barbarian king, because of the bellicose and unwarranted attacks he often launched at his undeserving employees. Although they rarely saw each other in person, they had all remained phone friends after Brooke left New York. "Anyway, I want you to meet my fiancé, Tom. He's a pilot, and he's going to fly us there. You can join us if you don't mind small planes."

"Okay. I'll go to the wedding. It sounds like fun. I think I'll fly there from here because it'll be easier and save some time. Let me check flights." Brooke sent in her acceptance and began to anticipate and plan for the trip.

After looking up their destination, and figuring that the quickest way to get there on her own would be by train, and rental car, Brooke called to accept Pam and Tom's generous offer to fly her there.

On that crisp clear day in September 2001, no one expected the attack on the World Trade Center. Everyone was nervous about the safety of flying after the attacks. Brooke and Ren discussed their relief that Brooke was not planning to fly on a commercial airline. She didn't want to disappoint Julie, but they were concerned about the trip so soon after the attack. When Brooke called Pam, she confessed that she and Tom had been discussing the same topic.

"We've been talking about air safety too," Pam said in an attempt to reassure Brooke. "Tom feels that we'll be fine and shouldn't be worried. After all, how much safer could we be from terrorism than in our own plane. I assure you, Tom checks the plane very carefully before each flight."

Somewhat reassured, Brooke agreed to the plans. "Okay, I'll meet you on Friday morning for the flight out."

Since she'd be in the city, she wanted to spend some time with her family before meeting Pam and Tom on Friday to fly out for the Saturday nuptials. "I guess it's from listening to all those people on television who either didn't get a chance to say goodbye to their loved ones, or who were talking to them on the phone when they died, I feel a need to see my family. From now on, I want to make the effort to see them more often."

"I know what you mean. Those scenes were emotionally draining for everyone. Why don't you ask your parents up for Christmas, if they can get some time off."

On Wednesday morning, Ren and Brooke took the boat over to the marina together, embraced and exchanged a quick kiss before Brooke closed the car door and rolled down the window. "Don't forget to miss me," she admonished.

"Not a chance. Call me when you get there."

Brooke nodded her agreement. With a jaunty wave, she pulled away.

True to her word, Brooke called when she arrived at her parents' home, and again later that night to talk to Ren about mostly nothing, as lovers do. They talked several times over the next two days. Before she got on the plane, Ren called Brooke. "You haven't forgotten that I love you, while I've been away, have you?"

"You know that could never happen. Give yourself a hug from me, and call me when you land. Okay, I'll talk to you in a couple of hours. Have a good flight."

"I love you."

She wanted to hear Brooke giggle, so she responded, "Ditto." They were both laughing when they hung up.

Four hours later, Ren answered the phone, eagerly expecting to hear from Brooke.

"Ms. Madison, I am Julie's father. There is no easy way to tell you this. Tom's plane crashed. No survivors. I'm so very sorry. We don't know why yet. It was windy here, and they suspect that wind shear may have been a factor in the landing."

***

Lindy handed her the box of tissues. "God, I'm a mess," Ren said after she issued a huge sniff and blew her nose.

"It's understandable. You've experienced a great deal of loss in your life. How long has it been since Brooke left you?"

"Today is four years." Ren exhaled an ironic humph. "You think I'm a mess today. You should have seen me after she died. I not only missed her, I felt guilty that it was me who had encouraged, almost insisted that she go to the wedding. She'd been reticent to leave the Inn in season."

Ren exhaled a long breath. "I managed to function through the memorial service in New York, shored up by the presence of my family and friends. Mallory, Piper, Carol, Nancy, Ben, and Joey all attended, along with a number of friends of Brooke's with whom she'd worked and attended school. Following the memorial service in Brooke's family's home church, a core group of close friends, including Brooke's parents and my family, all made the trip back to the island where we scattered Brooke's ashes near the flat rocks at the foot of the path where she and I used to sit and watch the ocean."

Ren sighed again, and Lindy reached for her hand, pulling it into her lap and grasping it in both of her hands.

"Joey and Ben, and Mallory and Piper remained with me through the memorial service in New York, as well as the one that was held here. I don't know how I'd have made it through without them. They never left me alone for one minute. Brooke's parents honored their daughter's request to have her ashes spread here on Sunset Island. We'd talked about our wishes for interment when Grandpop died, agreeing that we didn't want to be able to look out of the windows of the house and see the spot. As a result, we settled on a location where we would sometimes enjoy going to sit together to talk and watch the ocean, on the opposite side of the island."

Ren used her free hand to blot her eyes. "Thank you." Ren gave Lindy a weak smile. "Heard enough? It's a harrowing tale."

"I want to hear everything you're willing to share."

"Okay. Here we go." Ren inhaled a deep breath, met Lindy's eyes and began again. "Brooke's family returned home the following day, my friends had to go back to work, and I went back to Jack's apartment and curled up in my old room. I couldn't bear to be here without her, couldn't bring myself to get out of bed for anything. I cried for two days—not a sobbing cry, just a silent leaking of tears that I couldn't stop. Although still dealing with their own grief, Jack and Marie were so concerned about me that they moved into the marina apartment, along with Laura, so I wouldn't be alone. The apartment was crowded with the four of us there. After a week, they made me get up, shower, and eat something then took me to Marie's house where we all did what we could to support each other. I sometimes forget that they loved her too."

"Yes, but it's not the same kind of love."

Ren shrugged. "Jack had the staff cancel all the restaurant reservations through the end of the year, unsure if we would be keeping the restaurant open without Brooke. Maggie took care of everything here at the Inn."

Ren ran her fingers through her hair and exhaled a deep breath, gathering strength to continue.

"Laura was the only thing that gave me any respite from my grief. I spent hours holding and playing with her. When I couldn't sleep, I'd sit in the rocker in Laura's room to watch her sleep."

Ren looked up to meet Lindy's eyes, encouraged by the empathy they conveyed. "I finally stopped crying. When I did, it was as if the tears that had refused to stop for nearly two weeks had simply drained all the life from me, leaving just a shell. My movements were wooden, my responses nearly monosyllabic. I couldn't bring myself to initiate or participate in idle conversation. At the end of the third week, I decided that I wasn't going to be better if I allowed myself to stay there and wallow. I announced that I was ready to go back home to the island. When Jack questioned me, I told him that I had to go back because I felt too far away from her off the island. I hoped that being here, closer to her, would help me feel less hollow."

"It took several months until I eventually began to be more functional. I was able to do my job, could be caring, patient, and helpful when dealing with the daily problems inherent to running the Inn, but I'd lost my interest in my art."

"In private, I mourned with my mind, heart, and spirit. When I was alone, I cried until there were no more tears left to cry. It was just impossible for me to process that such a senseless accident had taken the woman I loved from me. I saw Jack, Marie, and Laura frequently, often babysitting for them when they had an obligation or wanted an evening out. Our first Christmas celebration took place at Jack and Marie's house because I couldn't bear to do it at the island house. It was a somber celebration for all of us with everyone missing Brooke. Only Laura demonstrated the joy of the holiday.

In January 2002, I tried to go back to my art, something that had always brought me joy before. I began to paint dark brooding paintings of the sea and of Brooke. No matter what I did, peace eluded me. The thing that troubled me most was that I could no longer remember how Brooke felt or how she smelled. It was horrible that Brooke was gone and worse still that the things I treasured about her were disappearing from my life, as well. I must have embraced and smelled Brooke's pillow and clothing so often that I'd extracted every ounce of Brooke's scent from the objects. In the end, the clothing became just empty reminders of Brooke's absence. I packed Brooke's clothes into boxes for donation to charity and sent the few articles of jewelry that Brooke used to wear to her mother."

Now that she'd started talking about her grief to Lindy, the feelings poured from her. The pace of her tale picked up and she pushed on to get rid of the emotions she'd held on to for far too long.

"In April, I began dreaming of Brooke. Sometimes, I would awaken at night swearing I felt Brooke's hands on my body. Other times, especially when I was painting, I would catch a whiff of her scent. Gradually my art took on a less somber tone, and knowing that the responsibilities of the upcoming season were too much for Maggie to handle on her own, I became more involved in the operation of the Inn, resuming my normal duties. Jack and I decided not to reopen the restaurant to the public. We promoted Brooke's assistant, whom she had trained well, to take Brooke's place in the kitchen."

"By May, eight months after Brooke's death, life had returned to what would become the new normal for all of us. Brooke was missed every day. In private, I still grieved and wondered if I'd ever be able to pull myself from the sadness that enveloped me. Through Marie, I met and began a counseling relationship with a therapist. The product of that counseling sits humbly before you today." Ren pretended to tip her cap.

Lindy smiled and rested her hand on Ren's knee.

"When Brooke was gone eighteen months, a local author contacted me looking for someone to illustrate her textbook on rug hooking. She needed someone who could draw pictures for the instructions, as well as take pictures of the finished project. It was right up my alley."

"Here at home, I moved into Grandpop's bedroom and converted my old bedroom into my studio. I treated myself to a new computer, an expensive printer, along with a popular photo editing program and illustration software suite of applications. Mastering the programs through reading and practicing at home proved too daunting a task. I admitted defeat and enrolled at the local college where I took courses to learn the software and began experimenting with using different effects and filters on my photographs. After mastering the drawing program on the computer I began marketing my skills on the Internet. Eventually, with all my responsibilities and activities, I became so busy that I began to heal from my loss mostly because I left myself so little time to think. Not that I forgot Brooke, but at least my heart didn't bleed anymore when I thought of her. I tried to focus on all the good things and happy memories I'd shared with Brooke, and less on the loss."

"To their credit, even when I was the most miserable of companions, my friends never gave up trying to encourage me to join them for social events. My core group, P and P and the guys, often refused to take no for an answer. If I declined their invitation to come over for a movie, they brought the party to me. Mallory and Piper called here every couple of days just to chat, trying to encourage me to become more socially active.

Penny and Peg tried to persuade me to begin to date again, often inviting single women to join us, hoping there would be a spark. I remained steadfastly disinterested. Although I'd really tried, I was simply incapable of letting go of the love I still had for Brooke."

I guess by...umm, around the end of 2003, I was beginning to feel a bit more like my old self. I'd regained my sense of humor, worked hard at my art, and managed the Inn along with Maggie's help. Here at the Inn, we shortened the months we were open to give me more time to work on my art. Jack and Marie came most weekends, bringing with them the light of my life, Laura. Besides reading fairy tales, we share a love of board and card games, and we often had fierce competitions in Chutes and Ladders. The kid plays a cutthroat game, trust me."

Lindy laughed, relieved that Ren seemed to be lightening after telling her the daunting tale of her grief.

"So, that's my sad tale—sad, longwinded and true. I'm learning that telling or, sometimes, even thinking about the past can be cathartic. I actually feel better having shared all of it. Now you know all my secrets and I know none of yours."

"How about we save mine for another day? It's late and we're both tired. It's been an emotional day." Impulsively, Lindy stood, pulled Ren to her feet and gave her a long hug. She pulled back and made eye contact. "Thank you Ren for telling me all of it. I know it wasn't easy. Despite all the pain, you were blessed with a great love. Savor that. Cherish that. It's not something everyone gets to experience—a great love."

"Have you ever been in love, Lindy?"

"In love, perhaps. But never like that." Lindy smiled and touched Ren's cheek with her palm. "I'll see you in the morning."

Lindy Caprini Journal

Today was emotionally draining. I learned so much about Ren and what has made her so sad. I was surprised at how open Ren was tonight as she told me her story. So raw and often in pain, she pushed through and told me anyway. We both cried, and sometimes laughed. By the end of the night, we'd definitely grown closer together. I feel so deeply for her loss. Still I envy that she had such a great love. When I look back on my life, I realize that I've never experienced anything like that. Imagine…she had that with another woman. I had no idea such a thing was possible.

I'd never given any thought to the possibility that Ren was a lesbian. I'm not sure it would have occurred to me if I hadn't seen the painting. I'm glad she told me about the joys of her relationship as well as being willing to share the pain of losing it. Maybe now that I know why she's sad, I'll be able to help keep up her spirits. I love it when she's feeling positive and cheerful. She has a wonderful sense of humor and is a genuinely wonderful companion. I am very drawn to her and like her more than I ever imagined I would.

Chapter 18: How Many Sets Of Eyes Do You Think I Have?

Ren had breakfast ready the next morning when Lindy came out to join her. She softly squeezed Ren's shoulder as she passed by her and took her seat at the counter. "Everything okay this morning?"

"Yes, Thanks. I'm actually feeling pretty good. Are we taking a run this morning?"

"Sure. Let's let breakfast settle. We can do some work and go for a run when we take our break."

The next few weeks found the two women following a now established routine of sitting together in the kitchen to share a light breakfast, followed by a few hours of work, a run--weather permitting--if not, a workout in the gym. After lunch, they'd each retire to their own workspaces. Ren was dependent on Lindy's production to give her material to work on, so sometimes she had to wait between stories. When she had some down time on their project, Ren worked on the drawing that she planned to give Lindy for Christmas. Although Lindy rarely appeared in Ren's studio unannounced, Ren always worked on the drawing with one ear attuned to Lindy's approaching footsteps, so she could quickly hide the piece under her worktable if she heard her coming. The drawing was a very different type of art for her--the kaleidoscope that Lindy gave her shortly after her arrival was the inspiration for the piece.

Ren treasured Lindy's gift and wanted her to have something in return of equal beauty and uniqueness. She also wanted it to have some kind of relationship to the gift Lindy gave her. The center of the canvas featured a drawing of the kaleidoscope. *That drawing was the easy part,* she thought. Surrounding the central picture of the kaleidoscope were six circles of equal proportion containing geometric shapes Ren created using ink and a pen with a thick nib. In each circle were patterns representative of the designs that the kaleidoscope displayed when held up to the light. Ren chose bright colors for the drawing. *This painting has been such a tedious piece that I can guarantee this one is definitely a one of a kind work of art.*

In the evenings, they spent time together, talking, playing cards, or reading. Neither was especially fond of television, although they did watch it selectively. Both enjoyed the news and weather, plus each had a couple of favorite shows.

Over several weeks, Ren did a number of sketches and drawings of Lindy's eyes and other individual features. She knew how the little furrow developed between her brows when she was concentrating and how that expression changed ever so slightly with the barely perceptible arch of her right eyebrow when she was even slightly dubious about what was being said. She was aware of how just the corners of her mouth turned up when she was pleased with herself or if she won a point in a discussion. It wasn't exactly what she would describe as a self-satisfied grin, but almost. She loved how her eyes crinkled and her lips separated into a full smile when she was happy to see someone. When she spoke of people she loved, her eyes softened and she always brushed her hair back from her forehead then drew her palm back around her ear, across her jaw and to her chin. It was almost as if whomever she was speaking about was giving her a caress. Once Ren could draw the eyes, and convey their expressions, the bodies always came easy.

"Lindy, I think it's finally time," Ren proclaimed one night as they sat in front of the fire. Ren's sketchbook was on her lap and she had been idly doodling in it for over an hour.

"Time for what?"

"Time for you to pose for me."

"Well, it's about time. How many sets of eyes do you think I have? You've been drawing my eyes forever."

Both eyebrows up, Ren knew Lindy was teasing her. "Only one pair but lovely ones."

"I wasn't fishing for a compliment. Thank you anyway."

"Besides, I've drawn your mouth too, and a pretty one it is too." A wicked grin and raised eyebrow accompanied her observation.

"Okay. Knock it off! What do I have to do? I do get to keep my clothes on, don't I?"

It did get her thinking even though she laughed at the question. Lindy had a very playful side to her personality that Ren really enjoyed and responded to with equal lightheartedness. "Whatever makes you most comfortable. I do have a bear skin rug around here somewhere, if you're ready to go Full Monty."

"No, that's not what I agreed to and anyway, with this weather, you'd need to spend another month learning how to draw goose bumps if you made me pose without clothes. Ask me again in July." She winked at Ren before she giggled.

"Well, that was mean, mean, mean. I didn't know you had it in you to be so cruel." Ren grinned broadly to let Lindy know she, too, was joking. She made a mental note to ask her again when the temperatures warmed up.

"You have no idea," she said with an evil grin. "I can be totally heartless."

"Right, I bet."

"Okay. What do I have to do? When do we start? Posing, I mean, not my being ruthless." Lindy's giggle made Ren smile.

"No time like the present. Why don't you get a book? Since I've watched you sitting here for some time now engrossed in your research or just reading your trashy romance novels for pleasure, I think that's the first sketch I'd like to do."

Once Lindy settled, Ren threw another log on the fire before she adjusted the light to get just the right effect, the perfect play between light and shadow that she wanted. "Are you comfortable?"

"Yes." After a few minutes of silence, Lindy asked, "Can I talk or do I really have to read?"

"What do you want to talk about?"

"Truth is, I don't want to talk. I want you to talk. I have a question to ask you."

"A question?"

"Yes, about dating."

Ren stopped sketching and looked up. "Go ahead."

"Haven't you had a desire to try to meet anyone else?"

"Why?"

Lindy started to turn toward Ren. "Ah ah ah," Ren admonished with a wagging finger. "Talking is okay...moving is not part of our deal."

Lindy resumed her original position. "Why? Well, it's simple really, because Brooke was obviously very loved by you and important to you, besides living here alone is very isolating. You had such a wonderful relationship before. Don't you want that again?" She tried unsuccessfully to get a peek at Ren's face out of the corner of her eye.

Lindy waited. She heard Ren exhale a deep breath before she heard the scratch on the paper as Ren started to sketch again. "Hmm." There was another deep breath. "Well, I would hope one day that I might. I tried dating a woman last year...unfortunately it didn't take. I was an abysmal failure at it. Honestly, I wasn't ready. Thankfully, neither was she."

"Why do you say you were a failure?"

"There was no passion in our relationship even though she was a lovely person. Do you know what I mean?"

Lindy nodded. "Sadly, I have to admit that I do."

Ren didn't comment on Lindy's reply. "I mean I liked her, but for some reason I just wasn't ready or willing to open myself to her. I never thought about a future with her. Rarely, in fact, did I think beyond our next date. In fairness, her head was somewhere else, too, although I take most of the responsibility."

When Lindy no longer heard Ren's sketching, she was able to turn a little to catch Ren's far away expression.

"You know how they say make up sex is the most passionate? I don't know about that. Brooke and I rarely ever even disagreed. And it only took one look from her to make me want her...crave her touch. Sounds corny, I know, but it was true. After she died, I used to dream of her. Sometimes I'd awaken, positive that I felt her hands on me, only to discover once again that she wasn't there. I'd have to live through the realization that she was dead, all over again." Ren stood up to get a tissue. She wiped away a tear, blew her nose, and paused when she realized how much she was revealing of her intimate thoughts. It felt okay though, to share this with Lindy.

"So, as it turned out, we were both still not over our former partners. She went back to her previous partner and we parted as friends. Obviously, I couldn't do that. So, that brings us up to current time."

Ren went back to sketching. "Ok, I'm done for tonight."

Lindy stood and crossed the few feet to where Ren was sitting near the fire. "Oh, Ren, it's lovely. You've flattered me."

"You're a beautiful woman, Lindy...inside and out. I just draw what I see."

Lindy reached out and wrapped her arms around Ren, pulling her into a hug. "Thank you for the beautiful drawing, and also for sharing all those difficult feelings," she whispered.

Ren pulled away and took Lindy's face into her hands. "No, I really should thank you." Dropping her hands, she smiled at Lindy "I know it's hard to believe from the weeping I do that it feels good telling you about her, our beginning, and our life together. I know it might not make sense to you, yet somehow all that good stuff lessens the pain of the one bad thing that happened to us."

"Good. You were obviously blessed with someone and something very special. No wonder you've grieved so hard for her loss. It's completely understandable."

"Lindy, you've been a very good friend to me, and I think your presence here has helped me."

Lindy arched both eyebrows, "Does that mean I have to leave now?"

Not paying attention to the clue indicating that Lindy was teasing her and feeling upset that she'd offended Lindy, she replied, "What do you mean? No, of course you don't have to leave. Why would you say such a thing?"

"Well, you first you said, '*You've been*' a very good friend to me...that could be interpreted to mean that our friendship is over, not you '*are*' a very good friend to me, like our friendship will continue to exist. After that, you said that my presence here '*helped*', using past tense, as if we were done. Don't forget, my dear, that you have a contract and I'm holding you to it."

It took a moment, for Ren to finally realize that Lindy was pulling her leg to get her to brighten up. "Oh, duh!" Ren laughed. "You really had me going there for a minute," she said patting her heart with her hand. "I thought you were a literature professor not a linguistics teacher. You certainly achieved your goal of not allowing me to wallow in my own self-pity, by scaring the crap out of me."

Lindy laughed. "Come on, let's raid the fridge. I've worked up an appetite with all that linguistic mumbo jumbo and I think you need ice cream, preferably chocolate ice cream, the soother of all souls."

"Okay, with one condition."

"Oh, come on. You can't hold me a conditional hostage over ice cream."

Ren just smiled and folded her arms across her chest.

"Ooohkaaaay," Lindy sighed feigning surrender. "What's the condition?"

"Next time, it's your life story including all the gory details about your love life, too. I'm eager to know how a catch like you is still single."

"Oh, that's easy, nobody wants me because I don't shave my armpits." She turned abruptly and made a dash for the kitchen. Ren's laughter trailed behind her as Ren chased her down the hallway.

As they sat at the counter together eating the chocolate-chocolate chip ice cream, Ren paused with the spoon half way to her lips. "So, tell me, do you braid it?"

"Ah, for me to know and you to find out."

LINDY CAPRINI JOURNAL

I posed for Ren this evening—it was a first for me. Whenever she is idle she drags out one of the many sketchpads she keeps in practically every room of the house. It's a strange feeling to see my own eyes staring back at me from the pages of the books she leaves open...just my eyes, not my face or body, just my eyes. Well, she did say she's drawn my lips too. I guess she must really believe that saying that eyes are the windows to the soul thing.

Tonight she spoke of passion—specifically the passion she felt for, and received from, her lover. It seems she dated only once since Brooke's death. She didn't talk too much about it, just said that she was an abysmal failure at the relationship because she wasn't ready. I can understand that. She seems, just now, to be starting to really deal with how much she's lost, balancing it out with how much she actually had. Which of us has been most blessed—she who had a great love filled with passion, or me who has never felt those emotions? Still, I see her enormous pain over the loss. She makes me want to wrap her in my arms and protect her from any more hurt.

Ren is so open when she answers a question or divulges a secret. She's the most honest person about her feelings I've ever met. Sharing her pain with me has, I think, helped her.

She's had these feelings bottled up for years now, just festering. As the feelings pour forth, she seems to be measurably growing lighter. She has a wicked streak, and can be a big tease.

Posing for Ren was an interesting experience. She is so intense when she sketches. I felt like I was under a radar beam of scrutiny as she focused her eyes on me. It evoked feelings of insecurity at first, until I saw the drawing. I was amazed at the beauty she sees when she looks at me. She captured a soft expression on my face. Was that the expression I was showing? How much of what she sees is influenced by how she feels about the subject? I thought I'd feel like a piece of fruit or some other inanimate object when she started to draw me. When she showed me the sketch, it felt like collaboration, an intimacy of sorts, between us. I actually kind of enjoyed it, although I'm not about to tell her that.

Chapter 19: I Could Be Naked Too

As the Christmas holiday approached, Ren dragged out the Christmas decorations. When they had guests through the Christmas season, the Inn was always beautifully dressed for the occasion. Now that it was just the two of them, Ren didn't feel the need to go overboard, but she did want to decorate the library. She loved the smell of the fresh cut spruce tree she set up in the corner of the room. Together she and Lindy decorated the tree and each placed their present for the other under it.

When Ren reached for her gift and gave it a shake, Lindy protested. "Hey! No fair."

"So when do we get to open them?"

"How about Christmas Eve? We're spending Christmas Day with your brother and his family, so let's do our celebration the night before."

Together they shopped for presents for Jack, Marie, and Laura. They chipped in to buy Laura *The Encyclopedia of Folk and Fairy Tales From Around the World.*

When Christmas Eve arrived, Ren asked Lindy, over breakfast, "What time do we get to open the presents?"

"How about midnight?"

"How about now? It is Christmas Eve, after all."

"No, it's not time yet. We haven't even finished breakfast. You're like a kid, Ren. You just can't wait to get into those packages."

Ren really wasn't as excited about opening her present as she was about having Lindy open hers. She was very pleased with the results of her labor on Lindy's gift. Ren had completed the kaleidoscope drawing the previous week and made a special trip to the art store where she picked a gold leaf frame that accented the gold tones in her drawing. The result was stunning, if she did say so herself.

Ren asked again, "How about after dinner?"

Finally, Lindy surrendered. "Oh, stop! Okay, after dinner."

They decided to take a walk even though it was cold and blustery. As they walked out the door, Ren started to turn left to go up to the high point. Lindy grabbed her arm and turned Ren to face her. "Don't you think it'll be too windy up there? Let's go this way and visit the flat rocks." Ren knew that the term flat rocks, was a euphemism for Brooke, and she loved Lindy for her thoughtfulness. She wanted to go earlier in the day, but it didn't feel right dragging Lindy there on such a special day.

Ren was satisfied with the short visit because it was just too cold to stay very long. They returned to the house chilled to the bone. Ren made hot chocolate and set the steaming mug in front of Lindy.

"Is it time yet?

Lindy laughed. "You are impossible. It's not even dark yet. Okay, if you insist."

They carried their chocolate to the library where Ren retrieved the packages and handed Lindy hers.

"Okay, you've been so eager all day...go ahead and open it." Lindy smiled and said, "Merry Christmas."

Ren tore the wrapping from the box and opened her gift. The card taped to the outside of the box said, "So you can join me when I read my trashy romance novels, Love Lindy." When she looked into the box to find six lesbian romance novels, she laughed heartily.

"How in the world did you find these?"

"Well, I am a literature professor. Thank God for the Internet...anything is available online."

"Well, thank you very much." Not really thinking about it she said, "I'll lend them to you as I finish them."

Lindy hesitated for a second before accepting the offer. "Okay. I'd be interested in reading them, thank you."

"Okay, now it's your turn."

Lindy could tell from the size and shape of the package that it was a picture or a photo. She wondered if her gift would be an autographed copy of the photos she'd bought the first day she spent in town. Ren had promised to autograph them for her as soon as she knew what she wanted to say. A gasp escaped her lips as she tore the paper from the drawing. "My God! Ren, it's beautiful! It's the kaleidoscope I gave you." She carried it to the table lamp to get better light on it so she could admire the intricate detail of the designs. Checking the back, she found the autograph, *'For my friend, Lindy, who has restored color to my world. Thank you for always listening and understanding.'* She set the picture down carefully before wiping the tears from her eyes.

Ren came to her and hugged her. "Come on, it wasn't supposed to make you cry. It was supposed to make you happy."

Lindy sniffed, "I am happy. What makes you think I'm not happy?"

They both laughed and exchanged a long hug. "Come on, Ren...help me hang it, please. I want it in the bedroom, where I can see it every morning when I wake up."

With the picture hung to Lindy's satisfaction and admired for way too long in Ren's estimation, she took Lindy by the hand pulling her toward the doorway. "There's plenty of time to admire it later. You don't want to wear it out." She added a grin that made Lindy laugh. "Let's go read. I can't wait to get into one of the books you gave me. It's been a long time since I read one of those lesbian romance novels. I still can't believe you ordered them."

They spent the rest of the evening reading their 'trashy novels' together. When Lindy turned in, Ren was still reading. Lindy was surprised, when she came out for breakfast on Christmas morning, to find the book Ren was reading the night before with a note tucked into it. The note read, *'Stayed up till 1:30 to finish it. I enjoyed it a lot, thank you again. When you finish it, it might be fun to talk about it, if you'd like. If I'm not up by 7:00, please wake me so we don't miss the munchkin opening her presents.'*

It was already ten after. Lindy knocked on Ren's bedroom door. She waited for a response. When she didn't hear anything, she considered the possibility that maybe Ren was in the shower, although she didn't hear it running. Feeling a little awkward, she entered the bedroom. Ren was sprawled in the middle of the bed with the sheet and comforter tucked tightly under her chin. "Ren?" She called.

When there was still no response, Lindy approached the bed. *Ren is beautiful*, she thought. She resisted reaching out to touch her cheek. Ren had a look of peace on her face that was rarely present when she was awake. *At least she has good dreams.*

"You need to get up if you want to see Laura open her presents. We're already late. Come on, I'm not calling you again." As Ren's eyes opened, Lindy said, "Up and at 'em' woman." With that, she grabbed the covers and flipped them back hoping the blast of cool air would encourage the sleepy Ren from bed. Lindy didn't know who was more shocked...she or Ren, who was completely nude. "Oh, my God, Ren, I'm sorry." Quickly, Lindy turned and hurried from the room but not before her eyes betrayed her by sweeping the length of Ren's naked body.

Ren got up, took her shower, and quickly dressed. She found Lindy in her office. She tapped on the open door and entered. Lindy was already apologizing. "I'm so embarrassed I did that to you. I don't know what I was thinking, I'm so sorry."

"Lindy, it's not a big deal to me. Honest." Ren approached, sat down next to Lindy, and took her hand into her own. Ren teased Lindy, hoping that humor would restore Lindy's equilibrium. "I knew it was a mistake to leave that lesbian romance for you. It was definitely hot. However, I had no idea it would affect you like that. Next time, instead of ripping off my covers, you could just come in, lie down, and ask." She waited for Lindy to look up and meet her eyes. When she did, they both laughed.

"I'm so sorry and so embarrassed."

"Embarrassed? No I think I was the one who was umm...bare assed." She chuckled. "Oh, excuse me. You said embarrassed--sorry, I must not have heard you correctly."

"Oh, it's too early in the morning for your bad jokes. This is to never be mentioned again—not to me nor anyone else. Clear?"

"What's it worth to you?"

"Anything."

"Anything? Really?"

"Word of honor. Name your price."

Ren's eyebrow arched. "Okay. You on a bear skin rug. You have to pose for me. You saw me naked. Now I want to have the same pleasure of drawing you naked."

"I saw you for a few seconds and there is no visual record of it."

"I'll take a picture for you. No, better yet, if that's what it'll take, you can go into the studio and look at the wall where you'll find a nude sketch I did of myself when I was in college. You can have it."

Shaking her head, Lindy groaned.

"You said 'anything'...then you gave your word of honor...Remember?"

"Okay, but you can't show my face."

Ren laughed. "You're going to be naked, and you don't want me to draw your face."

"Exactly. I'm a respectable woman. Lord knows where the picture could show up."

"I could be naked too, if it would make you more comfortable."

Lindy covered her red face with her hands and dropped her head to her desk. "Oh sure," she mumbled, "can't you tell that seeing you naked isn't something that makes me more comfortable?"

"Come on, I won't tease you anymore." She pulled Lindy to her feet and gave her a quick hug. "Let's go, your audience waits. The munchkin will be tapping all ten toes."

Lindy knew she was referring to Laura who always expected Lindy to tell her a new and different story every time she saw her.

They arrived a little late. "What held you up," asked Jack when Lindy and Ren came through the door loaded with packages.

"Ask Lindy," Ren said. She laughed when Lindy curled her lip then stuck out her tongue.

When Lindy replied, "Ren had an alarm clock malfunction," Ren laughed so hard she nearly choked.

"What's so funny?" Marie wanted to know why they were laughing.

"Beats me...these two are making no sense at all." Jack answered.

"Hey, Munchkin! I hear Santa came to see you. I think he got confused though. He left some packages under our tree for you, too." Ren started to distribute gifts for her niece.

Everyone enjoyed spending the holiday together. When Ren and Lindy returned to the island that evening, Ren curled up on the chair near the fire with the second book from the box Lindy gave her for Christmas. She was surprised when Lindy showed up and took the remaining chair and opened the lesbian romance that Ren had finished earlier that morning. Ren was ready to ask Lindy if she thought it would be necessary to lock her door tonight, until she saw the defiant glare Lindy sent in her direction that caused her to bite her tongue to stop herself from teasing.

LINDY CAPRINI JOURNAL

What an embarrassing experience this morning. Ren hadn't appeared by the appointed time, so I went in to rouse her. When I stripped back the blankets, I discovered she sleeps au natural. Worst part about it was that I knew I should look away...I just couldn't make myself do it. Even though I apologized numerous times, at the end of our discussion she'd succeeded in what I called 'bribing' me into posing nude for her. She used the terms 'convincing' and 'persuading.' Yes, that's right—nude. In exchange, I get a nude self-portrait Ren painted in college.

She teased me all day. I have to admit that I like it when she's playful and light hearted. She seemed to really be having fun with this. I enjoyed it when I posed for her before—it was somehow a very intimate experience, and she finds beauty in my face that I don't see. I'm sure that experience will pale in comparison to posing nude for her. Maybe she'll forget about it, or I will. I'm anxious to see this self-portrait she did of herself that I'm getting as my 'payment' for posing. I do like her work, still...nude...

Chapter 20: May I Ask You Something?

Things seemed to have returned to normal by the next morning when they both showed up for breakfast. A cold wet snow was falling. "I guess we'll miss our run this morning," Lindy said.

"Looks like."

"We could use the gym."

Ren pursed her lips as she considered Lindy's suggestion. "I think I'm going to be a lazy bum today and just lie around and finish my book. We've been working hard and we're ahead of schedule. I feel like I need a break. How about you?"

"I agree. I'm ready for a lazy day too. We've worked almost every day since I arrived. We've done something pretty much daily, even most weekends. It feels good to be ahead of schedule, though, doesn't it?"

"Come on, I'll stir up the fire and throw on a couple of extra logs. We can read, and there may be a nap in my future."

After stoking the fire, Ren settled into the chair opposite Lindy. The room was silent except for the turning of pages as they read. Ren wondered what Lindy thought of the lesbian romance she was reading. It was a good book, better than most she'd read previously, and it had three or four very explicit and sexy love scenes in it. She glanced up to watch Lindy as she read. She would finish soon. There were only a few pages left until the end, where the final love scene went on for several pages. Sensing she was being watched Lindy glanced up and met Ren's eyes. *Was Lindy blushing?* Ren wondered as she quickly returned her gaze to her book.

Less than five minutes later Lindy closed the book and placed it on the table between them. Ren waited.

"May I ask you something?"

"Of course."

"In this story, the two women were older and both had been involved with women before, so they knew they wanted each other. They never doubted for a minute exactly who they were or what they wanted despite the fact that they were both involved with other people when they first met although that fact did delay their getting together. I just was wondering though...is it possible to figure it out later in life...you know, that you're a lesbian I mean?"

"It happens every day. People are people and chemistry is chemistry, I guess. I know a female couple, friends for over twenty years. Both were married to men, got divorced at forty-something and began a relationship. They're are now in their sixties and they're still happy today."

"Married?" Lindy's brows furrowed. "Do people just switch teams like that?"

"Nowadays? Yes, sometimes. Although there are still difficulties for women today, in the past it was even more problematic. Times were different, as were expectations. It used to be that women married because that was what was expected of them. The option to remain single, or to be involved with another woman, was accompanied by strong disapproval and censure from society. In general, women didn't work, but if they did, it was often part-time. In addition, their pay wasn't equal to salaries men received and was therefore insufficient to allow them to be independent, to live alone. Another factor to consider is that, in those days, it was common for women to be virgins when they married, with little sexual experience. By the time they recognized they were attracted to women, it was too late. They were already married with two point five kids and few options other than to stay with their husbands. Today, there is a lot more awareness of sexuality, more experimentation before marriage, and as a result, more awareness of one's own sexuality than there used to be and less societal pressure too. Today, I think kids, especially, identify much younger and have a more fluid sexuality. Wouldn't you agree that women are more independent now, with more choices open to them?"

"Ren...how did you know you were a lesbian?"

"I don't know what to tell you exactly, except at some point I just realized I liked girls. I guess the simple answer would be that when I was growing up, I guess I was about twelve or so, all my friends were talking about boys and how wonderful it was kissing them. I didn't think kissing a boy, or even kissing anyone, was anything the least bit interesting until I'd kissed my best friend, Beth. Finally I understood. She was concerned her boyfriend of the moment would think she was inexperienced. Go figure..." Ren chuckled. "So we tried practicing on each other. It's probably how any number of young lesbians finally figure out their true identity. When I kissed her, it finally dawned on me why I wasn't interested in kissing boys. I knew I was in love with her at that moment when our lips met. I waited all through high school for her to see the light, even though she never did." Ren held up the book she was reading. "You might find this one more interesting. It deals with two neighbors, one a lesbian, the other straight and married to an abusive husband."

"You never told her how you felt?"

Ren shook her head. "Nope."

Lindy turned and stared into the fire.

"You know, you owe me that life history." Ren turned towards Lindy. "How about now?"

Lindy shrugged. "Not much to tell. I was born and raised in Pennsylvania, outside of Philly. I lived near so many good universities, that I never went away to school. I always commuted. I had a few steady boyfriends throughout college and just broke up with someone before I moved here. End of story." Lindy paused. "I'm sorry you lost Brooke, yet I envy you what you had with her. I've never had a love like that."

"What about the guy you just broke up with...what happened with him? Why did you break up?"

Lindy debated about how much she wanted to reveal. She felt that Ren had always been open and truthful with her so she felt that she owed her honesty. "I couldn't give him what he deserved from me sexually, and I didn't want him to settle for a life without passion. I think our lack of sexual compatibility would have become a bigger issue in the future if we'd stayed together."

"Maybe you didn't love him."

"I did love him. I sometimes wonder if I was in love with him. I can tell you that I never looked at him the way Brooke was looking at you in that painting in your studio. Although I found him handsome I've never felt that kind of desire." She shrugged. "I don't seem to be wired that way."

Sensing Lindy's reticence to share more, Ren dropped the subject. They continued enjoying their time together until the fire died and they both retired for the night.

The next morning, when Lindy came to the kitchen for breakfast, she noticed that Ren had left the second book on the counter.

Ren said from the doorway, "I feel like a poor host. Normally, by now, you'd have met my friends. With that virus that's doing the rounds, everyone I know has been sick at some point. I know we've gone out alone, and we've seen Jack and Marie. Still we've missed several of the movie nights for one reason or another—weather, people getting sick, whatever. I had lunch with them around Thanksgiving, when you were sick, and that's all. I think it's time we kicked up our heels and had a little fun."

Lindy turned and asked, "What do you mean?"

"Didn't you tell me you brought one slinky black dress with you?"

"I don't know about slinky, though I do have a dressy black dress with me. Why?"

Ren sat at the counter next to Lindy. "I used to date this guy in high school..."

Lindy groaned. "Oh, no, you aren't going to fix me up."

Ren crossed her two index fingers in the shape of a cross and extended them out in front of her. "Heaven forbid!" She laughed. "No nothing like that. On New Year's Eve I usually get together with Joey and his partner Ben and our friends Penny and Peg. How would you feel about joining us? My treat. No date, no fix up—just a group of friends celebrating the New Year together. We'll have dinner first then go dancing."

Lindy had to admit that she was starting to feel a little house bound. It would do both of them good to get out of the house for a dress up night. "Okay, sounds good. Though, I think I need to go to town one day to do some shopping. How dressy should I be? Will a plain black dress do?"

"Why not? Won't a little black dress go anywhere? Anyway, don't worry about it. You don't have to impress anyone." She wiggled her eyebrows. "Except maybe me."

"Yeah, sure. I won't worry about that. You've seen me in the mornings at my worst and still like me."

"That I do. I have to go to town tomorrow. You should probably give your car a good run anyway, maybe head out to the mall so it gets thoroughly warmed up and the battery gets charged up."

"Maybe Marie can join me. I'll give her a call."

Marie couldn't make it, so she gave Lindy the name of the hair salon she used and Lindy immediately called for a hair appointment. She wanted a change and now was as good a time as any to make one.

Lindy knew that the black dress would do, although for this special occasion, she wanted to add to its appeal. She found the perfect jacket-- with sparkles not sequins. It was a deep, forest green, with black accents, and she felt that it would be perfect over her black dress. The cut of the jacket, the sales woman told her, would elongate her torso, making her appear taller. Next on the agenda was her hair appointment. When she left the shop, her shoulder length hair was trimmed to a stylish ear length cut, feathered in the back, which gave added emphasis to her beautiful eyes.

The bell on the back of the door of the marina office sounded as Lindy pushed it open to enter. Ren glanced up then gave a long slow whistle. "Well, look at you." Ren added an appreciative smile. "I love your hair short. You look like a million."

"A million what? I was kind of going for sexy," she laughed. "Did I succeed?"

"Well, I have to say it works for me, and the guys won't count. So, I guess you succeeded. Hmm. Would you like to come home with me?" Ren wiggled her eyebrows.

Lindy laughed. "Might as well." She glanced around the vacant office. "It would appear that yours is the best offer I'll get today."

LINDY CAPRINI JOURNAL

We're going out for New Year's Eve with Ren's friends, so I went shopping and bought a new jacket to go over my 'little black dress.' Oh, and I got my hair cut. I haven't worn my hair short in years and had forgotten how much I like it this length.

Ren asked about my life. It wasn't until I started that I realized how little there is to say about it. I don't mean my professional life. After all I've been successful as a teacher, have good relationships with my students and the other staff members. Personally, I have little to boast of in comparison to Ren's personal achievements. I mean, we're both in our thirties, but her life has been so full and filled with passion. She has passion for her photography, her art, her former lover, this island, and any number of other things.

Although Ren is my size, she seems so much larger when she enters a room. It's not only about that dark haired, blue-eyed beauty of hers, it's just that there is something about her personality that just draws me in and makes me want to hear what she'll say or do. I love the way she can focus so exclusively on her 'subject' and I especially love it when that subject is me.

I watch her mesmerize her niece whenever they get together. Jack and Marie hang on her every word. There's just something about her that makes people attend to what she has to say. I can't speak for others, but when she focuses on me, I feel special. I'd never let her know it for fear of the consequences...I actually like it when she teases me, and it gives me pleasure when she laughs when I tease her in return. It seems that since she told me about Brooke and talked out all those feelings that she's happier, calmer, less taciturn, and there's a lightness to her personality that wasn't there before. She's a joy to be around. I'm looking forward to our 'date' for New Years Eve and to meeting her friends.

Chapter 21: Wonder If She Really Has That Tattoo?

On New Year's Eve, Ren was waiting in the kitchen for Lindy. As Lindy walked down the hallway, she could smell the fresh and soapy scent of Ren's perfume. When Lindy turned the corner and Ren saw her, she uttered the only thing that came to her mind. "Wow! Beautiful, just beautiful."

A quick smile of appreciation for the compliment flashed on Lindy's face. "You're looking quite lovely, yourself," complimented Lindy. Ren was wearing a very dressy, black pants suit made of velvet. She wore a white lace camisole beneath the jacket. They helped each other into their coats and left to join Ren's friends.

They pulled up in front of Joey and Ben's house, parked, walked to the front door, and rang the bell. Joey and Ben answered the door and each greeted the women warmly. After introductions were made, they ushered their guests into their beautifully decorated living room where wine, cheese, and crackers awaited them.

Taking Lindy in tow by the arm, Joey said, "These lovely ladies on the sofa are Peg and Penny whom I lovingly refer to in my own mind as "Peg Of My Heart" and "Penny For Your Thoughts". As I've gotten older I tend to need memory aid devices to help me with people's names."

Peg spoke up. "Lindy, if I were you, I'd be insulted. Our knight in shining armor here, although meaning well, just intimated that we have all arrived at such an advanced age that you need help with your memory."

"I intimated no such thing."

Penny jumped in. "Okay you two, don't start." Laughing, she added, "It's like having spoiled toddlers with these two around. Welcome, Lindy. It's nice to meet you. We're glad you could join us tonight."

"Thank you for inviting me. It's nice to meet Ren's friends."

"We have about a half hour before we need to leave for the restaurant. Addressing Lindy, Joey added, "We were so glad you could join us. We're even happier that Ren finally has a date for New Years' Eve."

Ren and Lindy looked quickly at each other. "I would certainly be honored if Lindy were my date." Ren corrected, "I can assure you that we're just friends. She's straight."

"That's all right, we'll forgive her. Who knows? Maybe before the night is over you'll get lucky and earn your toaster oven." He winked at his old friend.

Puzzled, Lindy looked to Ren for an answer. "What toaster oven? What are you talking about?"

"Do you remember when Ellen DeGeneres came out on her show? There was a comment about earning a toaster oven for turning Ellen gay."

Lindy's expression was still indicating that she was drawing a blank.

Peg offered, "Maybe you didn't see it. The toaster oven comment was a reference to an old joke among gay men and lesbians where the joke is about us recruiting straight people that ends with the punch line, something like 'if I convert one more straight person I get a toaster oven.' The story is that you earn a prize if you meet your 'quota' of straight people you've converted. For straight people who think we're interested in turning them gay, the joke is meant to illustrate how ridiculous that idea is."

"Oh, I understand." Turning to Joey, Lindy said, "What makes you think that I'm not here to convert you into a heterosexual?" With a straight face, she added, "Straight people get real, full sized ovens for that."

"Touché." Joey flashed a wide grin. "Great comeback."

"Yeah, good luck with that endeavor." Ben chided.

Everyone laughed good-naturedly. Joey squeezed Lindy's arm. "No offense meant, Lindy."

"None taken. It would be good if Ren had a date. I agree."

"Hey, stop talking about me like I'm not here."

Dinner was an enjoyable experience for everyone. The band started playing at nine-thirty. The guys took turns dancing with each of the women in turn. Ren, who only drank a single glass of wine, stopped drinking at ten, knowing she would be driving the boat back to the island as well as driving the guys home. Peg also limited her intake of alcohol, since she was driving as well. At midnight, the guys briefly hugged each other and kissed each of the women. When Lindy slipped into Ren's arms, she kissed her lightly on the cheek. Feeling just a little buzzed, Lindy leaned against Ren with her arm around her waist as the crowd sang Auld Lang Syne. Ben helped Lindy on with her coat, while Joey, Ren and Peg settled the bill.

It was nearly two o'clock when they entered the Inn. Lindy went to the fridge for some cheese and crackers she'd prepared before they left. She poured them each another glass of wine.

Concerned that Lindy might be hung over the next day, Ren asked, "Are you sure you want more wine?"

"Why not? You're still sober. I'm keeping you company." She turned on the radio and tuned it in to an oldies station.

"Okay. Don't ever say I didn't warn you."

"Oh, this is one of my favorite songs. Come on, let's jitterbug." She pulled Ren to her feet and started to dance with her. At first, they had a hard time coordinating their moves, since neither was used to leading. They laughed their way through the song as they each showed the other their favorite dance moves. As they danced, Ren drank one glass more of wine. Lindy finished the rest of the bottle.

The music switched to a slow song. When Lindy wanted to slow dance, Ren begged off, saying she was too tired.

"Have I told you that you're no fun?"

Ren wanted to say something like 'I could be a lot more fun than you can even imagine.' Instead, she settled for, "Come on, party girl, time to get you to bed." Ren turned everything off and led Lindy by the hand down the hall towards their bedrooms. "Will you be okay or do you need help?"

"I'll be fine. I had a good time. I like your friends very much. The women were very nice, and the guys, especially, were great fun. Thank you for asking me."

Ren turned to go to her room. She looked back at Lindy who was still standing at her doorway watching Ren's progress down the hallway toward her room. There was an odd look on Lindy's face. Ren had never seen the expression before. "Are you okay?"

"Yes, I think so. I just feel a little," she paused searching for the word, "I don't know, I guess lonesome, maybe a little sad. I tend to feel sorry for myself when I have too much to drink."

Ren turned and strolled back to Lindy's doorway. "Come on, let's get you into bed. You're going to have a whopper of a hangover tomorrow. You should drink some water before you go to sleep. I'll get it. You get ready."

Ren returned to Lindy's bedroom with two large glasses of cool water only to find Lindy sitting where she'd left her, still fully dressed.

"What's happening?"

"Nothing."

Ren laughed. "I can see that. Thought you were going to change. Here drink this first."

Lindy compliantly drank the glass of water as directed. Taking the empty glass and placing it on the night table next to the full one, Ren pulled Lindy to her feet and helped take off her jacket. She turned Lindy around to unzip her dress and pull it over her head. When Ren turned back after hanging up the outfit, she found Lindy sitting on the edge of the bed. "What do you sleep in? Pajamas? Nightgown? Where is it?"

"Bathroom. On the hook."

Ren noted that Lindy's speech was not slurred, just very slow, and excessively precise. Ren retrieved an oversized tee shirt from the bathroom and returned to the bedroom where she found that Lindy had managed to remove her slip and pantyhose. She was sitting on the edge of the bed trying to unhook her bra.

"Here's your night shirt. Can you manage from here?"

Lindy shrugged.

"Okay, stand up and turn around." Lindy did as directed. Ren made quick work of unhooking the bra, resisting her urge to place a kiss at the base of Lindy's neck. Lindy turned to face Ren and waited. Ren slipped the bra off. Lindy raised her arms like a little kid whose mother was helping her undress. Ren grinned as she tugged the huge shirt over the tipsy woman's head, stooping to pull it down over Lindy's body.

Wrapping her arms around Ren's neck as she stood up, Lindy rested her head on Ren's shoulder. She giggled, a sound that always brought a smile to Ren's lips. "This could be a scene from one of those lesbian novels we're reading."

Ren laughed. "You think so?" Ren gave Lindy a quick hug, flipped back the covers, and helped her settle into bed. "I don't think I read the one where the unscrupulous lesbian takes advantage of the inebriated straight woman."

"Yeah, I guess you're right. I couldn't be a participant anyway. I've been told I'm frigid, you know--no passion. I'm a broken toy...no fun to play with."

Now she understood better what Lindy was talking about a few nights ago when she said, 'I couldn't give him what he deserved from me sexually, I'm not wired that way.' *Oh boy. I hope she doesn't remember any of this tomorrow.* "You're not broken. You just haven't met the right person yet."

"I hope you're right," Lindy responded sadly.

Pointing to the glass of water on the night table Ren said, "When you get up during the night, drink more water. It'll help with the hangover you're going to have tomorrow."

Ren reached for the light switch at the doorway. When she glanced back at Lindy, she was already asleep.

***

The next morning, knowing holidays were sometimes difficult for people alone, Ren had made it a point to call Mallory for every special holiday since Piper died. When Mallory answered, Ren said, "I called to wish you a Happy New Year."

"Happy New Year to you, too."

Ren could tell from Mallory's voice that she was smiling her beautiful smile. "Did you go out last night?"

"No, did you?

"Yes, I took Lindy with me when the guys, P 'n P, and I went out for our traditional New Year's Eve celebration."

"Oh, nice. How did that go? Did the guys behave?"

"For the most part. You know Joey. He can never resist an opportunity to embarrass me, although for the most part he was on his best behavior. Besides, I think he's met his match in Lindy. She can give back as good as she gets." Ren told Mallory about their initial exchange regarding the toaster oven comment.

Mallory laughed. "I think you're right. Sounds like she's a good match for him. She certainly bested him in that exchange."

"We really did have a lot of fun. I can't remember having so much fun with anyone since, well you know, since Brooke. Truth is…" Ren paused.

"Go on. You know you can tell me anything."

"I know. It's just that the thought that ran through my head kind of surprised me and made me feel almost disloyal to Brooke."

"So tell me. Let's talk about it."

"I was going to say that truth is, I think Lindy is more fun than Brooke. Although Brooke had a good sense of humor, and could always make me laugh, you know how serious she was most of the time. Lindy is always full of the devil. She lightens me somehow. I know it's said that another person can't make you happy. It's just that when I'm with her, it's like I want to be happy, so I am."

"Ren," Mallory paused wanting to be careful how she worded her concern. "It sounds like you might be falling in love with her. If Lindy's straight, you have to be careful, sweetie."

"I can't argue with the fact that she'd be easy to love. I admit that I'm really enjoying her companionship. We work well together, are companionable housemates, and she's been a good friend to me. But, I'm realistic. I know it's not a possibility that we could ever become a couple, so don't worry. I know it won't happen."

"Where is she now?"

"Ha! When we got home, Lindy had a bit too much to drink, so she's still sleeping. I don't think she'll be her usual chipper self this morning."

"Oh, poor thing. Don't tease her. She'll not be in the mood for it."

"It will be hard to resist...but I promise I won't. How are you doing?"

"Okay. I'm thinking of applying for another job. Actually, it's closer to you. Administrative position, Director of Nursing, outside of New York, near Harriman."

"That'd be great. Maybe we could see each other more often. Why are you leaving where you are? I thought you liked your job."

"I do, I love nursing. The new job offers better money, I like the area, it's more rural than here. I think a change would do me good."

"Well, good luck if it's what you want." After a few more minutes of conversation Mallory said, "Okay, I've gotta run, I'm late. I'll talk to you soon. Thanks for the call."

"Bye." When she hung up Ren thought about Mallory moving. They'd been friends since college, and the fact that they'd both lost their long-term partners drew them even closer together. Ren wondered if Mallory was looking to escape the previous life she had with her lover, Piper or if she was really seeking advancement in her career. *I guess a change is good. Look at what it's done for me.*

***

Lindy didn't surface until just before noon. Ren was making herself lunch when Lindy emerged. "Good morning. Ginger ale or cola?"

"What?" Lindy sat at the kitchen counter and put her head in her hands.

Ren repeated her question.

"Oh, cola, I guess."

The drink appeared along with a thick slice of buttered bread and a hearty bowl of soup that Ren made earlier that morning after her call to Mallory.

"I know you won't want to. I promise if you eat this, it'll help."

Lindy compliantly did as directed. "I shouldn't have finished that bottle of wine last night after we got home." Lindy's face flushed red as their eyes met, which answered Ren's unasked question about how much she remembered of the night before.

"I hope I wasn't too much trouble."

"Not at all. Finish your soup and we'll take a walk. The fresh air will do you good. When we get back, I'm going into town for some supplies. There's a big snow storm predicted."

After she ate, Lindy's coloring was better and she was moving less like she was walking on eggs. "Feeling a little better?" Ren asked when they came back inside after their walk.

When Lindy nodded, Ren said, "I'm heading out. Why don't you jump into the sauna or the hot tub while I'm gone? It might help you feel better."

"I'll think about it. Maybe I'll just take a nap once I warm up, instead."

"Okay, whatever you think works for you. If you rally, I did a couple of illustrations this morning. They're in my studio. There's something...I don't know, I just don't like something about the one on top. I'd appreciate your opinion and advice about what you think I should change."

After Ren left, Lindy forced her body to move. *Might as well look at Ren's sketches.* She headed down the hall towards Ren's quarters. Entering Ren's studio, she once again found her eyes drawn to the wall displaying Ren's work. She searched for the nude picture that Ren told her was there and giggled when she saw it. It was a self-portrait of Ren standing nude at her easel, back facing the viewer, paintbrush in hand and another firmly clenched between her teeth. In the drawing on the easel, Ren was facing the viewer, and the sketch was only partially completed. Lindy thought the illustration aptly demonstrated Ren's wit and quirky sense of humor. The pen and ink picture of the back view of Ren was all in black and white. The only color in the drawing was a tattoo, on the right shoulder of the artist, of a paint palette with the colors of the rainbow in individual dollops of paint arranged in a semicircle. She fell in love with the painting, and knew she had to have it.

Wonder if she really has that tattoo. Lindy returned to the drawing table to study the drawings there. She left a note. 'I like them, but I think the eyes need to be a little more sinister. Maybe just a little more dark shading under the brows?'

Lindy Caprini Journal

I'm finally feeling better after my walk, the lunch Ren fixed for me, and a nap. What was I thinking? I don't think I've been drunk since my college days. I was surprised when Ren didn't tease me this morning about drinking too much. Last night and today she was kindness personified. When she undressed me last night and put me into bed, for a moment, I wanted her to crawl in there with me and hold me. That's all. Just hold me. At least I think that's all I want.

I told her last night—told her that I'm broken. I wish, just for once, I could experience that passion she's had the luxury of having. She told me I just hadn't met the right person yet. It's nice that she has faith in me, unfortunately she doesn't know me—doesn't know how I am.

I went to her studio today while she was out. She asked me to look at some of the work she's done on our most recent story. It was a luxury for me, because I had an opportunity to study her work without her eyes watching my every reaction. She is so talented. She pours her feelings into each piece of work she produces. The drawings of her grandparents and family show her reverence for them in each stroke of her pen or brush. Then there is that painting of Brooke. I actually love that painting, not only for its beauty, but for all that it represents. After searching, I finally found Ren's self-portrait. It's the smallest painting. Somehow it's the epitome of her, filled with her sense of her warmth and humor. I have to have it. The cost is high, though. I have to pose naked for her—no, she always corrects me on my choice of words, nude—not naked. I have to think about it a bit although I think I might pay up in order to get that painting. I just love it.

Chapter 22: Where's My Sketch Pad When I Need One?

The snow began in earnest sometime during the night. By morning, at least eight or nine inches had accumulated on the ground. Ren found Lindy on the porch looking out the window at the falling powder. Coming up behind her, Ren put an arm around Lindy's shoulders. "How do you feel today?"

"I've decided I'll live after all. Thanks for asking."

Ren stepped back and held up the illustration she'd been working on the morning before, the one she'd asked Lindy's opinion about. "Thanks for your advice. I think it was spot on. What do you think?"

"Yes, perfect." Pleased with the result she continued. "We do make a good team, don't we?"

Ren nodded her agreement.

Lindy glanced up at one of Ren's paintings of the Inn. "This is an interesting painting. It's a different technique, isn't it?"

"Yes. It's egg tempura. It's not a medium I'm particularly fond of since it is so painstaking to do. Brooke liked the technique. I used to tease her that she liked it only because of her vocation as a chef."

Lindy's brows furrowed. "I don't understand."

"I took her to see a display at one of the museums back when we first met, on our second date. I think I told you about it. I thought the show would be of special interest to her as a chef, paintings done in egg tempera. I figured that, with her vocation, she would enjoy this use of the lowly egg in making the paint in those pieces of art. I pointed out the luminosity, the linearity common to that method of painting. I showed her how you can see the many different layers of paint the artist applied."

"Egg tempera. Does it really involve eggs?" Lindy asked.

"Yup." Ren grinned. "That's the exact same question she asked me. Actually, only the egg yolk is mixed with color pigment and water. When she asked me, 'What about the white of the egg, does that get used too?' I managed to keep a straight face as I told her, 'No. I would expect that each artist who used that medium had a close relationship with a chef who liked to make meringue.'"

"It took a few seconds for Brooke to realize that I was kidding. When she did she replied in kind saying 'Here I thought you wanted me purely for my body. Now I discover you're only interested in me for my meringue making ability.' She lowered her shoulders and tried her best to look dejected until we both burst into laughter. It was one of my favorite days with her."

"You have such lovely memories of your time together with Brooke. You're lucky."

"Yes. You're helping me to recognize and appreciate that."

"I'm glad." Lindy turned back towards the window. "It's lovely out there. The snow is beautiful, and the wind has finally died down a bit."

"How about a walk in the snow? I should probably clear off the path and some of the entryway so we'll be able to get the doors open. I think we're supposed to get well over a foot all together."

"I'll get my boots and coat and meet you at the basement door."

Ren was just finishing putting on her heavy clothes when Lindy showed up. Together they shoveled out a path around the door and down to the dock. "I like to keep it clear, just in case there's an emergency. Usually Bob would do this. Unfortunately for us, he and Maggie are visiting her family over the holidays and they won't be back for a few days."

After working as a team to finish the chore, they carried the shovels back to the house. It's just beautiful, even though it's cold," commented Lindy. "Is it time for our walk now?"

Because Ren was more familiar with the path, Lindy followed in her footsteps. They were both quiet, enjoying the crisp air and the sounds of their boots crunching in the snow. Suddenly, Ren realized that hers were the only footsteps she heard. She turned and looked around, discovering she was alone. Quickly scanning the area, she didn't see any sign of Lindy, until she noticed a trail of footsteps leading off the path to behind a large tree. When the breeze blew, the tail of Lindy's scarf was visible as it fluttered in the wind, confirming her location.

Moving very quietly, trying to make as little noise as possible, Ren snuck around the tree all set to surprise Lindy. However, the intended victim, who was lying in wait for Ren, turned the table when she grabbed Ren and stuffed a fist full of snow down the neck of her jacket then took off.

Jumping and dancing to try to get the melting snow to fall through and out the bottom of her jacket, Ren yelled, "You'd better run fast. You're dead meat when I catch you." She took off up the trail after Lindy. When she lost sight of her, this time she was ready for the snowball that sailed over her head. Using her hand to fend off the barrage of snowballs Lindy tossed her way, Ren ran full speed ahead and wrestled Lindy to the ground where she straddled her, restraining her hands with her own. Using the weight of her body Ren gained the upper hand. She splashed snow at Lindy until she yelled, "Uncle! I surrender."

Laughing, both women lay panting, Ren lying on top of Lindy.

"Thank God you finally surrendered. I don't think I could have gone on much longer." Ren sobered when Lindy adjusted her position so that her firm thigh met Ren's crotch sending a jolt of arousal through Ren's body. Suddenly realizing the intimacy of the position they were in, Ren rolled off, stood up, and helped Lindy to her feet. They dusted the snow off each other as best they could, an activity that did nothing to help the sense of arousal she felt. "Come on, we'd better get out of these wet things."

They hurried down the trail and entered the Inn through the basement door.

"I'm frozen to the bone," said Ren. She stripped off the wet clothing down to her underwear and hung everything on the line inside the laundry room. Lindy did the same. Ren pulled two terry cloth robes from the shelf and tossed one to Lindy. "Let's jump into the hot tub and warm up."

They made their way down the hallway to a room next to the gym. Ren flipped the light on and uncovered the hot tub. Quickly she dropped her robe on the bench, slipped out of her underwear, and entered the steaming water.

Lindy tried not to stare, despite finding it hard to turn her eyes away, as she watched Ren climb the stairs, step over the edge and slip into the tub. *Well, that answers that question. She really does have a tattoo on her shoulder.* Lindy turned her back, dropped her robe, and removed her bra and panties. Wishing she had a towel, she self-consciously climbed the stairs and entered the hot tub. She could feel Ren watching her as she entered the tub and settled in a seat.

"Where's my sketch pad when I need one?" Ren asked as her eyes appreciatively swept over Lindy's body.

The tension released, both women laughed. "I suspect that it's right where you left it next to the bear skin rug."

"You shouldn't be shy or modest. You have a beautiful body and you keep it in good shape. As an artist, I lost all those inhibitions years ago. We here in America are very hung up about nudity, I think. In Europe they are much more liberal than we are."

"Well good for them. I grew up here, so I have an excuse."

"See, I got your mind off of how cold you were." Ren smiled at Lindy. She set the timer for fifteen minutes.

"I forgot this was even here. Do you use it often?"

"Not really. I used it after the first time we ran when I was so sore and sometimes at night when I can't sleep."

Ren adjusted the jets to a more vigorous level. The two women fell silent, enjoying the warmth and the massaging effects of the water. When the timer sounded, Ren turned the jets off and stood up. Lindy exited first, put on her robe, and turned to face Ren. "Okay, let's go find that bearskin. I'm warm, and I'm already naked, so you might as well get your sketch now."

Lindy led the way to Ren's studio. When they arrived there, she asked, "What do I have to do?"

"You don't have to do this, you know."

"I know. When I came in to look at the drawing you were having trouble with the other day, I saw all the sketches you've completed of me reading. They were only complete down to the shoulders. I guessed you were waiting for the body." She walked across the room to Ren's self-portrait and plucked it off the wall. With a smile curling her lips, she challenged, "I think you promised me this. So let's go, I'm ready."

Ren laughed with delight and shook her head. "Well, I did promise it to you, I guess."

"Hope you have one the same size to fill up that unsightly hole on the wall."

"I don't right now, although I will have one in a few hours." Ren raised an eyebrow and tilted her head in Lindy's direction.

Lindy's mouth dropped open in shock at the thought of her nude portrait hanging on the wall for Ren to view every day.

"Don't fret. No identifiable face, I remember. Come on." Ren grabbed the sketchpad, a drop cloth, and her pastels and led Lindy back out to the library. As she threw several logs onto the fire she joked, "I've not mastered drawing goose bumps yet." She turned the chair, tossed a throw over it, and demonstrated the pose she wanted. "Just sit and draw your knees up like this." When Lindy moved to sit Ren stopped her. "The robe needs to come off first."

Lindy removed the robe and looked around for a place to lay it.

"I'll take that," said Ren holding out her hand.

Wanting to make Lindy more comfortable, in the hope she could persuade her to pose again, Ren arranged the robe across Lindy's bottom so that it draped across her hips, then she spread it up the chair. "May I touch you? I want to position your hand."

"Don't you find it strange to ask my permission to touch me since I'm sitting here nude in front of you? Wouldn't permission be sort of implied?"

Ren moved into a very formal, professional demeanor now that she had begun the portrait process. "No, not at all. I respect your personal space. Just because you've agreed to model for me doesn't give me the right to touch you." She opened and placed a book in Lindy's left hand, which she leaned against the arm of chair, and tilted Lindy's head so it too rested on the back of the chair. "Please drop your right hand down and relax your shoulder for me." Ren checked the pose from various angles. She didn't want to get pastel dust all over, so she spread her drop cloth and placed the hassock on it before sitting down. "Turn your head into the chair more please, and drop your right shoulder a bit. Good. Are you comfortable?"

"Yes, I think so. Am I allowed to talk?"

"In a little while. Let me get this sketched as quickly as I can first."

"You could talk to me." Lindy could hear the scratch of the pastel stick against the paper.

"Okay. What shall I tell you about?"

"How about when we met?"

"Give me some time to get this under way, okay? Then I'll talk." Ren worked quickly for about forty-five minutes before she started talking. "Well, I knew I would like you even before you got here, because we'd already become friends on the phone. You're a very beautiful woman. In the beginning, when we first started to talk on the phone about your project, I wanted to know what you looked like so I could picture you when we spoke and exchanged e-mail. I'm not a shallow person. Really, I would've liked you even if you weren't attractive. Still,

I am a visual person. I was curious, and I looked you up on the university's website."

"You did?" Lindy tried to talk without moving her mouth making Ren smile to herself.

"Yep, I confess. I have to admit though, that the day you arrived here, when you pulled up, you stepped out of the car and stretched...the web photo certainly paled in comparison. Your body was silhouetted against the sea, and the minute I saw you I knew I wanted to paint you."

Ren worked quietly on the drawing for a few minutes before she continued. "I sat there behind the window watching you. You know I have this thing about eyes. You turned, stuck your glasses on top of your head, and looked in my direction. I was disappointed when you saw me, because I had to stop watching so I could go greet you. Here we are four months later, and I'm obviously still not tired of looking at you."

"Well, that may be true, although now you're looking at considerably more of me."

Ren joined Lindy in laughter. "See, I just knew you couldn't be quiet for more than five minutes." Ren stood and came closer to the reclining woman and smiled down at her. "Do you need a break? Want to stretch? Water?"

"No, I'm okay."

Ren noticed that Lindy was finally relaxed into the chair and seemed less posed. *Good. I'm ready to go to work now.* She returned to the sketch. As she began to add detail, she realized Lindy had drifted off to sleep. Now more able to concentrate on the task, Ren began to make faster progress. She started to add details to the sketch, using her finger to put in light accents and shading to add dimension to the drawing. When she used her finger to blend the color on the breast area in the sketch, she admitted to herself she wished her fingers were really tracing the warm contours and softness of Lindy s breast instead of touching the flat, cool texture of the drawing paper. *Stop,* she reprimanded herself. She imagined a little angel sitting on her right shoulder saying, "What's the matter with you? She is your friend, and she's straight." The little red suited guy with the pointed tail on her left shoulder was still whispering in her ear saying, "Yeah, but just look at her..."

Ren started when Lindy spoke. "Done? You're just sitting there staring at me."

"Sorry, I was thinking about if I wanted to change anything," she lied, fearful that Lindy might ask what she was thinking about. "Yes, all finished. Want to see it?"

Lindy swiveled her legs around and moved to a sitting position. Ren extended the sketch to her. "Oh, Ren, it's beautiful. I'm surprised though, because you spent months studying my eyes, and you can just barely see one of them. The most detailed parts of my body in the sketch are my breasts. Maybe you should have spent months studying them." Her eyes widened in shock when she realized what she just said. The two of them laughed until they had tears in their eyes.

Ren said, "Remember who you're talking to here. What self-respecting lesbian would turn down an offer like that?" She placed the sketch on the table and said, "Come on, let's get your robe on. You've made giant strides today. This morning you were embarrassed to get into the hot tub with me without your clothes on and now you're sitting here totally nude talking to me as if you are wearing a three piece business suit instead of your birthday suit."

Lindy smiled. "Don't you find it just a little weird that I'm sitting here nude and you're there fully clothed staring at me? Anyway, what's the point in covering up what you've been staring at for the past couple of hours?" She winked at Ren, stood up, and made a production of putting on the robe.

"You are an evil woman, Lindy."

Lindy smiled demurely, "Only in your dreams."

Ren gestured to the recently completed sketch. "Do you really like it?"

"Yes, I do. Although I'm just reclining there, sleeping, there's something very sensual about the drawing. It's not the way I view myself at all."

"Well, you should look at yourself more closely. I can see that woman very clearly. Why can't you?" Tapping her finger lightly on Lindy's heart, she offered, "She's in there somewhere."

LINDY CAPRINI JOURNAL

I did it! I posed nude, in the buff, in the altogether, naked as a jaybird. It was fun. Ren made me feel comfortable—so comfortable, in fact, that I fell asleep.

She's very professional when she's working. When I awoke, she was just sitting and staring, a wistful expression on her face. She said she was deciding if she wanted to make any changes, even though it seemed that she'd been finished for a couple of minutes. Was she admiring her work or me? Which would I prefer? I wish I could know what's on her mind sometimes, what she's thinking. She is really very genuine and quite open about her feelings about many things, however, I'm never sure about her private thoughts concerning me. Today it was fascinating to learn her recollections about the first day we met.

Hmm. Before, she said that when she painted me, she could be nude too, if I'd be more comfortable. It's an intriguing thought.

Chapter 23: I'm Watching You And You're Cheating

The huge snowstorm lasted two days and, by the end, it deposited nearly two feet of snow on the ground before leaving the area. The wind continued to howl nearly the whole time. Earlier, when Ren heard shovels on the path, she knew Maggie and Bob were back and working to clear the path to the dock. Maggie met Bob when Ren hired him to do some maintenance on the property four years earlier. Ren was so pleased with his work that she ended up offering him full time employment supervising the maintenance of the buildings and grounds. Previously, she'd hired several different people to do the work. Keeping track of everyone and being sure that everything was taken care of as it should be had been a chore for Ren. It was especially demanding in season when she was busy dealing with the Inn and its problems along with the work she did at the marina.

Now, together under Ren's supervision, Maggie and Bob managed the facility and grounds. Maggie was in charge of all housekeeping and kitchen staff, as well as helping Ren, during the active season, with the management of the Inn. Bob was able to do most of the maintenance work independently and, for the work he couldn't accomplish on his own, she set a budget so he could hire the extra people he needed. Bob was a hard worker. He kept himself busy, proactively maintained the property, and reported to Ren once a week on what he'd accomplished. It was during those meetings they discussed any unexpected problems that he'd dealt with since their previous meeting. It was an arrangement that pleased Ren. She felt that she was able to remain on top of any maintenance issues related to the property while not being directly responsible for dealing with them.

The previous summer, when Bob and Maggie announced their engagement, Ren offered them the smallest cabin for their private quarters when the season ended in September. Bob and Maggie painted and decorated it before they moved in together just before Halloween. Having both of them on the island full time was proving to be a good decision. She was enjoying the luxury of not having to deal with any number of people to do the upkeep work on the property and she didn't have to do all the shoveling herself.

"I think the wind is finally slowing down," Lindy said, peering into the nearly blinding whiteness outside the window. They'd finished lunch earlier and were playing cards on the porch when they started to feel chilled. They sought the refuge of the library where it was warmer because of the extra heat generated by the stove.

Ren finished the final paragraph of the third novel Lindy gave her for Christmas. She closed the book and put it on the table between the two chairs they usually occupied knowing that Lindy would probably want to read it.

Lindy was standing at the window enjoying the scenery below. Ren stood and crossed the room to join her. She resisted a fleeting urge to slip up behind and encircle Lindy in her arms. She wrote it off to still being somewhat aroused by the final love scene in the book she'd just finished and chose, more rationally, to instead stand next to her to enjoy the magnificent view below them. The phone rang and Ren walked over to the desk in the corner to pick up the extension, Lindy returned to her seat by the fire.

After Ren finished the phone conversation she put another log on the fire. "That call was from two very old friends of mine that I met the same day and at the same dance where I met Brooke. They're coming for a visit the first week of March. I think you'll enjoy them. They are wonderful people and have been good friends. I don't normally see them all that often. Our predominant interaction usually consists of phone conversations several times a year. I visited them in the city just before you came here and invited them up. Don't worry though. I'm sure I can still keep up with whatever drawings you need me to do on the project. They'll probably want to do some of the touristy things in town on their own."

"It's not a problem for me at all. We're a good bit ahead of schedule. By the time they arrive, I'm sure I'll be ready for a break anyway, and my brain will be ready for a rest. While your friends are here, I'd like to do some work on the children's story I'm writing called Flint's Follies."

"What? That's the first you mentioned writing something other than this text we've been working on together."

"It's really what I love to do, make up my own tales, you know, like I do sometimes for Laura. For me, writing the more scholarly text we're working on, doing the research and the analysis for the book, is work. Writing about Flint in my spare time is pure pleasure. It makes me happy, probably the same way your art gives you pleasure."

"What's it about?

"It's a book for kids, young readers really, who can already read independently. It's a story about an elf tasked with the responsibility of ensuring the wellbeing of the people of this mythical village of Talleymora, in Ireland. Flint's been banished to earth to make up for a youthful indiscretion that angered his king. His penance is to help the villagers realize their dreams and overcome their hardships. Flint's further challenged when he's prohibited from using any of his magical powers, disclosing that he's an elf, and the people are not permitted to know of his involvement. He continually has to invent clever and creative ways to assure that people achieve their goals and overcome their difficulties. Sometimes he meets with failure because he's been so accustomed to solving problems using his magic in the past. Now that he can't use his powers to help him, sometimes his plans go horribly wrong with very disastrous results. I try to write it so that the reader is kept in the dark too, along with the villagers, about some of the details of his plans until his plot is sprung. So there's a little mystery for them as well as the sometimes humorous and, in the end, heartwarming results when things finally go right."

"What does this elf look like?"

"I imagine him to be a light elf."

"Which is?"

"A light elf is like the elves popularized in J. R. R. Tolkien's *Lord of the Rings Trilogy* and the exact opposite of a dark elf which is often depicted as a dwarf. He doesn't look like one of Santa's elves. I think I imagine him looking a bit like that actor in the movie we saw last week might have looked as a teenager or young adult, only with slightly pointier ears."

"May I read what you've written so far?"

"Really?" Lindy was amazed Ren would be interested in her story. "You really want to read it?"

"Of course. Why wouldn't I?"

"I don't know. No one else has ever asked to read anything I've written, not even my best friend at home, Terry. I'd welcome your opinion and would appreciate it if you would circle any errors or other problems you find as you read. Please be tough. I value honest criticism."

"It's too bad Laura is a little young yet to read it on her own since it's geared to an audience a bit older than she is. Someday, maybe we can test a little on her?"

"Well, we know she'll be honest. I'll go get it for you."

Lindy returned in a few minutes with a loose-leaf binder filled with printed pages. She handed the book to Ren who took it to the library, opened it, and began to read. Lindy sat down in the chair across from Ren. Her heel started to tap on the floor as she watched the fire and she kept stealing side-glances at Ren as she read the book.

When Ren giggled, Lindy immediately said, "What part are you at, what's funny?"

"Listen love, you can't ask me every time I laugh or groan or whatever I'm going to do as I read your story or I won't enjoy it. I've already added a note in the margin that says 'cute—made me laugh,' so you'll know what I'm feeling as I read. How about you read this," Ren said handing her the lesbian novel she'd left for her on the table. "I'd bet this book would definitely take your mind off children's stories."

Grasping the book that Ren offered, Lindy opened it to the first page. "I'm sorry. It's just that it is very important to me that you like it."

"Relax. I like it already. Now hush so I can read."

The two read in companionable silence for nearly an hour. Ren stood up to stretch, carefully placing the manuscript on the chair. "I'm going to go carry in some more wood."

"Need help."

"No, I don't think so. Thanks for volunteering though. I'll just get a couple of carrier loads full for tonight. Maybe tomorrow we can stack the wood box up here on the balcony. I'll only be gone a few minutes. After I get the wood, perhaps we can think about dinner."

"Are you sure you don't want help. I'm more than willing."

Ren shook her head. "I know. Really, I'll be fine." She got her jacket and stopped back to tell Lindy, "Tomorrow, I need to go over and clean off the cars. I should help my brother walk through the marina and make sure everything is okay over there. Want to come?"

"Absolutely!" Lindy's eyes lit up at the thought of going to town. "Think we can have dinner out? I'm sort of sick of my own cooking--yours too, for that matter." She snickered. "Maybe something ethnic, like Chinese?"

"Sure, I'd like that."

When Lindy could no longer hear Ren's footsteps, she reached for her manuscript and flipped it open to the first page. She howled when she saw the note there. Beneath a quick sketch Ren had made of her own eyes, printed in large letters, she read, 'I'm watching you—and you're cheating.'

She knew she'd not be able to hide the fact that she'd been caught cheating. Still chuckling, she decided to go start dinner. Ren soon joined her in the kitchen. All Lindy had to say to make Ren crack up was, "Very funny."

Chapter 24: You Are A Vision In Flannel And Wool, Miss Scarlet

The next morning, the two women planned the rest of their day agreeing that they would work until lunch, eat at home, do what was necessary at the marina, and spend some time walking around town before having dinner.

Ren called her brother to tell him she'd be there to help. "We'll arrive around one to help you check out things at the marina. By that time, you should have the parking area plowed, and we can help clean up and dig out the cars and check on the boats. As soon as we're done, we plan to wander around town for a while, before we grab some dinner."

"Ok, sis. I'll see you there."

Back on the mainland, the town was still digging out from all the snow. Lindy started to clean off their cars and dig out around them while Ren did a quick survey of the marina. She met Jack coming back from the far end where he'd been checking the docks. Despite the high winds, everything seemed to be intact. Ren waved to Lindy as she and her brother were walking toward the parking area where Lindy worked on cleaning off the cars. Jack put his hand on Ren's arm to stop her for a moment.

"I don't want to intrude into your personal life, even though I worry about the relationship that seems to be developing between the two of you?"

Ren, a smile curling her lips, was watching Lindy remove the last of the snow from her car. When she heard what Jack said, her head snapped around and she fixed her gaze on him, her smile replaced by a furrowed brow and an intense expression. "What do you mean, relationship? What do you think is happening between us?"

"Nothing, I guess. It's just that the two of you seem to have chemistry together. Don't get me wrong, I love seeing you like this, you know, happy. I just don't want to see you get hurt again by falling in love with another woman who isn't available."

"Jack, you're talking nonsense and are wrong on so many levels. First, it wasn't Melanie's fault our relationship ended. I just wasn't ready. Second, nobody is falling in love." A thought struck her like a shot to the forehead. *Did I just lie to Jack?* Quickly shaking off the idea, she added, "Where'd you get that lame brained idea anyway? She's straight."

"Precisely. Unavailable."

"Not unavailable, just not interested. I swear we're just friends, close friends, just not in a sexual way. I will admit that I've been happy with her sharing the house. I like her company. We're very compatible, get along very well, and have a productive work relationship. That's it. Period."

"Just be careful, Ren." He pulled her into a loose hug. "I love you."

"I love you, too, even if you are an idiot." Knowing he was speaking to her out of concern for her wellbeing, she softened giving him another quick hug. "Don't worry, everything is under control. We're just friends."

"Let's help her finish digging out the cars and the two of you can come over and help us. We promised Laura we'd build a snowman when I got back."

When Ren asked if she'd like to go to Jack and Marie's, Lindy was thrilled with the change in plans. The threesome made short work of freeing the cars from the snow. They started them and let them run while they finished shoveling out around them. Work completed for the day, they locked everything up before hiking back to Jack's house.

Marie and Laura were thrilled to see Jack return with Ren and Lindy and even happier that they agreed to stay and help. Of course, there was a snowball fight. Later, after everyone finished brushing off, Ren and Lindy mentioned they were going for Chinese food and invited Jack and his family to come with them.

Everyone wanted the food, except Marie who was reluctant to take the wound up Laura to a restaurant. "Maybe it would be easier to do take out. Would you mind?"

"Whatever works for you two is fine with us," Ren replied after Lindy nodded her agreement.

Marie phoned in the order and Jack went to pick it up. After dinner, Lindy and Ren wished Marie and Jack a good night, and started their walk back to the marina. The wind picked up again and it was bitter cold. Ren turned up her collar and stuffed her hands in her pockets. As they walked side by side down the sidewalk, Lindy slipped her arm through Ren's and pulled in tight against her. Ren was no longer cold. She stopped walking.

"Is this okay?" She tugged on Ren's arm with her own linked one. "I'm so cold." Lindy spoke through chattering teeth.

"It's fine by me, although if people see you, it could ruin your reputation. Most people around here know I'm gay. If they see you holding onto me like this, they'll make assumptions about you."

"Let them assume what they will. None of them is my mother and they don't pay my bills. So what they think about me is totally irrelevant. Besides, gay or straight, I'm always proud to be with you. So let's stop talking about this nonsense and get home. I have a great lesbian novel waiting for me there." She giggled, a sound that was always music to Ren's ears.

Ren laughed and pulled Lindy's arm closer as the two fell into step towards their destination. Ren was sorry she had to let Lindy go when they arrived at the marina. *Damn you, Jack! Now you have me thinking that innocent gestures have some hidden meaning. We're just friends--that's all.* She vowed to put his idiotic concerns aside. She knew Lindy was straight and could limit her feelings for Lindy to appropriate boundaries. She wasn't going to let Jack's doubts ruin her close and comfortable friendship with Lindy. She knew in her heart that she could easily let herself feel more than friendship for the beautiful and charming woman. She also was very aware of Lindy's sexual orientation, despite her liberal attitudes. Ren treasured their friendship too much to risk losing that, knowing when Lindy finished the book they were working on, she'd return home to her straight life. Ren had to hold back her feelings so she wouldn't be hurt when Lindy left. *No matter how much she wished their relationship could be more.* The final thought and what it meant shocked and sobered her.

By the time they arrived home they were both chilled to the bone. "Hot tub or fire?" Lindy pointed one finger towards the library and one towards the basement where the hot tub was.

"Ooooh. Tough decision. I think fire and sherry. If we do the hot tub, it means I have to get naked and I don't think I could possibly bring myself to remove one item of clothing, let alone all of it." *For more reasons than the obvious.*

"Oh, okay" Lindy replied, "I'm going to go to my room and put on my flannel jammies and my slippers. It'll take the fire a few minutes to get up to speed. I'll be back before it gets really toasty." She disappeared down the hallway to her bedroom.

Twenty minutes later she appeared in the library dressed in her red and black-checkered flannel pajamas, red wool slippers, and a red flannel robe, Ren looked her up and down from head to toes and chuckled. "Why, you are a vision in flannel and wool, my dear Miss Scarlet."

"You're just envious because you don't own such distinctive homespun finery." Lindy opened the robe to give a better view of the pajamas and pirouetted twice around as she added, "You may admire if you must." She strolled provocatively over and made a show of picking up the lesbian novel she was reading before she saucily sat in the chair.

Ren burst into laughter, joined shortly thereafter by Lindy. The two women laughed until their sides hurt. Slowly Ren gained enough control to pour each of them a sherry, serving the amber liquid to Lindy before she went to stand near the fire enjoying the heat, glass in hand staring into the flames.

Ren looked at Lindy and smiled. "May I be serious for a moment?" When Lindy nodded, Ren said, "I love how we laugh together. I can't remember how long it's been since I laughed like a child, from my heart and not from my head. I don't know if that makes any sense to you. I'm sorry, I don't know how else to explain it. When you watch a child laugh, their joy just bubbles out of them as laughter. For so long I've felt...well, let's just say, not quite my old self. Your being here has been good for me. You've brought that joy, that laughter back into my life. The work we do has given me purpose and a consistent outlet for my creativity--also good for my soul. Your presence here and your friendship have provided me companionship and kept me from being lonely. I don't want to be maudlin, I just wanted to say thank you. I hurt a whole lot less since you've come into my life, and you've helped me find my joy again."

Lindy couldn't stop the tears from welling up in her eyes. Ren had just opened her heart and shared her soul with her. She stood, approached Ren, and slipped her arms around her. "I have a few more months here to see if we can't get you to a point where you don't hurt at all." She leaned back and using both hands she brushed Ren's hair back, turned her head from one side to the other, as she placed a kiss on each cheek. "I would say that you have, without a doubt, given me more." Lindy pulled Ren to her for another quick hug. "I'm going to turn in. I'll see you in the morning."

Lindy Caprini Journal

It's been a strange and wonderful few days. We've laughed so much and have had some wonderful times together. I feel so totally comfortable with her—being with her, no matter where, is like being...what? I guess like being home. You know that feeling of how you miss being home when you aren't there? I feel that way about Ren. I seem to be hyper aware of her absences and when she returns, it generates a feeling like, well I guess it's like that feeling of coming home. It's beyond comfortable. Her smile lights me up, and her laughter inspires joy. Tonight she told me more or less the same thing, and it made me cry. I'm feeling things I've never felt before. It's a little bit scary and a lot exciting.

I like it when she touches me, and my hands are drawn to touch her. Before I recognized this...craving...this desire I have to have my hands on her, it was a completely unconscious thing. Now that I'm aware of it, I can't get enough physical closeness to her. These are feelings I've never experienced before and feelings I don't completely understand yet.

Oh yeah, one more thing. I kissed her tonight. I kissed each cheek and had to stop myself from kissing her lips. I think I'm reading too many of these lesbian novels, or maybe...No, I'm just letting my imagination run wild, that's all.

There is one question though that I have about reading those stories. Something I need to ask Ren about.

Chapter 25: You Could Get Your Toaster Oven After All

Lindy was sitting at the kitchen counter just ending a phone call with her friend Terry when Ren came in to pour herself a second cup of tea. "Hey, good morning sleepy head. I missed you this morning. I've been up and have half my work done already. The water is hot if you want tea."

"Oh, hello. I guess I'm off to a slow start this morning."

Lindy was generally bubbly in the mornings. Puzzled by Lindy's subdued demeanor Ren inquired, "Is everything okay back home?"

"I just got some interesting news. I've been puzzled by the last few conversations I've had with Terry, my best friend and landlady, and another close friend from home, Karen. They have been...I don't know, what's the word? I guess reserved would kind of describe it. You know, just not as free and open as usual. When I talked to them in December and last month, I chalked it up to the rush of the holidays. This morning, when I couldn't shake the feeling that something was wrong I asked Terry what was happening. Anyway, Terry gave me some information I didn't expect. Remember I told you that five months ago, just before I came up here in September, I broke up with Jim, the guy I'd been dating somewhat seriously before I came here? Well, Terry is now dating Jim."

"And that upsets you?"

"I don't know...it just makes me feel uncomfortable. I guess if I didn't have to see them together on a daily basis, it wouldn't matter. I mean, my bedroom is on the floor above hers, only eight feet away. For some reason it all just feels a little incestuous to me. More importantly, I used to share confidences about our relationship with her, and now..." Lindy shrugged. "I guess I'll adjust and get used to the idea of them being together. It's just that the thought of returning home to face them certainly makes me less homesick."

"We all like to think of home as a stable place. I think it is always shocking to come home and find that things are different, and that 'home' hasn't just stayed in suspended animation while we were gone."

"Who knows, six months from now, after you're back home, the world may have righted itself again and they'll have moved on." Ren joined Lindy at the counter. After taking a sip of her tea she smiled. "Try to not let it bother you too much."

Brighter now, Lindy admitted, "I'll try. Could be this will all pass...if not, I'll get used to the idea. I do love them both and, as much as I hate to admit it, they'll make a great couple."

Lindy looked over at Ren. "You seem pensive today. What's up with you this morning? Something on your mind?"

"I was wondering, if you'll be my 'plus-one' for the wedding next Saturday?" Ren hoped that Lindy would keep her company. She didn't want to go alone and knew she'd have much more fun with Lindy there.

"Wedding? You mean Maggie and Bob's?"

When Ren nodded, Lindy gladly accepted the invitation. "I just have one condition. I'll need to go shopping."

"My chariot is at your disposal. Let me know when you want to go. By the way, I finished reading Flint's Follies. Want to see my notes?"

"Now? Oh yes, absolutely. Where? Your place or mine," she grinned.

"Why don't you come to me? I have something I want to show you anyway."

With her first step in the door of Ren's studio Lindy's eyes naturally gravitated to what should have been the empty spot on the wall where she'd removed Ren's self-portrait. It was no longer empty, the nude portrait Ren drew of her was in its place. "You can wipe that smirk right off your face, Miss Thing. You didn't waste any time getting me hung up there, did you?"

"It gives me pleasure to look at you whenever I want. I had a wonderful time with you that day and doing that portrait was just part of it. I get warm...uhh, thoughts every time I look at it." With a devilish twinkle in her eye Ren continued. "Now that I've had practice at drawing your eyes and drawing your body, if only I could put everything together in the next portrait all would be right with the world. When will you pose for me again?" She waited for the response she knew would be coming. She was not the least bit prepared for it when it did.

Lindy walked over and started looking at the wall.

"Picking out the next picture you'll take in exchange for posing?"

"No, not this time. I know I only did it once, but lying around nude while you're fully clothed studying me, like a squirrel stares at the last acorn on the oak tree in November, just won't work for me this time. As I recall, last time we talked about this, you said you'd do anything to get me to pose for you. I believe your exact words were, 'I could be naked too, if it would make you more comfortable.' You asked what it would take and that's it. We'll see how you like standing around naked while someone stares at your business for hours on end. Oh yeah, don't forget the bear skin rug. That ought to put the thought of another nude portrait out of your mind," Lindy said, satisfaction evident in her tone.

"Hey! Where're you going? I thought you wanted to review your book."

Lindy paused at the doorway torn as to which was more important, making a dramatic departure after her defiant speech or finding out what Ren had to say about her book. Vanity and curiosity won out and she returned, a sheepish smile on her face. "Okay, I'll pose again, just not until it's warmer."

"Well, I'll certainly vote for that now that we're going to be wearing matching goose bumps." Ren grinned.

Equanimity restored, they bent to read the comments Ren wrote in Lindy's book. With Ren sitting at her drawing table, Lindy put her hand on Ren's back and leaned against her as she read over Ren's shoulder while Ren explained the comments she had made in the margins of Lindy's book. Ren was acutely aware of the contact as Lindy's breast pressed against the back of her upper arm or her shoulder as she leaned in to read the comments along with her. Ren could smell the fresh, light musky aroma of the perfume Lindy wore that Ren had come to identify as her scent. Lindy seemed blissfully unaware of the effect that she was having on Ren.

Most of the comments about the story were positive such as, 'I like this,' or 'Good point.' A couple of times she wrote, 'Too large a clue. It feels like you should keep the reader guessing a while longer.' The last comment was, 'This story was a great read so far, when can I read more?' When they finished discussing all the notes, Ren closed the loose-leaf and presented it to Lindy.

"Thank you, Ren. Your review was very helpful. I appreciate the amount of serious effort you put into reading my book."

"It surely wasn't an imposition. I enjoyed it. Oh, by the way, I wanted to show you this. I hope you can use it somewhere in the book. If you can, consider it a gift." She pulled a drawing from beneath the desk and presented it to Lindy.

"Oh, my God! That's Flint. That's him exactly." She threw her arms around Ren and pulling her close, leaned in to kiss her cheek. At that instant, Ren turned her head to say something and their lips met briefly.

"It was an accident," Ren stammered quickly, her eyes large. "I'm so sorry, I didn't mean..."

"Sorry for what?" As if to prove her point, Lindy grabbed both of Ren's cheeks in her hands and placed a quick kiss on Ren's lips. Lindy laughed, perhaps just a little too nonchalantly. "See, no harm done." Putting the picture on top of the notebook, Lindy backed away until she got to the door where she paused. "Ren, you are so kind to me. You captured him exactly. I may decide to illustrate Flint's Folly after all. It could be our next project together. Let's think about it."

Ren did think about it, a little sadly. Her lips still tingled from Lindy's kiss. She touched them with her fingers and recognized how much she would miss Lindy's presence in her life. Ren also knew that she would never initiate a relationship with Lindy, even if Lindy were willing, for all the reasons she'd already identified. Uppermost on her mind was the fear that Lindy would want to return home both to her job and to her heterosexuality. She shook her head. If she were to illustrate *Flint's Folly*, it would mean that Lindy would be gone, back to her home and they would again be working through e-mail and over the phone.

***

Later that night, as they sat together in the library, Lindy inquired, "What do you think I should wear to the wedding? What are you wearing?"

"Come on, I'll show you." Lindy followed Ren to her bedroom. Ren opened her closet and pulled out a beautiful dark blue knee length sheath with a long fitted jacket. "Will this do?"

"It's a beautiful dress. It will bring out the blue of your eyes."

"Speaking about eyes, I can lend you this one that compliments yours, if you don't mind wearing my dress. We're about the same size. It should fit." She pulled out a dress from the closet and raised the plastic wrap exposing a beautiful deep green dress.

"It's lovely. May I try it on?"

Ren worked to remove the plastic dry cleaner's film placed over the dress after it was cleaned. Ren unzipped the dress and turned to find Lindy standing in her bra and panties waiting for her. Ren slipped the dress over Lindy's head and turned her around to close the zipper for her. Ren again squelched the desire to place a kiss at the base of her neck as she zipped the dress. The dark green sheath fit Lindy like a glove. Because Lindy was maybe just a bit less than two inches taller than Ren, the skirt ended just above her knee showing off Lindy's shapely legs.

Lindy studied her reflection in the mirror, noting Ren's momentary pause before she zipped her up. Her back tingled where Ren's fingers brushed her skin as she worked to close the zipper.

As Ren locked the tab into place, her eyes raised, met, and held Lindy's in the mirror.

Lindy pulled her eyes away and turned to face Ren. "I love this dress. I don't know though...I'm worried that it might still be too cool to go in a sleeveless dress. Wait a minute, come with me!"

Ren followed Lindy to her bedroom where Lindy rummaged in her closet. Pulling out the jacket she'd bought to wear with the black sheath for New Year's Eve, she pulled it on and held out her arms palms up to say, "How's this?"

"Perfect, the color is almost exact. What you think is more important." Ren closed the bedroom door so Lindy could view her image in the mirror behind the door.

"I'm sold. I hate to wear black to a wedding, and it's all I brought. I don't want to buy anything new, because I must have ten things at home I could wear. Thanks for lending it to me."

LINDY CAPRINI JOURNAL

I kissed her this afternoon—twice, actually. We were very close physically, working on 'Flint's Folly.' I was leaning over her shoulder. Being near her, touching her, working together—it felt good. Quite accidentally, as I went to kiss her on the cheek in gratitude for the picture she'd made of Flint, she turned at the same time, and our lips met. For me, it was electrifying, but she was so apologetic. I suspect she thought I'd think she was making a pass at me and that I'd be upset if she had. I wanted to show her that the kiss didn't upset me, and to be honest, I wanted to experience it again. So I took her face in my hands and kissed her on the lips.

Lindy put her pen down and recalled the moment, fingers to her mouth, enjoying the sensation of Ren's soft lips on her own again for about the tenth time that day.

I liked it. There, I've said it. I liked it, and I'd like it to happen again with more participation on her part next time. I need to think about what that would mean for my future and for hers. The last thing I want is to hurt her. Am I a lesbian? Am I one of those 'late bloomers?' Do I love her? Would being physically intimate with her be different than it's been in the past? Judging from the way I feel when I'm with her it would be. I can't be sure without, well, without being intimate with her. Even without that, somehow, I feel different. Before, I used to get physically involved because it was expected. To be considered normal, it was expected that I would want to be intimate. With Ren, I feel like I want to be physical with her, because I want it, not because it is expected.

Sometimes I think of the painting of Brooke that Ren has in her studio. I think I grow to appreciate that piece of art more each time I see it. I can identify with how Brooke felt about Ren. I think I want Ren too, in the same way Brooke did. I'm amazed that I have these feelings. Yet, to my surprise, everything feels so right. For once I feel like I imagine other people feel, what motivates them to want to be physically intimate with someone. Having desire for another human being makes me feel normal. At last!

What is Ren feeling? She seems to hold herself back. She welcomes any touch I offer, but doesn't usually initiate physical closeness. Is that because she doesn't feel the same way—doesn't want me? Is she afraid of my reaction, or is it because she's still not ready? Do I just confess how I feel? I'm terrified to tell her how I'm feeling even though, normally, we have such open communication. I think that if I confess my attraction, I might scare her away.

So many questions—so few answers.

Chapter 26: Someday She's Going To Learn She Can't Outsmart Me

The day of the wedding, the last Saturday in February, the women went to their rooms to dress then met in the kitchen. Lindy joined Ren who was already dressed and waiting at the kitchen counter with a small box grasped in her palm. "Okay, here I am. I'm finally ready." Lindy smiled, "How about you?"

"Just one more thing." Ren stood, opened the box, displaying for Lindy a beautiful necklace of gold. The pendant was an artistic rendering of the tree of life. At the base, where the roots of the tree emerged, there was inset a gorgeous emerald. "The tree of life symbolizes the unity of all living things. The emerald, the salesman says, represents the fertility of life." Ren turned Lindy around so she could put the necklace on for her. "However, to me the beauty of the necklace is representative of you—grounded, and incredibly beautiful."

When Lindy turned to face Ren there were tears in her eyes as she clutched the necklace in her hand. "And I'm supposed to be the writer. That was a beautiful sentiment. I'll never forget it or you and your generosity." She pulled Ren to her and held her close. When she pulled away, she put her hand on Ren's cheek. "Thank you doesn't even begin to convey what I'm feeling. You're too generous."

"No, I saw it and knew it would be perfect for you. I'm pleased you like it and I want you to have it."

"I'll treasure it always. And you."

Ren took Lindy's hand in her own and kissed her palm. "I'm pleased you like it. Quickly she turned away, got Lindy's coat and helped her put it on. Lindy reciprocated the gesture for Ren. With both of them finally ready, they left for the wedding.

After the church ceremony, seated at a table with Jack and Marie, they had a great time at the reception. They danced all the standard dances including The Chicken Dance, The Hokey Pokey, The Macarena, and YMCA. Jack took turns dancing the slow dances with the three women. They teased him mercilessly when they noticed that he danced twice as often with Marie. By the end of the evening, Ren and Lindy were dancing all the fast dances together. After a few drinks each, Lindy leaned over and whispered to Ren, "Do you think anyone would notice if we danced a slow dance?"

Ren looked around at the crowd. "Yes, I think they would. If you can wait, Ben and Joey usually have a party before winter ends. The people who come are either gay or gay friendly, so we'd be able to dance there if you're still in the mood. Brooke was taller than I am, so she always led...I don't know how. Anyway, you're taller, so you'll have to lead, otherwise no deal."

Always up for a challenge, Lindy thought, *Hmph. She thinks she just got off the hook. Hmm, I wonder who I can ask to teach me to lead in the next month. Someday, she's going to learn she can't outsmart me.*

✳✳✳

They drove to the marina and changed to the boat to navigate out to the island. They were totally chilled from the trip in the cold car then the cold boat. Back home at ten, by ten-thirty they were nestled in their PJ's in front of a roaring fire. Lindy was still reading the third lesbian romance novel, while Ren worked her way through the fourth. Ren glanced over at Lindy "That book is really steamy. Maybe you'd prefer this one. It's a bit more romantic. More story and less sex."

"Well, these two are on each other like rabbits." Lindy raised an eyebrow, shrugging one shoulder. "I'd like to finish it. It's very educational." She winked at Ren as she went back to reading.

They were again quiet as they both read, with the crackling of the toasty fire and the flipping of the pages the only sounds in the room. Lindy mustered her courage to ask the question she'd wanted to ask for some time. She'd never found the right moment before and decided that this would be a good time. "Ren?"

"Yes." Ren inserted her bookmark, closed her book, and looked up.

"I'm curious about something." When Ren blushed, Lindy declared, "Don't worry, it's not about sex. After reading this book, what possible questions could I have about that?"

"Okay, shoot, what is it?"

"Well, I was wondering...you know the novels I brought with me, the ones I think you referred to as my trashy romance novels?" When Ren nodded, Lindy asked, "Do you read that type of book ever?"

"Sure. Of course I have. Sometimes. When I'm alone, I more often draw rather than read. Occasionally though, I have read them. Why?"

There was a long pause as Lindy gathered her courage to ask her embarrassing question. "Do they ever turn you on?"

Ren laughed. "Sure, sometimes they can turn me on. Not like these do. Still, I can get a little horny from reading them. Why? Is that lesbian novel getting you hot and bothered?"

Face pink, Lindy nodded. "Whew! Well it stands to reason then, that I would respond to this type of novel. I thought I was turning into a lesbian, and maybe you'd be able to get your toaster oven after all." She smiled when Ren chuckled.

Ren considered asking Lindy if she could ever be romantically involved with another woman. However, when Lindy said she seemed relieved that she was not turning herself into a lesbian by reading the books, Ren already had her answer. She was surprised at how disappointed she felt. Maybe Jack wasn't wrong. *On some level I've been secretly hoping there could be something more between us. Well, now I know it's not possible--she's definitely straight and intends to stay that way.* Ren's disappointment caused her eyes to brim with tears. She looked away forcing them back, willing them not to flow. No longer able to deny her feelings, her acknowledgement of them caused her to gasp. *When did I fall in love with her?* Cautioning herself that she could not have what she wanted, she decided to enjoy the remaining time with Lindy that she could have and accepted that she would have to deal with another loss and the associated pain when Lindy returned home. *Maybe it won't hurt as much this time because I'll be better prepared for it.*

LINDY CAPRINI JOURNAL

I finally asked Ren the question about the books turning me on and she reassured me it's a normal response. I'm not so sure. I mean when I read 'my' trashy novels I do get a bit excited. It's different when I read 'her' trashy novels because I feel things I've never felt before...they flat out make me horny. I yearn and have desire I've only dreamed about. I confess that there are times when I look over at Ren sitting there so completely oblivious to my feeling, and I want to jump up, race across the floor and, as they say in the novels, 'have my way with her.'

Lindy rested her chin on her hand as she thought about what she'd just written. As the realization struck her she could feel her pulse beating and her breath coming more quickly than it should for someone resting in a chair. Picking up her pen, she committed her feelings to paper.

I love her. There, I've said it. Something even more amazing, I want her. I think it's taken me a while to recognize my feelings because I've never felt like this before. I've never felt desire before. No doubt, I want her. I want to touch her. I want to please her. And I want her to touch me. That's the part where I've always been a disappointment before. I would die if...

Well, it's never going to happen anyway, because she hasn't shown any interest in anything other than friendship with me. We have a wonderful friendship. I want more, yet I don't know how to let her know this without just throwing myself at her. She seems to not want anything more than the close friendship we have.

One thing does bother me though. How could I live well into my thirties and not know this really important thing about myself—that I can be attracted to a woman, that I can desire a woman?

Chapter 27: Those Two Left Feet Of Yours Are Stepping On My Toes

Ren and Lindy continued their steady progress on the manuscript and were several weeks ahead of the schedule Lindy had laid out for them when they began the project. The weather turned a bit warmer, so the two women were able to get off the island more frequently. They saw Joey and Ben a couple of times for dinner, attended movie night at Peg and Penny's where Lindy met some of Ren's other friends, saw Jack and Marie, went to the movies, and had fun dinners out, just the two of them.

Early in April, Ren prepared for Carol and Nancy's visit by stocking in extra supplies of food and drinks. She bought some recently released videos in case they couldn't get off the island. Sometimes, this time of year when rain or ice storms hit, the trip to the mainland became more difficult to navigate, so she wanted to be prepared in case they couldn't get ashore for a couple of days.

Carol and Nancy arrived bringing a whirlwind of hugs and kisses for Ren and Lindy alike. There was no way not to like them. They were witty, energetic, smart, and fun. The first day they were together seemed to fly by. After dinner, they retreated to the library. Ren and Lindy had already rearranged the seating in the library so that the loveseat and two chairs faced each other straddling either side of the wood-burning stove. Carol and Nancy sat on the loveseat holding hands. Lindy sat in one of the chairs while Ren opened a bottle of wine and filled their glasses before taking her seat. Carol held up her glass. "To Brooke, gone, but never forgotten."

Lindy joined in the toast after she glanced at Ren to see her response. She was relieved to see that Ren was still relaxed and smiling as she raised her glass. The toast was just the beginning of a walk down Memory Lane. Ren held up for a little over an hour as her two friends told 'remember when' stories about Brooke then laughed about the good times they'd shared with Ren and her first partner.

Somewhat abruptly, Ren stood and declared, "Well, I'm sure you two have had a long day. Tomorrow, we'll get up early and I'll take you to town and drop you so you can do some shopping." By way of explanation, she added, "I have some work to do at the marina."

"Can I come to town, too? I want to stop in at the library." Lindy said as nonchalantly as she could manage.

"You're welcome to come shopping with us," Carol and Nancy offered.

"Thanks, I can't. I have a few things I need to research."

Lindy noticed Ren's furrowed brows at her interest in visiting the small library. She had signed up for a card when she first arrived, but had expressed no interest in returning there since. She finished cleaning up the glasses and snacks as Ren showed her visitors to their room.

Finished in the kitchen, Lindy noticed that Ren was nowhere around. She was curious about why Ren ended the evening so abruptly before disappearing without even saying goodnight. Lindy padded down the hallway to her bedroom. She wasn't ready to sleep yet so she went into her office. Ren kept popping into her head, so she decided to check in on her. Watching her tonight had been like watching a balloon with a slow leak. Ren had begun the evening excited about the visit from Carol and Nancy, and ended it early by hustling them off to bed. Lindy wasn't sure why.

Lindy tapped gently on Ren's bedroom door. There was no response. On her way back towards her room, she noticed a light under the doorway of Ren's studio. Again, she knocked with another soft tap. This time she heard a soft reply. She found Ren sitting on the loveseat in her studio staring up at the picture of Brooke. She looked over at Lindy and patted the empty loveseat cushion next to her. "Come, sit with me." Then in a barely audible voice, she added, "Please."

Lindy sat down and Ren reached over and placed her hand on Lindy's arm. "I'm sorry," she said. "They didn't mean to be insensitive."

"I enjoyed their stories. I'm surprised you didn't appreciate hearing some of those stories about the good times they had with Brooke before she met you. I felt I got to know her better."

"I was just sitting here trying to figure out exactly what it is I'm feeling and then why I'm feeling this way."

"So, have you come to any resolution?"

Ren released a long sigh when Lindy slid over closer to her. She reached for Lindy's hand, pulling it over to rest on her thigh, still gripping it with her own. "Well, I think I've come to the conclusion that I feel like I do for a variety of reasons. Part of it is that I'm feeling a little sad that Brooke is gone. I think it's a feeling that will remain with me probably always be a part of me, no matter how accepting I become of that loss. So, that's really the least of it." She looked at Lindy and smiled a bit weakly. "If I'm honest I think I'm mostly just annoyed."

"Annoyed? At whom?"

"Well, I don't know if annoyed is the right word, really. Maybe upset is a better word, I guess. I mean…of course, it's natural they would mention Brooke. The four of us had a history together. Brooke is mostly what we have in common. I thought they'd be over this, especially after my last visit with them last fall just before you arrived. However, I guess I was wrong."

"And what about tonight upset you?"

"Tonight, I became more and more distressed when they just wouldn't let go of the past. I tried to change the topic several times while they doggedly kept coming back to me and Brooke."

Lindy waited holding Ren's hand and allowing Ren the time she needed to work through her feelings, trusting that she would share more as soon as she put the pieces together.

"I guess I feel that they should have respected your presence here in this house and here in my life as well. I mean, they know we're not lovers because they asked me. Still, I told them you are important to me. Knowing that, they should have at least tried to learn something about you...about us and what we're working on, perhaps shown some interest in our project." Ren shifted her weight drawing up a knee and sliding back farther into the cushions. She turned more towards Lindy. "I've worked very hard to release Brooke, to leave her behind. Despite years having passed since she died, she was an important part of my life. As much as I didn't want to and resisted it when she first died, I've finally moved forward. She is my past, but she will always be loved. Over the past few months, with your help, I've moved forward into a happier place. Now I'm content being in the present. You've helped me get here. What I'm doing with my life, the relationship we've developed, my life now, that's what is important--my present, our present. I'm proud of what you've created and what we've done together on the textbook. They could have at least asked about our lives, the present, instead of just dwelling on the past the whole time. The *whole* time."

Lindy felt the tension in Ren's body and heard the frustration evident in her voice. "You know they love you. Maybe they just don't realize that you've made progress in your life and that you've found a better state of mind. Be patient. As they spend time here, they'll see you're happier than you were last time they saw you."

"I know, it's just that they tried to drag me back to what was and I don't want to return there. Where I used to be is a dark and dreary place. I've worked too hard to get back to the here and now where I'm actually happy. I don't know if that makes any sense." Ren looked at Lindy for an answer.

Lindy nodded and gave Ren a smile. "Tomorrow will be different. Wait and see." Lindy slid her hand up Ren's arm to encircle her back then drew her friend's head down to her shoulder.

Ren allowed Lindy to comfort her. "You know, I used to think about Brooke hundreds of times a day. I would dream about her at night, feel her hands on me. It took years to get to where I was when you first came here. You helped me get through another anniversary of her death. I don't know how to explain how I felt...I think it was like I was always holding my breath before."

Ren sat up and turned to look into Lindy's eyes. "After you came, just by your being here and our working together, I felt like I started to breathe again. I know no one else can make me happy. I hope it makes sense when I say that I feel like you inspired me to be happy. With you, I found work I enjoy and companionship that brings me peace. You're a happy person, and I wanted to be happy with you—for you. It's not like I don't think of Brooke. She gestured to the large portrait on the wall. "I mean, there she is, right there, staring down at me every day. Now, when I think about her I'm able to give her a more balanced place in my thoughts, have placed her importance in my life more in proportion to how she relates to my present. She'll always be treasured." She collected her thoughts before continuing. "Maybe it's the artist in me, but it seems to be all about scale. She's become integrated with all the other people I've loved and lost, like my grandparents and my parents. All of them were important to me. I loved and I still miss each of them deeply. They're all gone and won't ever come back to me."

Lindy patiently waited for Ren to complete her thoughts.

"So, I've made up my mind. Tomorrow, if they haven't shaped up, I'm going to have to say something to them."

Ren stood up and pulled Lindy into her arms to give her a tight embrace. "Thanks for listening and thanks for checking on me. It means a lot." Arms wrapped around each other's waists as, side-by-side, they walked out of the studio. They paused at the threshold while Ren turned off the light and closed the door. Each turned toward her own bedroom, stopping only once to look back at each other before they continued to their separate rooms.

***

The next day things did change. They were dramatically better. To Ren, it almost seemed as though someone had replaced Carol and Nancy with two entirely different people. She was grateful that her visitors must have figured out that they had trod a little heavily on 'Memory Lane' the evening before.

Conversation over breakfast was animated. The couple asked numerous questions of Lindy in an effort to learn about her background and more about what she was writing. After Lindy mentioned the wonderful art that Ren was creating for the book, they asked if they could see some of the illustrations before their trip into town. Lindy, in turn, had an opportunity to learn some basic information about them.

Ren seemed refreshed and relieved by the fact that no one mentioned Brooke's name even once. Ren suggested that they might all want to catch dinner and a movie later that evening, since they would already be in town.

In a familiar gesture, Ren touched Lindy's arm. "Maybe we should ask Joey and Ben to join us?"

"I'll stop by and ask them on my way back from the library," Lindy volunteered.

Ren didn't have a clue that Lindy had called the guys and asked them to teach her how to lead during a slow dance. Lindy did not intend to waste any time at the library. She was heading straight for their house the minute Ren was out of sight. In case Ren happened to stop in at the guys' house, she now had a reasonable excuse she could use to explain why she was there. She and Ren had spent several evenings with them since New Year's Eve and she felt they were now her friends, too.

Ren dropped Carol and Nancy off in the center of town for their day of meandering through the quaint shops. They agreed to meet at The Anvil Restaurant for an early dinner at five-thirty. Planning to drop Lindy next, Ren made the turn off the main street. Lindy said, "You don't have to drop me at the library. I found the information I needed on the Internet. You can take me straight to Ben and Joey's house. I'll hang out with them for a while until you finish up. It'll be fun."

"Maybe I'll come in with you and say hello."

Lindy hid her feeling. Trying to sound as if that were the greatest idea ever she replied, "Oh good. I'm sure they'll be glad to see you." Lindy hoped that by being nonchalant Ren would change her mind and not come in. She was fearful that Joey or Ben would forget the purpose for her visit was a secret and would spill the beans about her dance lesson. Her concerns included worry that they would think something was humorous like teasing her by calling her Ginger Rogers or something similar. As they pulled up at the guys' house, Lindy was relieved to see that Ren must have changed her mind.

"You know, I think I'll get right down to the marina and start on the paper work I have to do there. If I can finish up quickly enough, want to come with me to stop by the mall and maybe check out that new coffee brewery place? Marie told me they have some nice imported teas there for me, too."

"Sure. I'd like that. Give me a call if you finish up early. That would be fun."'

Lindy exited the vehicle then turned to wait for Ren to pull away. Before she did, Ren lowered the window. "I feel a little silly. Despite knowing that I'll see you in a couple of hours, I'll miss you."

Lindy thought for only a few seconds before she realized that she felt the same way. She smiled then reached into the car to touch Ren's arm, delaying her departure. Her gaze held Ren's eyes. "I'll miss you, too." She watched Ren pull away. It was true, she admitted, she would miss her. She'd never felt so comfortable or compatible with anyone ever before.

When she first arrived on the island, she'd been concerned that it would be difficult to adjust to the lack of having other people around with whom to converse. It hadn't been. Ren was excellent company. They had similar work schedules, liked to take breaks around the same time, and enjoyed many of the same leisure activities. More important than all the work related and personal compatibilities, they simply had fun together. She had never once been bored with Ren's company or her conversation.

During their five months of having spent nearly twenty-four, seven together they had grown to be very close, sharing their innermost thoughts and fears. She knew that if she asked Ren something, she would always respond with a completely open and honest answer. A feeling of sadness washed over her when she thought of leaving Ren and the island to return to her former life. She felt tightness in her chest at the thought of not seeing Ren every day. Things at home felt different for her now that Jim and Terry were dating, but it wasn't only that. If she were honest with herself, she'd have to admit that she'd grown to love living with Ren. Now, when she thought of home, her first thought was of the island and Ren, not of her apartment and the university.

Ben's voice drew her back. "Hey, Ginger, plan on standing out there all day? Or should we call you Fred since you plan to lead?"

Ben and Joey were standing in their doorway watching her. She laughed, snorting air out through her nose and muttering 'ha' under her breath. *I should have made a bet that they'd called me Ginger. It was a sure win.* The thought never crossed her mind that they'd call her Fred. "Okay, which of you is the smart ass?" She meant which one had yelled to her. She had to laugh when both of them raised their right hand. *This was going to be fun.*

Joey was the first to try to teach Lindy how to lead in a slow dance. He demonstrated some fancy steps, even dipping her at one point. Then he tried to instruct her by dancing with his partner, returning in the end for another attempt with Lindy. After several painful encounters where his feet ended up under Lindy's, Joey muttered, "I think your two left feet are standing on my toes."

Ben gently led his partner to the recliner. "Sit," he ordered. Then turning to Lindy he laughed. "Okay, my turn. Enough of amateur hour...let an expert show you how it's done."

"Lindy, you're trying to do too much with all these fancy steps. If your intention is only to win a bet with Ren, you don't have to do all that fancy footwork the Fred Astaire wanna be over there is trying in vain to teach you. If you really want to learn how to dance with her, then the two of you should take lessons together. If you're just trying to prove your point, all you have to do is hold each other and do a simple box step. Do you know how?"

"I think so."

"Look, come here." He stood next to her and demonstrated.

She fell into step with him, duplicating his simple movements. "Oh, I can do this," she said, a relieved grin on her face.

"Okay, keep doing that." As she danced, he smoothly turned to face her and fell into step with her, not yet touching her. As they danced in step, he slowly moved closer until they were finally in dance hold. "There you go," he encouraged. "See, nothing to it."

She hugged him closer and kissed him on the cheek.

"Hey watch it," teased Joey. "That's my honey you're mauling." He made a grand show of standing and tapping Ben on the shoulder. "May I cut in?" Nudging Ben in the ribs, he added, "I'm ready for my turn."

Lindy swapped partners, leading as they danced through the end of the song then relaxed a few seconds waiting for the next song to begin. When the Platters began to sing *My Prayer*, Lindy exclaimed, "Ooooh, my favorite song."

She pulled Joey closer and started to dance with him. "Now, this is fine, if you just want to win a bet and show her you can do it. If you want to get her engines revving, just slide your hands into her back pockets and pull her hips nice and close, then you whisper something sweet in her ear and nibble on her earlobe."

Lindy couldn't imagine herself doing that. She laughed and pushed Joey away. "I think I've learned enough for today." She helped the guys put the coffee table back in place before they all went into the kitchen for hot chocolate. They were just in time too, because it was at that precise moment that Ren knocked on the door.

"Hey! It's Ren," she announced gleefully. Then, quietly to her cohorts in crime, "Don't forget, the dance lessons are our secret."

Ren came in to visit briefly before she invited Ben and Joey to join them on their shopping expedition. "Thanks anyway, we can't possibly...we have to wash our hair."

Ren laughed at their corny joke as she grabbed Lindy's hand, tugging her towards the door. "Let's go then, we're getting short on time if we want to make it to the mall and back before we meet Carol and Nancy." She turned to her friends. "Want to join us for dinner?"

"No. Thanks for asking. We have plans for later. We'll see you at our party though, if not before. The invitation is in the mail."

"Great!" The two women left and walked to the car as the guys watched from their doorway. Although unable to hear what they were saying, they both noticed the closeness of the women's bodies as they walked down the sidewalk together and the familiar way Ren touched Lindy's back as they separated to get into the car.

Joey looked at Ben. "How soon do you think it'll be until they figure it out?"

"I don't think it'll be too long now. I like Lindy a lot and I think she's good for Ren, don't you?"

Happy about the budding romance that he was convinced neither woman had yet become fully aware of, Joey responded. "Yes, I like her, too, and I agree with you that she's good for Ren. I haven't seen Ren this relaxed, and dare I say happy, in years, since...well, you know"

"The party could prove to be an interesting evening." Closing the door, the two men smiled at each other saying nearly in unison, "Can't wait!"

Ren and Lindy headed for the mall. "I'm glad you finished early."

Ren reached over and gave Lindy's hand a squeeze. "Me too."

They had a good time at the shop, 'Coffee, Tea, or Bee.'

"What an awful name," observed Ren. They had both giggled when they discovered that the shop had a very good selection of organic honey from the local area. "Now I get it," admitted Ren, pointing at the neatly stacked containers of honey. "I think I'll get some to go with my tea."

With their purchases safely stored in the back of the SUV, they drove to the restaurant. Carol and Nancy were already seated. They were extremely excited about all their bargains and they expounded on the wonderful stores they found in town.

"There is even a shop that sells a ton of Christmas stuff," Nancy observed excitedly.

After dinner, the group returned home to watch the news and weather report. There was a special Nor'easter forecast that the weathermen projected would arrive early on Thursday bringing with it another big snowstorm. "I wonder if we should consider heading home early," Carol said. Turning to Ren, Nancy asked, "What do you think Ren?"

"I hope the storm won't be a problem," Ren replied. "We'll definitely keep an eye on it."

"If the weather looks like it'll be really severe we might leave earlier than we planned so we can avoid the bad weather on the drive home. We hope you won't mind," Carol said.

"Of course I don't mind. I'd rather see you safe and not have to worry about you getting home in one piece."

Chapter 28: Will You Tell Them I'm a Lesbian?

The next couple of days passed quickly as the women relaxed together. Now that Ren's visitors seemed to understand that Ren didn't want to constantly speak about Brooke, their visit became much more pleasant. Lindy liked them a lot and the four women had fun together.

Lindy begged off, saying she had some work to do when Ren, Carol, and Nancy took a walk to explore the island and to visit the flat rocks near where Brooke's ashes reposed in the sea. "Thank you for asking, but you should have some private time there."

After their walk, Carol and Nancy decided to use the hot tub, which offered Ren an opportunity to visit privately with Lindy. She told her friends she'd see them later and came upstairs to find Lindy.

"Come in," Lindy responded to the soft tap at her office door. Ren entered and settled at one of the chairs near the window. She smiled when she noticed the display of her artwork on the wall in front of Lindy's desk. The framed set of photos she bought on her first trip to town hung there, as did Ren's self-portrait that Lindy had taken from the wall in Ren's studio as part of their deal for her posing. "How'd it go?"

Without mentioning specifically what 'it' was, each knew they were talking about the visit Ren, Carol and Nancy just made to the flat rocks. "It was okay. Don't be worried. I'm fine.

It's been good seeing Carol and Nancy again." Ren paused again, organizing her thoughts. "Our visit got off to a rocky start. Fortunately, it's been fun the past several days. Still sometimes, I still get the impression that when they look at me they see what's missing, as though it took Brooke and me together to make a whole. Now that she's gone it seems that, in their eyes, I'm less than she and I seemed to be as a unit. It feels like they expect me to be incomplete forever--the walking wounded, for want of a better term."

"And how do you perceive things?"

Ren considered the question seriously. "I think that I thought of myself the same way for a long time. At last, I'd say that's changed or at least is changing, now. It's hard for me to explain it verbally because I'm such a visually oriented person." Ren paused again, briefly. "From my point of view, Brooke was a piece of me that made me a whole person. I've learned that when she died, that piece of me didn't disappear, it's still here." Ren touched her heart. Needing to solidify her thoughts more in her own mind than for Lindy's benefit, she elaborated. "The way I think about it is like this." Ren stood and walked to Lindy's desk and pulled a sheet of paper from the printer. She picked a red magic marker from the container on the desk.

"Say I start with a canvas this size." She drew a large red circle in the center of the paper then filled it in so it was solid. "The paper represents me as a whole person. The circle represents Brooke's importance in my life." She smiled. "I was young when we met, so the canvas isn't too big, because I'd only lived through a limited number of experiences up to that point in my life. Therefore, Brooke had a large place in my canvas, in my life. The present represented most of my canvas. Everything, most every thought was in the present because my life was mostly comprised of the present, since there was little past. The intensity of my feelings for her, combined with my limited canvas, amplified her importance to me."

"Okay, I think I understand...and now?"

"Well, now, I'm older and I need a bigger canvas to represent my life and things that have happened in my life." Ren gestured to the wall. "Now, my canvas is this size." She placed the piece of paper with the circle on it against the white wall. "Now, if you look at the circle, Brooke is still there, still a whole piece of me and no less important. I've come to realize that in this larger canvas that is my life," Ren gestured in a circular motion, "there are compartments here, in an organized life. At least that's how I've come to visualize it." She took another piece of paper to draw on. "Let's reduce the scale to something more manageable."

After drawing a line down the paper dividing it into a larger section taking roughly three quarters of the sheet, and a smaller section taking up one quarter of the page she said, "The whole paper is the area representing my life currently. Imagine the present is the bigger of the two because it houses all my active and probably what should be considered as the more important thoughts.

Ren drew another line to bisect the past then labeled the top half 'sad.' "Brooke is no longer in the present because she died. Her loss combines with my loss of my parents and grandparents, the failure of my relationship with Melanie and any number of other sad things in my past. They are now compartmentalized in this section right here, the sad section." Ren, more animated now, raised her eyebrows, tilted her head slightly, and raised her index finger. "But, and that but is in all capital letters, here's the good thing."

Writing the label 'happy' into the bottom half of the smaller section, she explained, "In the past there is another section for happy things as well. If we're lucky, the happy section is crammed full, filled with joyful memories that can balance out and make up for the sad things. Sure, Brooke is gone and, of course, that's sad. However, I'm lucky that I had many happy years with her."

Ren made some squiggly lines in each of the two sections, happy and sad. My grandparents are gone, too." she added squiggles to illustrate her points. "Again, I have many happy memories of my childhood with them over here in the good memories place." She added more lines. "Mom and dad here...to balance out for my lack of good memories for them since I was too young to have any when they died, I have the fact that I was raised by wonderful grandparents and a have great memories of growing up with an equally loving brother. For me, I think I suffered so much because I struggled with transferring Brooke's memory into my 'past compartment' where memories are easier to deal with. It's taken me a while to get a handle on all of this, but thinking things through this way has helped me achieve a better sense of balance. Now, Carol and Nancy...they seem to keep trying to drag Brooke back here, into the present, and she just doesn't belong there." Ren stopped to look at Lindy. "I hope you understand what I'm trying to explain so poorly here."

"Yes, very clearly. You've obviously given this a lot of thought."

Ren paused staring at the huge red spot on the paper where she'd started. "Another thing I've realized..." Ren picked up the paper and tore out the red circle from the center of the page after which she again held the paper against the wall. "With Brooke gone, this is the way Carol and Nancy look at me, as if Brooke has been removed, leaving me missing a huge part or portion of myself. I've come to recognize, to understand and believe that she's not gone. She's just been relocated here."

Lindy pointed to the sad past memories, then to the happy memories section on the smaller paper where Ren had drawn the squiggly lines. "From here to here?"

"Exactly!" Ren exhaled and gave Lindy a smile then nodded to indicate her satisfaction that Lindy really did understand what she was saying. "Exactly. I'm still whole, Brooke is still here," she placed her hand on her chest, over her heart, "in a safer place and not always front and center in my minute-to-minute and day-to-day thoughts."

"I understand what you mean. Give them some time. Look how long it's taken you to get all these thoughts straight in your head and in your heart. They'll come around. You haven't seen them enough since she died, for them to have seen you as a bigger canvas." Lindy put her hand on Ren's, drawing her closer so that she was standing right in front of her. She took Ren's other hand in her own. "They're a wonderful couple who love you. They want to help you, and maybe they think sharing remembrances is what you need. Eventually, with some gentle redirecting on your part, they'll figure out what you need from them. Someday, you will find someone else to love, and will be happy with her. Despite some rocky spots, they'll come to understand and will see you differently once they understand that you've moved on. They've been your friends a long time." Lindy tapped her finger on the paper Ren used to explain her thoughts to her, "Remember, they're seeking their own balance, too"

As Ren became aware that Lindy's hands still rested on her own, she looked Lindy in the eyes and knew that she had already found someone to love. *It's not fair that I can't have her now that I've finally found and fallen for her.* She resisted her desire to pull Lindy to her, into an embrace, to confess her love. Instead, she swallowed down the words and her emotions, reluctantly pulled her hands away, and returned to one of the chairs near the window. Lindy sat opposite on the other chair. For a while, they just sat quietly, enjoying sharing the comfortable quiet with each other.

"I've enjoyed having you here with me." Not wanting to allow herself to become depressed after all the serious conversation, Ren sought Lindy's help. "Got any good news?" Ren winked at Lindy. "I'd sure like to hear some."

Lindy thought for a minute then smiled. "As a matter of fact, I do. I went through the mailbag while you were with your guests. We got the invitation to Joey and Ben's party."

"Are you sure you're comfortable going to that party"

"Why wouldn't I be comfortable? It's just a party. In fact, I'm looking forward to it. It should be a fun time. Oh, by the way, it said 'clothing optional' on the invitation."

Ren's head snapped around as she said, "What?" Her voice was louder than she intended. "What the hell are they talking about?" It was at that moment she saw her face and knew Lindy had once again used her mischievous sense of humor to brighten their lives. She felt her mood lift as they shared the laugh together. "We'll be talking about this moment again, I'd imagine."

"Oh, you can surely count on it. I'm sure it'll be mentioned when I call to accept for us. Or would you rather respond?"

"No. You do it. Maybe you'll get it out of your system before we see Jack and Marie."

"Not a chance." Lindy giggled as humor danced in her eyes.

"What can I do to bribe you?"

"Hmm. I'm not sure. Let me think about it."

"I'll do something nice for you. Name it."

"Oh, I can't even think. You do nice things for me all the time."

Ren looked at the warm, comfortable room. Lindy's personal touch was evident everywhere, transforming the plain space into a cozy and cheerful workplace. As her eyes traveled around the comfortable room, Ren's gaze came to rest on the framed photos on the table next to her. "Your parents...it's nice that you're close to them."

"Yes, very."

"You said they live in Florida. It must be hard not seeing them for such a long time."

"It is, even though I talk to them on the phone often. I figured when we finished our project, I might go see them for a couple of weeks for a nice visit."

"Do they like to travel?"

"They usually take a trip once a year. In fact, they just got back from a cruise. Why?"

"I don't know," she shrugged, "I do have an idea for my penance so you won't tattle."

"That's not necessary. I swear I won't tell. You're absolved from all debts."

"Deal. Still, I do have an idea I'd like you to think about."

Unsure about Ren's sincerity Lindy warily asked, "What?"

"I know you can't go to them right now, we're going to be busy catching up after Carol and Nancy's visit. However, you could invite them up here for a couple of weeks early in May just before the start of the season. I'd love to meet them and you would get to spend some time with them. May is usually a lovely time of year here. If they're willing to make the trip, I'll open one of the cabins for them and they can have a romantic little get away along with a visit with you. We can take them sightseeing. I haven't done all the touristy things in the area in years. And you can spend some time showing them around."

"Really?" Overwhelmed by Ren's kind offer, Lindy's eyes filled. "That's very sweet, and extremely generous of you. I do miss them," she confessed. "This year I missed my usual Christmas visit." Lindy thought for a moment, smiling in remembrance. "My mom loves to take photographs and my Dad loves to add little things into the background without her knowledge. Once he put someone streaking far in the background of the photo she took of some garden they toured. She threatened to kill him over that one. Secretly, I think she loves it, despite being unwilling to admit that."

Ren studied the photos carefully. "You look like your mother."

"I do, but I have my father's mischievousness," she confessed.

"Why don't you give them a call and invite them? Let me know if they accept and when they'd like to come so I can make the arrangements for the cabin, stock in some extra food, and get the kitchen staff in early."

"We won't need a kitchen staff. We'll all cook. After all, it's just the family. Maybe one Sunday Jack, Marie, and Laura could join us and meet my parents. Maybe we could invite Joey and Ben, too. It would be fun...our first party."

Lindy's furrowed brow indicated she was seriously thinking about something. Decision made, she nodded. "I know they'll like you very much."

Ren sat quietly for several seconds, finally deciding to ask the question. "I'm curious, will you tell them I'm a lesbian?"

"Would you want me to?"

"It's not something I worry about for the paying guests, since I maintain a fairly casual relationship with them. However, since I'll be spending more time interacting with your parents socially, on a more personal level, it might be easier if you told them. I'd probably be more relaxed if they knew, not having to be on guard about what I say--especially if you want to include Joey and Ben. How do you think your parents would react to having a meal with fifty percent of the attendees being gay?"

"My parents are very liberal people. They raised me to think for myself and not to be excessively concerned about the opinions of others. I can't imagine them having an issue with you or anyone else being gay. I mean really, can you imagine a pair of bigots raising someone like me?"

Ren smiled, a kind expression gracing her face. "I can only imagine parents who were no less than perfect raising you." Ren's expression conveyed the sincerity of her compliment. "Call them and let me know if they accept our invitation."

"Thank you, Ren. I'll call them later."

"Good." Ren checked her watch. "Damn. I'd better get out there to my guests. Will you come with me?"

"Sure." Lindy stood to follow Ren out the door. "Maybe we can find a movie to show them or a game?"

"That would be good." Ren started to go find her guests then turned to Lindy. "Thank you is such a simple phrase to express such a deep and profound sense of gratitude. Please know that I mean it."

"No need to thank me. All I did was listen."

"No, you've done much more than that. You lift me up every day and make me look forward to tomorrow. Ren cupped Lindy's face in her hand. She wanted to kiss Lindy, to show her physically what simple words, in her mind, failed to convey. She clamped down on her desire and led the way down the hall.

LINDY CAPRINI JOURNAL

I thought for a moment today Ren was going to kiss me. She held my face in her hand and her lips were just inches away. Seconds later, she pulled back and turned away. I know she cares, and I'm pretty sure she wants me, too. I think she's afraid—I guess it stands to reason, doesn't it? I have several strikes against me. Historically, I'm a straight woman. I am only here for a few more months, and I live several states away where I have a job and a life. She has to suspect that, even if she did allow herself to get involved, all too soon I'd be leaving her. Another loss. Even though she's much stronger now, I'm not sure that she could stand to allow herself to love me, assuming that I'll be leaving in a matter of months. I know that if she'd love me back, I'd never leave her. Unfortunately, she has no way of knowing that. I think I would scare her away if I just come out and told her I love her. She needs more time. I'm reasonably sure that the feelings are there, but she needs to come to me. I just need to let her know that I won't turn her away. Maybe there is a way I can prove it to her. I have an idea.

Chapter 29: What Do You Have On Our Agenda For Today?

Wednesday morning over breakfast the group listened to the weather forecast for the next few days. The meteorologist was predicting a very bad Nor'easter with high winds and possible blizzard conditions. Forecasters suspected there would be at least a foot of snow in many areas of New England although it was still too early to predict accumulation amounts exactly.

"Ren, Nancy and I talked it over last night. We've decided to leave today, before the storm hits, if you don't mind. Could you run us over to our car once we gather up everything? We figured that if we left this morning we'd be able to take our time and not feel pressured on the trip home."

"I understand. You certainly don't want to have to drive home through this storm, so you either need to get out in front of it or wait till it's done and leave then."

"That's what we thought too. I have to be back at work on Saturday, so we can't wait it out. We think this is the safest option."

"I can take you whenever you have your things together." Carol and Nancy left to pack while Ren and Lindy cleaned up after breakfast.

Lindy finished drying the last plate as Ren wiped her hands on a paper towel and leaned against the counter. "We have some found time today. Feel like taking a day off just for us, to do something different? After they leave, we can spend the rest of today on the mainland and think of something fun together, if you'd like."

"That sounds like a great idea. Do I need to put on dress clothes?

Ren shook her head. "Be comfortable. I think jeans will do, and dress in layers. We can eat somewhere casual." Ren grabbed her coat from the hook near the back door. "I'm going to go warm up the boat so we don't freeze to death on the way over. When they get their bags together, can you have them bring them down to the boat? Wear something warm and water proof. It'll be raw today."

While everyone was packing, Ren returned from the boat to check the house and make sure everything would be secure during her absence. She normally wouldn't have to worry about it. Because Maggie and Bob were on their honeymoon and no one would be around, she took extra precautions. Satisfied the Inn would be safe, she went down to warm up the boat.

The ride over to the mainland was rough. The winds were starting to kick up already. Carol raised her voice above the engine noise, "I think it's a good decision to leave early." Nancy nodded her agreement and slid her hand into her lover's.

With the goodbye hugs and kisses exchanged, Carol and Nancy waved as they started on their journey home. Lindy and Ren watched until the car disappeared around the corner then headed for their cars parked in the marina. Because they had not run Lindy's car for a couple of weeks they agreed that they should use it. Ren drove, as she knew their destination.

"I'm curious, what do you have on our agenda for today?"

"Well, I thought I'd like to show you the park, unfortunately some of the roads are closed this time of year. I'll take you on a little tour first of the areas we can get in to see, then stop for a visit with my friend at the sanctuary. They have a nice museum there. Then, we can have a little lunch. We'll find a place that has a great view and some good food. If there's time, we'll stop at the museum in town. I love to check out their gift shop every now and then. They have a wonderful assortment of baskets. We have several at the house."

Ren continued driving out of town stopping now and again to point out a landmark of interest. When they arrived at the sanctuary, they toured the museum before observing some of the birds housed there for rehabilitation.

"Feel like a little stroll through the woods?"

"That would be lovely. It's so beautiful here."

They started down one of the pathways, enjoying the scents of the forest, trees, and crisp air. As they walked, Lindy slipped her arm through Ren's as she had done before. Ren felt herself respond, heat spreading outward from her core. *If only*. She wished with all her heart that she could speak her heart to Lindy. Too afraid to risk their friendship, knowing she couldn't bear to lose that, she kept mum.

They both jumped as a deer darted across the path ahead of them. "We must have scared her." Lindy said. "She was so beautiful."

Ren nodded. "Getting cold?"

"Mostly just my feet."

"Let's head back. We'll get warmed up in the car and then get some lunch."

On the way back to town, Ren drove through the local college. "This is a place worth exploring. You should look it up, maybe schedule a visit when the spring comes. I think you'd find it interesting."

They found a cozy little restaurant that specialized in seafood on their way back into town. Ren requested that they be seated near the fireplace where they both finished thawing out.

"I'm sorry we can't tour more of the park today. So many of the roads are closed for another month or two. There are so many beautiful places there to see. I regret that we didn't go earlier in the season, when you first arrived. We were so eager to get started on the project, I really neglected my duties as a good host."

"No, everything is perfect as it is. We're seeing it now."

"Depending on what's open when your parents come to visit, we can do more of the park then. We'll take them on a tour of the area and I'll arrange for a special brunch for us at a restaurant near here owned by a friend of mine. You go there and they have four rooms where they serve the meal. Each group has their own dining room and the food is something you'll remember forever."

"My mother would love that. I can't wait."

After lunch, they'd planned to go to the museum. When Ren mentioned her concern about the weather, Lindy responded, "I don't mind going back early so we can see better on the trip home. I've seen a few flurries already. Like you, I think I would feel more comfortable going back now."

Ren smiled. "Wise woman. Let's do that."

On the trip home, Ren analyzed her feelings for Lindy. There was no doubt that she was attracted to her. However, there were numerous reasons why she felt she was in a hopeless situation. *First consideration, Lindy is straight and she'll only be here a few more months. She has a job and friends back home. We could always just have a fling. Lindy might be capable of that. Then she could go back home and pretend it never happened. She seems like she could be open enough to it. She admits that the novels turned her on. I wonder if that really means anything? I wouldn't want to be the one to bring her out if it is only an experiment for her. I can't let myself love her that way if there's no chance she'll love me the way I'm prepared to love her. Face it, especially if we go to that level my heart will shatter when she leaves. Yeah, like it won't break now*, she thought wryly.

"You're awfully quiet. What're you thinking about?"

Ren was usually very honest with Lindy. Still she didn't think sharing the truth about what she was thinking would be of any benefit so, instead, she prevaricated slightly. "I'm thinking about what a nice time we had today. Spending time with you is always so easy. I really enjoy whatever we do together, even work. Speaking of work, how is Flint's Folly progressing?

"I've put it on hold for a little while. I got another idea for a novel, and I've been picking away at it."

"When can I read it? What's it about?"

"I don't want to share the plot until I'm more confident about how it will end. I'm still working on developing the story. When I finish the plot outline, I'll let you read that. Deal?"

"Deal."

Chapter 30: She's Trying To Make Ren Make The First Move

After their short break from daily life, Ren and Lindy went back to work with renewed enthusiasm. Ahead of schedule, they were making great progress on their book and expected to complete everything as planned, possibly before their planned deadline. When Lindy's parents accepted Ren's offer for them to come for a visit in May, at Ren's suggestion, Lindy agreed to relax their work schedule during their visit. Lindy's parents wrote, sending a warm note of greeting to Ren expressing their appreciation for her generosity and for allowing them to enjoy an unexpected visit with their daughter.

For the most part, their routine remained unchanged with the exception that, after dinner, Lindy would return to her room for an hour or two to work alone to complete her plot outline and eventually to work on writing her book.

Lindy joined Ren in the library one evening and after a brief time, she closed the book she was reading and announced that she'd just finished the last of the romance novels from her Christmas gift to Ren. They talked briefly about the story then sat quietly enjoying the fire and the companionship. Lindy noticed Ren studying her. Finally unable to stand it any longer Lindy asked. "What's wrong?"

"Not a thing. When are you going to pose for me again?"

"You know when."

Ren recalled their last discussion regarding Lindy's posing for her. "Oh yeah, I remember--the bear skin rug. Right."

***

Ren and Lindy each showered and dressed in preparation for Ben and Joey's annual St. Patrick's Day party. Earlier in the week, after the guys declined their offer to help set up for the gathering, saying everything was under control, they'd agreed to make a night of it and have an early, light snack in town before joining the festivities at Joey and Ben's place.

By the time they arrived at the party, it was in full swing. They finally found a parking place over a block away. Lindy linked her arm through Ren's as they made their way to the house. Ren enjoyed the feeling, always pretending, even if for only a moment, that they were a couple and heading off to their destination together.

Joey greeted both women warmly after he opened the door. With hugs and kisses exchanged and coats hung Joey announced, "Drinks are at the bar downstairs. Ben is playing DJ tonight."

"Are Peg and Penny here yet?" Ren asked.

"No. They called me yesterday. Penny's parents decided to pick this weekend for a visit, so they're not coming."

"Oh, that's too bad. I was looking forward to seeing them again." Lindy added. "Maybe we can all get together again for dinner in the next couple of weeks."

"Ben and I would enjoy that."

"We'll give them a call and arrange it. When do the parents leave?"

"Monday, I think. You'll have to check with them to be sure." When Ren nodded, Joey led them to the cellar door. "Go on down and have some fun."

Ben had compiled his own music for the party. The disco beat was thumping as they descended the stairs. Wanting to be able to entertain, the guys had turned the full basement of their large ranch home into their 'party' room. There was a small bar at one end of the open space. The furniture arrangement was fluid. Chairs, tables, and sofas could be repositioned according to need. For the party, they had made small groupings of furniture to allow people the opportunity to sit and socialize in intimate groups. There were fewer seats than people so once a seat was vacated, someone else slipped into it quickly. It was an idea the hosts thought of so people would rotate and get to know or visit with everyone at the party. Snacks were set up near the bar. Later in the evening when they brought out the food, they would set up folding chairs and tables so everyone could sit and eat the meal.

Ren and Lindy made their way through the crowded room to the bar to get a drink. Ben was having a great time as the DJ and was playing the several disks of music he'd created especially for the party. For the most part fast and line dances were first up. He'd already been successful in his goal of getting people out on the dance floor. Several couples were already dancing at the area at the far end of the room reserved for that purpose, and it was still early in the evening.

There were several men and women standing at the bar when Lindy and Ren approached to order their drinks from the bartender. The room was noisy and it was difficult to hear.

"Where are you from?" A tall woman with cropped red hair leaned in close and spoke in Lindy's ear. "You must be new in town. I thought I knew all the lesbians who live here." She put an arm around Lindy's shoulders and drew her closer to her. "Come on over here nearer to me so we can talk."

Before Ren could intervene or correct the brash woman's assumption that Lindy was a lesbian, Lindy pulled away from the woman's embrace and slipped her arm through Ren's. "Yes, I'm a newcomer. I'm Lindy. Have you met my partner, Ren?"

"Yes. Yes, I have. Hi, Ren. Sorry, I didn't know. How long have you two been together?"

Lindy snuggled closer to Ren and even though the woman addressed her question to Ren, Lindy's eyes twinkled mischievously as she replied, "Just a few months now, right honey?"

Getting into the harmless charade Ren smiled at Lindy. "Whatever you say, dear. You're the one who keeps track of all our anniversaries." Ren picked up their drinks. "Excuse us, Toni. We're going to try to find a seat." They found two chairs near the dance floor.

"That's Toni. If she were a man, I'd call her the biggest letch in town...also the biggest gossip. I'll be having a call from Jack and Marie tomorrow morning wanting to know why we didn't tell them we're a couple."

"Would you be ashamed to admit it to them?"

"That we're a couple? Of course not...not if it were true. I'd be proud to announce it on the front pages of the Times if it was true, but it isn't."

"No, it isn't. Look, don't worry about it. We can explain the situation to Jack and Marie tomorrow." Taking Ren by the hand Lindy said, "Come on, let's dance and have some fun."

They danced the next two fast dances before returning to eat some snacks and have another drink. Enjoying the opportunity to socialize, Ren and Lindy met and talked with the party guests. Ren introduced Lindy to several friends that Lindy had not yet met. With the food served, they filled their plates and went upstairs to find a quiet place to sit and enjoy their meal.

Lindy popped a stuffed mushroom into her mouth umming her appreciation. "Yum! The food is amazing. I'm having a great time, aren't you?"

"Yes," responded Ren a slow smile spreading on her face. "I've already had about five people congratulate me on being able to land such a lovely partner. They all wanted to know where I'd found you. I told them I had to import you because no one here was worthy of me." Ren winked.

"Truer words were never spoken." Lindy laughed. "Come on, I hear the music starting up again. I'm ready to dance some more."

They danced several fast dances before Ben announced over the mic, "It's time to slow it down a little. Our first number is a very old standard, *My Prayer* by the Platters. Come on all you love birds." Ben's eyes sought Lindy's. He winked in conspiracy.

Lindy extended her hand to Ren, leaned in closer, and said. "May I have this dance?"

Recalling their agreement about them slow dancing, Ren asked, "Who's leading?"

"Me." Lindy grasped the hand Ren extended and led her to the dance floor that was already crowded with other couples. Lindy pulled Ren to her and started to lead using the simple steps Ben and Joey had taught her. As she gained confidence, she pulled Ren closer. They were moving in a rhythm now, both comfortable with the simple steps. Ren could feel her nipples harden as they pressed against Lindy, and as she became aroused, the seam of her jeans began to put pressure in a very sensitive area. She knew she should pull away and stop herself from enjoying the way her body was fitting with Lindy's. *I'll be okay...the song is almost over.*

The next song on the dance mix was another Platters song, *Twilight Time*. Lindy put her lips to Ren's ear and said innocently, "I can't believe it, my two favorite slow dance songs right in a row." She held her lips as close as possible to Ren's ear. Ren shuddered against her.

The words were innocent enough but the effect of Lindy's lips moving against her ear made Ren literally groan aloud. She covered her response by clearing her throat. *Oh, Lord! I'm in trouble here.* When she tried to put some space between her and Lindy, she felt Lindy's hands slip into her back belt loops. By pulling against them, Lindy maintained enough tension to keep Ren's hips pulled tightly against her. "I'm so glad we came to the party. I'm having a great time dancing with you," Lindy murmured into Ren's ear.

As the song finally ended, Ren mumbled, "I'm about to spontaneously combust." She wiped her palm across her forehead. "I need a drink. Aren't you hot?" She didn't wait for a response. Instead she pulled Lindy back to the bar to get them each a beer.

"I think I'll use the restroom. It doesn't look like the line is too long now." Lindy touched Ren's shoulder as she squeezed behind her chair. The light brush of Lindy's fingers across her neck as she pulled away did nothing to calm Ren's excited condition.

Joey slid onto the stool next to Ren and leaned closer so she could hear him. "Watching you two dance...um, I think you look good and fit together very nicely. If I didn't know better, I'd say that you two were already doing the deed, you know, were lovers. Are you sure she's straight?"

"Yes. Unfortunately. So, don't get any ideas. She's straight. If we got involved, it would just be a little stroll on the wild side for her. Anyway, I don't want a quick romance. If I get involved with someone again, I want a forever. She has a home and a job in Philly. That doesn't leave any room for me to be a permanent part of her life. Believe me, I've given it serious thought, although I just don't see it happening."

"Have you told her that's how you feel?"

"No. I'm not sure exactly what it is I'm feeling. Under different circumstances, I could easily fall in love with her. I have to keep reminding myself not to go there. I don't want to lose her friendship, it's very important to me. I've been enjoying just spending time with her so much that I don't want to screw up, to complicate, the last few months we have together before she heads home."

"You know, Ren, she's a great person who cares for you very much. I think you should talk things out with her. You may be surprised to find out that she's feeling exactly the same way you are."

"No, I don't think that's a good idea. It's better we leave things as they are and remain friends. In a few more months, she'll have to go back to Philly and that would break my heart if I allow myself to care for her as anything other than a friend."

"Are you sure that hasn't happened already?" Joey asked.

Ren just looked at him then glanced across the room to watch Lindy as she made her way across the room towards them. Joey got his answer just from the look in Ren's eyes, as she watched Lindy's approach.

***

I can't take any more dancing like that. One more dance like the last one and I'll have to take her upstairs, find an empty room, and qualify for my toaster oven.

Part of her wanted to stay snuggled into Lindy's arms forever. When the rational side of her won out, with regret, she told Lindy it was time for them to head back to the island. "Come on, it's getting late. We'd better head home."

As Ben and Joey watched Ren and Lindy leave, Ben asked his partner, "Think it'll happen tonight?"

"No, I don't think so. There's obviously chemistry there, Ben. It's almost impossible to believe, that Ren still thinks Lindy is straight and would only be interested in her for a quick fling or as she put it, a walk on the wild side. She just can't accept the possibility that Lindy might be having the same feelings she's having. Ren figures Lindy might just want to experiment with her then return home at the end of the summer. I don't know Lindy well enough to know what she's feeling for sure. Either she's an incredibly big tease or she has genuine feelings for Ren, who was just about jumping out of her skin every time Lindy touched her tonight."

"What about Lindy?" Ben asked his partner. "Lindy surely can't be oblivious to the reaction Ren is having to her. I mean...she'd have to be blind not to see that Ren pretty much self-combusts every time Lindy touches her."

"You're right. No, I think Lindy's trying to push Ren's buttons to get her to make the first move. Ren has recognized that something is happening between them that could be more than just friendship, but she's concerned and too afraid to take things further. So, she's holding the line at friendship, too afraid, I think, to risk anything more out of fear."

Ben absorbed the information Joey shared. "It's obvious that Lindy cares for her. Still, maybe Ren is right to be cautious. She's finally feeling good again. She's happy. What would happen if they get involved and Lindy goes back home at the end of the summer? If Ren allows herself to fall in love, it'll devastate her again if Lindy leaves. Lindy could very easily think she's really in love with Ren, then decide she isn't a lesbian."

"Absolutely. You just verbalized exactly what Ren shared with me."

"Still it seems that Lindy genuinely cares for Ren. She didn't look straight while she was dancing with her tonight."

"I know. We know from experience that recognizing you're not who you thought you were is a difficult admission. Lindy is dealing with that all alone. She really didn't share exactly what she's feeling with us," Joey said. "I don't know. I guess it's possible she's just looking to experiment but I don't think so."

"I hope not, for both their sakes. Besides, Lindy knows Ren very well—at least well enough to know that if she declared her feelings, Ren might just give her that, 'I'm not ready yet,' knee jerk reaction. I like Lindy, and like you, I trust that she has Ren's best interests at heart. I still think she's trying to push Ren into making the first move."

"Well, Lindy's either really innocent, unaware of what she's doing to Ren, or she's really clever. I'm not sure which it is. If only they'll allow themselves to trust that it would work, they'd be great together. I just hope they figure it out before one or both of them end up getting hurt."

Chapter 31: For Now, Forever, And For Always

As they left the party, Lindy linked her arm through Ren's as they walked to the car. "That was fun."

"Yes, it was."

They parked at the marina. Handing Lindy the key to the office, Ren requested, "Can you get the mail while I warm up the boat?

"Sure." A few minutes later Lindy returned to the boat carrying a large cardboard box and a bag of mail.

"Who's the box for?"

"Me."

"More books," Ren asked hopefully.

"Nope. If all goes well, I guarantee you'll enjoy it as much as I will."

Ren furrowed her brow. "Well, I can't wait to see what's in the box if I'm going to enjoy it so much. How about a hint?"

Lindy shook her head. I'll show it to you when we need it...no sooner."

"Now I'm really curious."

No matter how Ren tried, Lindy wouldn't reveal the contents of the box even though Ren guessed and coaxed for the duration of their trip back to the island. She still knew no more when they arrived back at the Inn than she did when they left the marina.

***

They relaxed at the kitchen counter, and while Ren made them each a cup of tea, Lindy switched on the radio to the oldies station. As she listened to the song playing, Lindy absently watched Ren putter around the kitchen as she waited for the water to boil. A smile teased her lips as she recalled her recognition early on, shortly after her arrival on the island, that she was attracted to Ren. The feelings that she initially wrote off to the power of suggestion after she discovered that Ren was a lesbian, she'd always assumed would pass. They hadn't. In fact, as she grew to know the wounded and sensitive woman, Lindy's feelings had intensified and deepened. As Ren began to heal, growing stronger during the time they spent time living and working together, Lindy sensed that they were both happier as a pair than either had been alone.

Through her actions and comments over the past couple of months, Lindy suspected that, left to her own devices, Ren wouldn't move their relationship to a more intimate level. The sudden clarity of this realization struck her, leaving no doubt in her mind. She felt a sense of peace come over her. Peace and another stronger, undeniable feeling—desire. She wanted Ren. For the first time in her life, she understood what it was to really want, to crave someone, and she was determined that she wasn't going to wait any longer for Ren to accept and believe that she loved her.

As a slow song began to play, Lindy stood and slid behind Ren and wrapped her arms around her. "Dance with me," Lindy whispered.

Ren turned around slowly. Lindy pulled her tight, and they began to dance, bodies pressed closely together. Lindy placed her cheek against Ren's and playfully whispered into her ear, "I love slow dancing with you, because I get to feel your body against mine." She brushed her lips softly along Ren's ear lobe and gently sucked it into her mouth.

Unable to deny herself any longer, Ren pulled her head back and sought Lindy's lips with her own. Passion exploded between them as their tongues danced together. Ren slipped her leg between Lindy's allowing them to press intimately together. For a moment, Ren's heart soared with pent up passion and love for Lindy. With a groan, she stopped herself and pulled away.

"Wait, Lindy, we should talk. I can't let this happen. You want me today. What happens when you want to go home in a few months. I can't face loving you now then losing you when you leave. I care too much for you already and can't face another loss like that, not again."

Not wanting to argue when she was so close to getting what she wanted Lindy said, "I have something I want you to read." She went to her office then quickly returned with the plot outline for *Sunset Island*, the book she was working on writing. She laid it on the counter and shoved it towards Ren. "Maybe you should ask me what I want instead of being a one woman judge and jury."

Ren reached for the document on the counter as Lindy turned to walk back to her room.

"This is hopeless," Lindy said aloud to no one. Back in her bedroom, she angrily stripped off her clothes and prepared to take a shower.

Ren started reading the plot outline for Lindy's book. As she read, she soon realized that the story was loosely based on the life that she and Lindy had been living over the past few months. Quickly, she skimmed down to the chapter dealing with the party, where slow dancing made the couple so sexually charged that they made love on their return to the island. Ignoring the rest, she flipped to the next page and read the summary for the final two scenes. The next to the last scene was the commitment ceremony the couple held on the cliff overlooking the ocean. The story ended with the new lovers settled in the library taking turns reading a published copy of the book to each other.

"My God, I'm an idiot," Ren uttered aloud. She hurried down the hallway to Lindy's room. Finding the door ajar, Ren pushed it open further and called Lindy's name. Hearing no response, Ren paused to listen--she could hear the water in the shower running. "Lindy," she called as she entered the bathroom and shoved the curtain aside. Their eyes met. "I'm an idiot."

Lindy pulled the fully clothed Ren into the shower with her. "Yes, you are, but you're my idiot. I love you, now and forever. I'll never change my mind. If you'll have me, I'm yours for as long as you want me."

"Good, because I'm never letting you go. I love you, Lindy."

In between kisses, they managed to get Ren's soaked clothes off so they could finally press their wet, warm bodies together. Their kisses left them breathless. Ren's hands traveled over Lindy's back. She slid her palm up Lindy's body cupping her breast. Lindy's hand stopped her causing Ren's eyes to snap open.

"What's wrong? I thought you wanted this, wanted me."

"I do. I want you more than anything, ever." Lindy closed her eyes and shook her head. Exhaling a frustrated sigh, she pulled Ren close. "It's just that I'm afraid it won't be different than before for me and I'll fail again. But I want at least this much. Please, let me make love to you."

"I promise you won't disappoint me, no matter what happens. I love you."

Ren leaned in for a slow kiss, the passion building quickly. Lindy pulled her lips away from Ren's as she began to explore her body. She turned Ren around as Ren braced her palms to the wall. Lindy wrapped her arms around Ren to fondle her breasts, softly pinching the already erect nipples until Ren cried out in pleasure. Lindy lowered her lips to Ren's tattoo and ran her tongue over it.

"I've wanted to do that from the first time I saw it."

Grabbing the bar of soap from the dish, Lindy began to lather Ren's breasts and stomach, slowly moving lower. She reached the thatch of curls between Ren's legs and moved her hand between Ren's legs, slowly sliding her slippery fingers down between the folds of Ren's body until she heard Ren gasp as she brushed over Ren's clitoris and slid into her.

"Yes, Lindy, don't stop," Ren panted.

After a few more slow strokes, Lindy slipped out and turned Ren towards her. Returning to her lips, she kissed Ren with long pent up desire. Again, she slipped her fingers inside Ren and began to stroke in and out while she stimulated her with her thumb. She dropped her lips to her lover's breast as Ren, eyes closed, began to tense around her lover's fingers. She heard Ren moan, "A little harder, mmm yeah, that's it."

Lindy felt the spasms surround her fingers as Ren climaxed, collapsing against her. They stood that way with Lindy supporting Ren until she felt steady enough to support herself.

Ren kissed Lindy softly. "I love you."

"I love you, too.

Ren reached behind Lindy to turn off the shower then led them both dripping into the bedroom. Lindy slipped into bed and Ren stretched out next to her. Linking her fingers with Lindy's, Ren pulled Lindy's arms up over her head. She kissed her lips before kissing her way down the inside of Lindy's arm and across her collarbone. She could feel the tension in Lindy's body. Lifting her head so she could see Lindy's face she asked, "Are you okay?"

"Yes, I love and want you. It's just that I'm so afraid I'll disappoint you. Uh, I...well, you know what I mean."

"You could never disappoint me." Ren kissed the hollow of Lindy's neck slowly placing kisses all the way to her ear. She traced Lindy's ear with her tongue and nibbled softly down her neck. Ren felt Lindy push harder against her leg with her wet center. A soft moan told Ren that Lindy enjoyed it when she licked her nipple then blew air across it. Sucking the now erect tip into her mouth, Ren teased one nipple with her tongue, as she ran her palm over the other breast to stimulate the other nipple into erection. Ren pressed her thigh harder against Lindy's core, as she felt Lindy begin to grind against her.

Her breath quick and shallow, Lindy whispered, "Touch me...please."

"I will." Ren delayed, urging Lindy's need higher. She nibbled her way down Lindy's body inhaling the scent of Lindy's arousal mixed with the fresh smell of her soap. She kissed Lindy's breasts, circled her navel with her tongue, and allowed her tongue to explore along Lindy's inner thighs until Lindy was squirming beneath her. She stimulated her lover to a higher level of passion than Lindy ever imagined herself capable of feeling.

Lindy managed to beg, "Please, I want you inside me."

Ren slid up and waited for Lindy to open her eyes. "I want to watch you come," she whispered as she slipped inside Lindy's slick opening. She started with a slow even pace, moving deeper with each thrust. Lindy was breathing as if she'd just finished running a marathon. She was on the edge. Ren just barely touched the swollen tissue beneath the hood when Lindy tensed and gripped her hand as she fell back onto the bed in release. As the spasms stopped, Ren stayed nestled inside Lindy's warm center. Once Lindy's breathing became more regular Ren again began again to move gently inside her this time using short quick strokes.

"Oh my God!" Lindy exclaimed, as she came again. She curled against Ren. "I love you."

"And I you. I promise I'll do everything in my power to make your dreams come true."

A smile of contentment on her face. "You just did," Lindy whispered, tears filling her eyes, before she kissed Ren softly.

They cuddled against each other. Ren asked, "Sleepy?"

Lindy managed a weak smile. "Not really sleepy, just not much energy left. When I thought about us being together like this and believe me I've thought about it plenty, I pictured it differently."

"Better?"

"No absolutely not. How could anything be better than what we just did?" Lindy was starting to warm to the topic of conversation. "I don't know. So far, we only made love using the techniques from the first two books. As a novice, I didn't think I was ready for, and couldn't imagine myself doing, some of the techniques they described in book three." She giggled.

Ren laughed. "So reading those lesbian novels was just research?"

"Not entirely. I read the first one out of curiosity. When I found myself turned on by them and I finally figured out that what I was feeling for you was more than friendship, I wanted to be ready when I figured out how to get you into bed. I didn't want to scare you away before you were ready to love someone, not someone...love me, specifically. Yet I wanted to be ready if, or when, you ever were. I could barely keep my hands off of you." With her head on Ren's shoulder, Lindy's hand idly trailed over Ren's body teasing each nipple in turn then stroking down her torso stopping to dip her finger into Ren's navel. Lindy smiled and kissed Ren lightly. "I never imagined it could really be this way. That I could ever be like this, feel like this."

Ren was teasing Lindy's nipple. "So when did you know you were in love with me?"

"In love with you?" She slid her hand down Ren's torso, coming to a stop with her hand tightly pressed against Ren's mound, "Or when did I know I wanted to do this with you?" Lindy began playing in the soft curls she found there then slid down over Ren's clitoris to dip her finger into the increasing wetness.

"Both," answered Ren hoarsely as Lindy added a finger.

Lindy slowly stroked in and out, pulling up far enough to make Ren think she would touch her now hypersensitive clit, stopping just short of making contact each time. "Well, I knew the first time you looked at me with those deep blue eyes of yours that you were something special."

Ren responded with sounds of enjoyment as Lindy increased her pace. She watched Ren's eyes close, her breathing deepen as her hips began to rise to meet each stroke of Lindy's fingers. Lindy was having fun, her dialogue, as she stimulated Ren, serving to distract her just enough to prolong her climb.

"Then, probably the first time I ever felt a physical response to you was when we were making the peanut butter and jelly sandwiches in the kitchen and I wiped the jelly from your lip. When was that, the second day I was here?" Ren's breath was coming faster now, her head thrown back, her eyes closed. "I didn't even know yet that you were a lesbian." Lindy stroked up between the soft, pink folds of her lover's body, but this time didn't stop short of touching Ren's center. When she slid up and over the engorged flesh Ren screamed in pleasure and came quickly and hard. Ren wrapped her arms around Lindy and pulled her close.

"Want to talk some more?" Lindy asked with an impish grin.

"Ummm." Ren sighed. "I like the way you converse."

"I'm so glad. I hope we can talk like this often."

"Yes. Me too," Ren chuckled and rolled over onto her side before kissing Lindy gently. "You are a very good lover, considering you're a straight woman."

"I'm not straight anymore. I'm yours. That makes me just as much a lesbian as you are."

"That you are. However, you're going to have to pay for teasing me like you just did. Payback starts right now." Ren rolled over trapping Lindy beneath her hungry mouth. She teased and stroked Lindy until she was frenzied with desire and begging Ren to let her come.

Lindy finally fell back onto the bed after her release. "I never imagined making love could be like this for me. I can't believe I want you again. You may have created an insatiable monster. I don't think I'll ever get enough of you."

"Do you promise?"

"For now, forever, and for always."

Chapter 32: Will This Do?

The next morning, the sound of the shower woke Lindy. She sat on the edge of the bed and waited for Ren to come in and join her. A few seconds later Ren emerged from the bathroom, came toward Lindy and knelt between her legs. She put her head on Lindy's thigh, pretending to search for something under the bed.

Slightly disappointed, Lindy said, "What are you looking for?"

"I lost my button."

"How could you lose a button? You weren't wearing any clothes."

Suddenly laughing, Ren slid Lindy's legs over her shoulders, spread them open, and as she leaned Lindy backwards, she plunged her tongue into her as deeply as she could, then dragged her tongue slowly up to flick it across Lindy's already erect clitoris.

"Ah," Ren grinned as she looked up, "there it is."

"Oh Ren, quit joking around and do that again," Lindy said as she pushed her fingers into Ren's hair, pulling her lover's mouth to her again.

It was after one by the time they finally made it out of bed, showered together, and dressed. They were sitting at the kitchen counter eating lunch and revisiting their conversation about when each knew she was attracted to the other and when they each recognized they had fallen in love. They were nearly giddy they were so happy.

"I can't even keep my hands off of you," confessed Lindy. "Oh, I nearly forgot, I have a present for you. Come with me to my room."

Lindy handed Ren the big box she brought home with them the night before. Ren was puzzled. "What's this for?"

"Just a little gift for you, in case you have nothing better to do this afternoon."

Ren laughed, a deep joy filled laugh, when she opened the box and removed a faux bearskin rug. "You're on. I'll go get my supplies." Before she left, she spread the rug on the bed. "I'll expect you there when I come back."

"That's fine. Don't forget your end of the bargain," Lindy said with a wink.

When Ren returned, she had nothing on other than her slippers and a grin. "I just couldn't bring myself to take off my slippers. Will this do?"

It took a while for Ren to get the pose set just the way she wanted it. Lindy, propped on her elbow, reclined on the bearskin as Ren spread a sheer drape across both of Lindy's breasts and draped it down between her legs. Lindy was reclining on her left side with her legs out straight. There was love in her expression and happiness in her eyes. Ren leaned over and kissed her before she returned to her stool to begin sketching. When Ren glanced up at Lindy, she saw a different pose, with one breast exposed and her right leg raised at the knee. Lindy's hand, now resting casually on her stomach, pulled the drape that was between her legs aside to give a much more intimate view to the artist.

Ren laughed. "Okay, very funny." Returning to her frisky model, she re-draped the fabric as it had been, and arranged Lindy into the more modest pose. Returning to her stool, she turned to see Lindy had reverted again to the more risqué position.

As Ren returned one more time to the bed, Lindy grabbed her arm and pulled Ren down on top of her. "Do you really need one more picture on your wall or do you need me to make love to you till you can't stand up?"

After kissing her lover deeply, Ren replied, "Let's see who won't be able to stand up."

"I think," replied Lindy, "if you want another painting completed, one of us needs to keep her clothes on. Just not right now."

They managed to surface for dinner around seven. The phone rang, and after Ren listened a few minutes, she said, "Wait a minute, let me take this in the studio."

Ren returned to the kitchen where she revealed that the call was from Jack. "It seems he ran into Toni, the big mouth, at the pizza parlor. She was bursting to get information from him about his sister's new lover. Damned old busybody."

"He's not upset about us is he?"

"No. However, he didn't appreciate it that he had to hear it from her instead of us."

"Did you explain to him that we just figured it out ourselves last night?"

"Not exactly in those words; however, I did tell him that at the time she learned of our involvement it wasn't yet true. He laughed when I told him the story and how you put Toni in her place." Ren came up behind Lindy and circled her arms around her as she buried her lips in her lover's neck. "He had questions. Things we'll have to settle between us before we can answer him. Like what happens now? Where will we live? All that stuff we haven't talked about yet. I told him we hadn't even begun to address those issues, we were too busy being in lust."

"What?" Lindy squirmed out of Ren's grasp and turned to face Ren, her face bright red. "No, you didn't say that to him, did you?"

"What, that we were in lust?" Ren laughed. "No, I think I used the word love. Anyway he's happy for us."

Lindy sighed. "Do we really have to face those decisions already?"

"No, we don't. When we do, I want you to know that I'll do whatever it takes to keep you happy, to have you continue to love me and be with me. If you want to keep working at the college, you can. I'll be able to be with you there during the winter months, and you can be here with me in the summer, or I could move down there with you full time. Or, you can quit entirely and stay here as my sex slave."

"Well, you are a silver tongued devil, aren't you? You know how to tempt a girl."

Ren hugged Lindy close. "You just need to believe with all your heart that I love you."

"I do."

"Speaking of 'I do,' let's have a commitment ceremony when your parents visit. Oh, wait. I'm moving a little fast. I'm eager because I never expected to find this happiness again. Ren took Lindy's hand in hers, "Will you marry me?"

"I would certainly do so if we could. We can't get married. We're two women."

"I know that. We can do a domestic partnership. It does give us some protections even though it isn't a legitimate marriage. At least, legally, we'd be considered each other's closest next of kin."

"Doesn't that mean you have to ask me to be your next of kin, instead of asking me to marry you?" Lindy chuckled.

"Boy, you're tough. I thought you told me you were a romantic. Okay, then, let me try that again." Ren smiled, "Will you be my next of kin?"

Lindy pulled Ren close, smiled lovingly, and then kissed her tenderly. "I'll do whatever it takes to be sure you and I can be happy like this forever."

"You have to have your legal residence in this state for one year, so we can't legally do a DP until September. We could still do a commitment ceremony. Let's try to see if we can do it while your parents are here."

Lindy took a deep breath and then exhaled a long sigh. "That all sounds fine and I do want to make a commitment with you. I think before that, I have to tell my parents I'm in love with a woman. One step at a time, please. I want to do the ceremony, but maybe we should wait until my parents get used to the idea first. "

"I'm sorry. I guess I'm so eager because I never expected this, you know, us. We'll figure it out. You're right, first things first." Ren started down the hall with Lindy's hand grasped firmly in hers. "So what do you want to do now?"

"How about we try something from book three..."

LINDY CAPRINI JOURNAL

Guess what? I'm not frigid. Oh yeah...she loves me. I'm delirious.

Chapter 33: I Took It Down—It's Time

Over the next few weeks, Ren and Lindy lived and loved. They went to visit Jack and Marie and stopped in to see Joey and Ben who were very happy for both of them. Ren did eventually get to work on the portrait. She wanted to capture the love Lindy felt for her, and at the same time, the mischievous side of her personality. She wouldn't let Lindy see the painting until it was finished. When the day finally came for Ren to unveil it, she asked Lindy to come to the studio. Lindy noticed that Brooke's portrait was gone and Ren had rearranged the other paintings on the wall where the large portrait of Brooke used to hang.

On the adjacent wall, hung the two portraits Ren had painted of Lindy. Arranged on either side of the portraits were a series of sketches Ren had done of Lindy's eyes that she'd sketched before doing the first portrait.

Lindy laughed when she saw the sexy pose, the eyes filled with love and in her hand a book titled *Book Three*. She loved the secret joke Ren incorporated into the portrait.

Lindy glanced at the other wall. "What are you doing? Where's Brooke's portrait?"

"I took it down--it's time."

"Ren, I love that painting. Every time I looked at her portrait, I saw in her eyes the way I feel inside when I look at you."

"Well," Ren admitted, "I wasn't sure what to do about Brooke's portrait. I mean we both know she was an important part of my life."

"Yes, and it's because of her that you became the person that you are today. Her love, her presence in your life, and then her loss all are parts of who you are."

"I wanted to try something out and see how it feels for both of us. Look again at the wall."

Lindy looked at the display of Ren's art more carefully this time. She finally saw it. There in a smaller size, was a miniature duplicate of the large portrait of Brooke.

"I felt her portrait should remain on the wall, which represents my life history through my art," Ren explained.

"I understand. Your art for you is like my journal for me."

"I guess, in a way it is. Still, Brooke needed to be placed into a scale more representative of the importance in my life she now represents. If this doesn't work for you, I can understand that. I can replace her smaller portrait with another picture."

"Honestly, I don't have a problem with the large portrait. It's been here since I came. I've loved you for many days while she has watched over us. Somehow, I feel she'd approve of our love. You need to do what you feel is right and what makes you comfortable."

"I wouldn't want to sell it, it's too personal. I think I'm comfortable putting it into storage for now. When I die, hopefully years from now, it can be donated to my old art school or somewhere else, wherever my art ends up."

**

Lindy was in her office working on her book when Ren came in and took a seat by the window. "How's the book coming?"

"I'm making progress on it. It's a little better than half way done." Lindy smiled. "Don't worry, you'll get to proof it before I submit it."

"Have you ever considered writing full time for a living?"

"Not really, because I was afraid I wouldn't be able to support myself that way. I took this year off because I inherited money from my aunt, plus I also got the grant. It's hard to give up a job I didn't mind doing, that paid enough for me to support myself in a comfortable fashion and was reasonably secure, for an iffy career as an author. I mean there are very few bestselling authors out there. I don't have that kind of confidence in my abilities. I thought I'd see how Flint's Follies did. I figured that writing would supplement my income rather than be my whole source of support."

"Have you given any thought to what you want to do, now that there's an us, besides try out everything from books four, five and six?" Ren grinned.

Lindy crossed the room to sit in Ren's lap. She draped her arms around Ren's neck. "One thing I know. I want to be with you. How we achieve that I don't know. Do you have any ideas?"

"Well, by now, you've probably figured out that I'm not poor. I work hard because I like to work and because my grandparents brought me up to be productive. To be honest, if we both quit work tomorrow we could still afford to live anywhere we wanted and be comfortable for the rest of our lives. So, now you have options that you might not have entertained before. If you could do anything you wanted to do, what would it be? You could write, travel, go back to the university, teach here at the college, work at the museum, or just stay home and love me."

"The last is a given. Short term, I'd like to finish our project and finish everything necessary to publish it. After that, I think I'll finish our story and see if I can get someone to publish it. I've changed some of the details and used a pseudonym to maintain our privacy. Next, I'd like to finish *Flint's Follies* and, if you're willing, I'd like you to illustrate it for me. When all that's done, I'd like the option to re-evaluate our plans depending on how successful we are with all those things."

"Sounds good. Don't forget I'll be a lot busier from May to September with the Inn."

"I know. We'll have less alone time together," said Lindy sadly. Then she brightened, "Would I be able to help you with those responsibilities?"

"There's always room for another set of hands in this business. We'll work it out." Ren knew that Lindy's kindness and warm personality would be an asset at the Inn.

"I love you Ren, It makes sense for us to be here where your business is. I can teach anywhere or write anywhere. You can't move the island there. So," Lindy winked, "looks like you're stuck with me."

They held each other tightly. "I'm glad that's settled," sighed Ren. "Now all we have to do is make plans for our commitment ceremony sometime while your parents are here."

"Well, that's not exactly all. First, we have to tell my mother and father that I'm in love with you."

Ren's brow furrowed. "I thought your parents wouldn't have any trouble with me being a lesbian."

"They won't have any trouble with you being a lesbian. Now, I have to figure out how to tell them I'm one, too."

Chapter 34: Come Here You Two And Give Us A Big Hug

It was almost May. Franco and Belinda Caprini were due in a couple of weeks so Ren began making plans for their arrival. Maggie and Bob were getting the cabins ready for the season. Unsure of their tastes, Ren asked Lindy which cabin she thought her parents would prefer. "Actually, I think they'd be happier staying in one of the guest suites in the house rather than having a cabin to themselves. Especially since the Inn won't be open yet."

Together they picked a bed and sitting room in the guest wing for Lindy's parents. Ren arranged with Maggie to place fresh flowers in their room regularly throughout their visit. Everything was in place for Franco and Belinda's visit.

With the weather warming up, Lindy and Ren began jogging again around the island. While on one of their runs, they chose the spot they wanted for the commitment ceremony. After discussing the ceremony further, they agreed to wait to do it at the same time they did the domestic partnership, in the fall.

"Although I really don't want to wait, I think it's probably a good decision." Ren said as they returned to the Inn hand-in-hand. "It might be too rushed to try to have the ceremony before the Inn opens."

"Yes. Plus postponing will also give my parents time to adjust to the idea of my new relationship. It'll take some pressure off of all of us."

"Good. We're agreed. Everything is all set then."

"Except for one minor detail. I, or we, still have to tell my parents about our relationship and then invite them to return in the fall to participate in the ceremony."

***

May third, the date Lindy's parents were to arrive for their visit, dawned crisp and clear. The light breeze commingled the fresh sea air with the scent of the evergreen trees. Ren and Lindy felt it would be best to meet Mr. and Mrs. Caprini at the airport. Ren wanted to be able to relax and chat with them on the trip back to the island and not have to attend to the driving. Lindy agreed to Ren's idea of renting a limo for the roughly forty mile trip. Although the flight wasn't due to arrive until late in the afternoon, Ren arranged for the limo to meet her and Lindy at the marina an hour earlier than necessary.

"We can spend the extra time in the airport bar plying ourselves with liquor." Ren teased.

"It's just my parents," mused Lindy. "I can't believe I'm so nervous."

"Well, it's natural I guess. It's not every day you get to tell your parents that you're involved in a lesbian relationship."

"Do you think I should have told them before they made the trip up here?"

"I don't know. Maybe it'll be easier for them if they see us together and get to know me a bit before you break the news. Sometimes the devil you know is easier to accept than the one you don't," she said with a smile.

They did have that drink at the airport before they met Lindy's parents, gathered their bags, and got everyone settled in the limo for the trip home. As they chatted in the car on the way back to the island, conversation was easy and relaxed. Ren liked Lindy's parents immediately, finding them to be funny and warm. They stopped for an early dinner at a seafood restaurant where Lindy's parents asked Ren questions about her home and background.

"So, our daughter tells us that you live on an island. I have a number of questions I'd like to ask you about life there."

Ren patiently answered every query. When he started on his questions about food supply, without realizing what she said, Lindy cautioned, "Dad, why don't you wait to see our home before you ask any more questions." Not thinking she gave Ren's hand a lingering touch as she told her father, "Ren has a brochure in her office that tells how the inn was built and some of the history and other details about it that you can study. I want to hear more about your cruise."

Dinner progressed at a leisurely pace. Lindy's parents told about their trip, and Ren answered a few questions about her family. Mr. Caprini directed his gaze at Ren. Our daughter tells us it was your grandfather who purchased the island."

"Yes, Mr. Caprini, my grandfather bought it when I was a little girl. My parents died when I was two and my grandparents raised me."

"Please call me Franco and my wife Belinda. No need for formality." His kind and welcoming smile helped Ren to relax a little.

"Okay, thank you."

"You are an only child?"

"No, I'm lucky. I have a wonderful brother with whom I'm very close. I was only two. So being an orphan was just an unfortunate fact of my life. I don't think I internalized the reality until I went to kindergarten and discovered that my family was different. It was harder for my brother who is ten years my senior. My grandparents made many sacrifices for us including selling the business and moving to the island to raise us. Between my grandparents, my brother, the Inn, the island...I believe I've been truly blessed to grow up as I have."

After dinner, they returned to the limo and made the short trip to the marina where the driver helped Ren load the luggage onto the boat. Ren paid him, giving him a generous tip for all the waiting he had to do during the day. The sun was setting as they pulled into the dock. Lindy's parents each commented about the impressive house and beautiful scenery.

"Let's get you settled in your room first," suggested Ren as they entered the Inn. "You can unpack and have a rest or come out to the porch for a drink and visit some more with us."

Lindy's parents exchanged a look and Lindy's father answered for both of them. "I think we'd like to get settled in, and then we'll take you up on that offer of a drink."

Ren led Franco and Belinda down the hallway to their bedroom where she left them to get settled.

Finally alone, Lindy asked Ren, "How do you think that went? Do you think they suspect that we're a couple?"

"I don't know. They did exchange a look between them when you called this 'our home' and I think your mother caught it when you pretty much held my hand in the restaurant. They might have an inkling."

Lindy fretted. "So, what do you think we should do? Should we tell them together or should I tell them by myself? I really don't know how to tell them about us. I thought this would be easier than it is."

"Give it a day or two and maybe there'll come a time when it feels right to tell them."

A few minutes later Franco and Belinda joined Lindy and Ren on the porch where Lindy made each of them a drink. The evening passed pleasantly enough. When Lindy started to talk about the work she and Ren were doing on the fables, she finally began to calm down and bubbled about their project. She glowed with pride as she showed them some of the illustrations Ren had done for the book. Her conversation was peppered with 'when we did this' and then 'we did that' as she described her past eight months on the island with Ren. "When we first started working on the project," she explained to her parents, "I was still in Philly and she was here. I thought it would be difficult, but we talked on the phone all the time and e-mailed. It was much easier than we thought it would be working long distance. We were already friends by the time I arrived here to work with her. We're going to finish our project ahead of schedule, aren't we?" Lindy looked at Ren, trying to keep the love she felt for her partner from showing.

They chatted for a little while longer as they enjoyed their beverages. Once she felt her guests had relaxed enough, Ren offered a tour of the house. They returned to the library when Ren finished showing them around. "Tomorrow, I can show you some of the island then if you'd like, we can go back over to the mainland and take a walk through the town."

"That would be wonderful," Belinda said. "If you'll forgive us now, I'm tired from our long day. We'll see you two in the morning."

Lindy hugged her parents before they went down the hall to their room.

"So how do you think it went?" Ren asked Lindy.

"I think they are having a good time. Tomorrow will be fun. It's been a long day for us too. Ready for bed?"

"Always," Ren answered a seductive smile tugging at her lips.

The next day everyone was up early, eager for the full day Ren had planned. After breakfast, they took a short stroll around the nearest parts of the island before taking the boat across to the marina. They shopped for a bit before having a wonderful early lunch of lobster rolls and French fries at one of the restaurants near the pier. Ren drove Lindy and her parents around the scenic countryside pointing out various highlights along the way and relating some of the history of the area. They strolled along the shore in one of the scenic coves then got back into the car for a drive through the local college.

Ren had made reservations at the restaurant she'd described to Lindy a couple of months earlier. They had a wonderful dinner filled with good food and spirited conversation. Ren finally relaxed and began to enjoy Lindy's parents. They were very funny people, and it was evident from their humor where Lindy got her playful personality. When they finished dinner, Ren drove everyone back to the marina where they boarded the boat for the return trip to the island.

They had consumed two bottles of wine during dinner and once settled in the library, cocktails in hand, they chattered about the wonderful day they'd spent. "I don't know how you can top today. We had a wonderful time, didn't we, Franco." Belinda said.

"Absolutely. What do you have on the agenda for tomorrow? We know you and Lindy are busy working on her book. We don't want to interfere with your project and don't want you two to feel that you have to entertain us every day. As much as we enjoy spending time together, we'd also love to just have time to poke around on our own. I'd like to visit the park and see more of what you told us about today, like the museum and the bird sanctuary. I'm sure you've been there dozens of times, Ren, so don't feel obligated to drag us around. Either we can borrow Lindy's car or, if she needs hers, we can rent one. Our only issue is that we're at your mercy to get us off the island."

"It's a pleasure, sir, not an obligation." Ren responded, meaning it sincerely. "Maybe tomorrow, since you showed such an interest in the workings of the facility, I can arrange for Bob, our maintenance supervisor to show you some of the more mechanical parts of our operation here."

"That would be wonderful."

"Mom, maybe you and I could spend some time together while Dad is doing that. I've told you about *Flint's Folly*...maybe you'd read some of it for me and tell me what you think, while I make dinner. Later in the week, we'd like to invite Ren's family over for dinner so you can meet her brother Jack, his wife Marie, and their daughter Laura." Lulled by the wine and the two cocktails she'd consumed since they returned to the island, Lindy was relaxed to the point that she was no longer on guard. "And I want you both to see Ren's artwork tomorrow." She turned to Ren and put her hand comfortably on Ren's leg as she concluded proudly, "She's a wonderful artist. Will you show them some of your work, Hon?"

It was as if the air was sucked from the room. Everyone froze in place until Belinda said, "Oh thank God. We thought you weren't going to tell us you're in love with her."

Incredulous, Lindy said, "What do you mean...how did you know?"

Franco chuckled, "You are of course referring to the period of time before you had your hand on her thigh and called her Hon."

Everyone laughed, finally feeling fully at ease with each other. Relieved they no longer had to try to hide their love or affection, Lindy reached for Ren's hand. "We didn't know how to tell you, Mom and Dad. How long have you suspected?"

"Well, our first clue was when you invited us up here. It was out of the ordinary enough that it made us aware of the little clues you didn't realize were giving you away. Your calls and e-mails told us you were happy, so we weren't worried."

"And it doesn't bother you that I'm a woman?" Ren asked.

"Bother us personally, no." Franco answered. "We want our daughter happy. We would love whomever she chose as long as that person makes her happy and values her as we do. To us, the fact that you love our daughter, will treat her well, and make her happy is what is important to us. From what we've seen so far, you are succeeding on all counts."

"Believe me, she does the same for me," Ren admitted. "I imagine this feels pretty sudden to you, but we've known each other well over a year now and have lived and worked here twenty-four hours a day, seven days a week since September. We've seen each other at our best and at our worst. We've taken the time to be sure about wanting a relationship and sharing our lives together."

Lindy nodded her agreement. "I'm in love with a wonderful person, and I know you'll love her too when you get to know her better."

They spent the next three days showing Lindy's parents around the island and the town. Ren acting as a tour guide provided Lindy's parents an opportunity to get acquainted with her. It was over lunch on the fourth day of their visit, that a nervous Ren cleared her throat and said, "Franco, Belinda, I've asked Lindy to marry me later this year in Canada and I'm asking for your blessing. In September, we'll have lived together for a year and we can file for our Domestic Partnership here in Maine. We've planned to have a commitment ceremony in the fall. Regretfully, it holds no legal significance. Still, the ceremony we have planned is important to us. Our friends, Joey and Ben, will conduct the ceremony and have completed their application for ordination by the Universal Life Church. We've already begun writing our vows. The only thing we need is your blessing of our union."

Franco and Belinda exchanged a look. "Of course you have our blessing," they said in virtual unison.

Belinda stood up, "Come here you two and give us a hug."

After the congratulatory hugs and a toast to the happy couple made by Franco, he stated, "It's unfair that you can't get married like other couples in love."

"Yes. We agree," replied Ren. "At our ceremony in September, we will make our personal promises to each other and really, aren't those the ones that count?" Belinda and Franco nodded. "Yet, we both feel it's important that we share our commitment with others. We can get a domestic partnership here, in September, but since neither gay marriage nor civil unions are legal yet in Maine, we plan to marry in Canada, when we take our honeymoon. We're still working out the details of what we want to do, and we hope you will return in September for whatever we decide. Our season, here at the Inn, gets underway after next week, so I won't be able to leave here until after we close in September. After that, our intention is to gather our closest friends and family here for the ceremony and then have a small wedding somewhere in Canada. Despite it having no legal significance in Maine, it's important to us that we do it."

"What a shame, three ceremonies and none have much legal significance for you," said Belinda.

"The domestic partnership will carry the most weight legally. Hopefully, it won't be too long before marriage will be passed for couples like us. I can't tell you how relieved we are, and how much we appreciate your support of our relationship." Ren took Lindy's hand. "I promise I'll take good care of her."

The following day, Jack and Marie invited everyone, including Joey, Ben, and the Ps over for dinner, so Lindy's parents could get to know everyone better. After the return trip to the Inn, while Ren lit the fire in the library Franco and

Belinda sat in the kitchen watching Lindy make tea for the group.

"Ren's family and your friends are all very nice people," Belinda told her daughter. "And Laura is a lovely little girl. She obviously adores her aunt and loves you too."

"Well, she certainly loves the stories I tell her."

While waiting for the water to boil, Lindy took a seat at the counter with her parents.

Lindy's mother studied her daughter's glowing face. "You're really happy, aren't you?"

"Yes, mom. I know this whole relationship is probably a big shock to you. I have to admit that falling in love with a woman, with Ren, surprised me too. I've never felt anything like this before. It's like I've been missing something all my life and with her, all seems right with the world." Lindy looked from her father to her mother to determine if she could discern their true feelings. "Does it shock you or embarrass you that your daughter...that I'm a lesbian?" She had struggled to accept and admit that fact to herself, but this was the first time she had said it aloud to anyone. It felt strange to say that phrase to anyone other than Ren, despite having no doubts that it was true.

Franco answered her question. "I think surprise is a more accurate description of what we feel." He glanced at his wife who nodded her agreement. "I mean all these years, since you were young, we thought you were happy dating men."

Not wanting to go into intimate detail, Lindy settled on saying. "I like men, but there's always been a critical element missing in my involvement with them. With Ren, I have the total package. We just seem to fit everywhere and in every way. Everything is so effortless. All I can say is that I feel complete and extremely happy." The water kettle began to whistle and Lindy turned her attention to pouring the water into the cups.

Lindy's mother chose to answer the question her father hadn't. "In regard to being embarrassed, I'm surprised you'd even ask that. We love you and are proud of you. And we are proud you chose such a wonderful woman to give your heart to. Why would we be embarrassed by your choice? You know we have always held liberal views on homosexuality and they apply to our family as well as anyone else's."

Lindy fought the tears in her eyes, resisting their attempt to overflow. "Thanks, Mom and Dad. I love you both. It means so much that you accept us and will support our relationship."

Ren entered the kitchen, oblivious to the serious conversation that had just occurred. "Fire's blazing, where's the tea?"

"Almost ready, sweetie. Help me carry it in." She would tell Ren about her conversation when they were alone.

Later, as they snuggled together in bed, Ren was pleased she had not been there for Lindy's discussion with her parents. "I'm so glad they approve. I like them very much and I hope they'll visit us often. They're lots of fun and I think it makes you happy they are here."

"True, yet not as happy as being here with you makes me. Come here and kiss me. My lips are lonely."

"Well, let's see what we can do to remedy that deplorable situation." Ren poured all the love she felt into the kiss they shared.

Chapter 35: If It Bothers You, We Don't Have To Make Love Tonight

A week after Lindy's parents left for home the season opened. It didn't take long for Lindy to find places where she could be useful. Lindy's innate ability to interact with people caused Ren to wonder how she'd ever run the Inn without her. Her quick wit and easygoing ways made her a natural for dealing with the guests' needs and complaints, freeing Ren for the more complicated management tasks and Maggie to better manage her housekeeping and kitchen responsibilities. The summer flew by. In Lindy and Ren's off hours, they finished the fairy tale book and Lindy finished both of her novels.

Several serious conversations resulted in finalized plans for their domestic partnership, commitment ceremony, and wedding plans. Of the three ceremonies, the domestic partnership was mostly a registration process, but it carried the most legal rights and benefits.

Ben and Joey were pleased that Ren and Lindy asked them to officiate at their commitment. They were so excited when they received their certificates from the online church certifying them as ordained ministers capable of performing the ceremony.

Lindy's parents returned for another weeklong visit before the ceremony in September. Belinda helped Lindy with the final arrangements for the celebration of their union, and everyone was emotional by the time the big day finally arrived.

Their commitment day weather was perfect, crisp and sunny. By two, when their family and friends gathered on the hilltop overlooking the ocean, the air was warmer and the breeze was less vigorous. Mallory, Peg and Penny, Ren, Lindy, and their respective family members gathered in their positions in preparation for the simple ceremony. Jack was escorting Ren and Lindy's father was escorting her. They had decided to walk up the path together, blending their own lives and symbolically joining their families together for their journey in life. "You look beautiful, sis." Jack whispered before they started up the path to the summit where the rest of their family and friends were gathered waiting for them. They wore suits in complementary shades of blue. Each man wore a boutonnière and the women each had a small bouquet of flowers.

They stood at the top of the hill, hands clasped. Ben and Joey officiated as Lindy's father and mother, and Jack and Marie stood to either side. Instead of saying, 'Who gives this bride' Joey asked the family members on either side of the celebrants, "Do you promise to support the joining of this couple?"

Both sets of family members responded, "We will." Lindy's mother squeezed her hand.

Ben asked, "Friends and family members please join hands and encircle Lindy and Ren to symbolize your commitment to love, support and protect them."

After the ceremony concluded, everyone walked back to the house where they enjoyed a meal together then spent the rest of the afternoon socializing.

"That was a wonderful ceremony guys," Lindy hugged Joey and Ben in turn. "Thank you. It was a lovely day. I loved the part where you asked our friends to support our union. That was a surprise, and a nice touch.

"We decided to add it last night. We were talking about how important it is to have the support of family and friends. You know, the whole 'it takes a village' idea."

"Well, regardless where you got the idea, it was great."

After celebrating for the rest of the afternoon, the guests finally left, and Lindy's parents bid them good night. Ren and Lindy lay in bed cuddling. "Maybe we should have arranged for us to go away tonight," whispered Lindy as she slid her hand up Ren's side to fondle her breast. "This feels a little strange with them still here."

"Why? Is it that much different from last night when we made love, or any other night this past week?"

"I guess not. It's just that last night they weren't completely sure I'd be making love with you and tonight they'll know."

Completely sure of the response she'd get to her ruse, Ren put her hand over Lindy's and pulled it to her lips snuggling her close. "Well, if it bothers you, we don't have to make love tonight." She kissed Lindy lightly on the nose and said, "Good night."

Lindy tickled Ren until she begged for forgiveness. Fortunately, Lindy's parents in the other wing of the house most likely didn't hear Ren's tickle-induced screams or any of the following sounds each of the lovers made as they satisfied their desire for each other.

Chapter 36: I Still Think The Last Words Should Be...

The next morning, two limos picked the wedding group up at the marina and drove them to the pier where they boarded the cruise ship. Ren had made all the plans for the wedding to take place onshore at their stop in Quebec. A month before the ceremony, she had flown to Quebec for two days to apply for the license and to make sure all the paperwork and the venue for the wedding was set. When the ship docked in Quebec, the family traveled to a little chapel where they had a beautiful ceremony attended by members of their family and closest friends. The festivity of the wedding was extended for the group by having over a week of cruising together to various ports from Boston to Quebec.

After the ceremony, back in their suite on the ship, Lindy asked Ren, "Do you feel any more married today than we did yesterday?"

"I don't know, I guess I do, or rather I will, at least while we're in Canada," Ren teased. "We'll get to do it all over again when we get same-sex marriage in Maine. To me, that's no problem. I'd be happy to marry you every day. We always have hot sex after the ceremonies."

"Like we don't have hot sex every day of our lives..." Lindy chuckled, just before she placed a loving kiss on Ren's lips.

Ren pulled back feigning a puzzled look. "What book are we on now?"

They both laughed until passion overtook them as they melded together.

***

Back at their home, in front of the fire, late in May of the following year, Lindy handed Ren a package. "What's this?

"Open it and see."

"Oh, your book, *Sunset Island*. I love the cover," Ren smiled, pulling Lindy onto her lap. "Congratulations."

Ren flipped to the end of the book to read the final paragraph. "Hmph" Ren grumbled, her tone teasing, her face filled with love. "I still think the last words should have been...and they lived happily ever after."

"Next book," Lindy promised as she leaned down to kiss the woman she adored.

The End

About AJ Adaire

Let me tell you a little about myself. Twenty years ago, I wrote my first book just to see if I could do it. The novel occupied space on my bookshelf, unread for nearly twenty years until one day, while in a cleaning frenzy, I considered disposing of the neatly stacked but now age-yellowed pages. As I began to read the long forgotten work, I was surprised to discover that the story was enjoyable! Editing and retyping the first book provided a new sense of accomplishment and additional tales followed. Completion of *This is Fitting* encouraged me to write four more romance novels. *I Love My Life* and *Sunset Island* were followed by *Awaiting My Assignment* and its sequel, *Anything Your Heart Desires*. *One Day Longer Than Forever* is now complete, and *It's Complicated* is in the hands of first readers before the first big edit.

Now retired, there is all the time in the world to write. I live on the east coast with my partner of twenty-eight years. Because we love a challenge, we provide a loving home for two spoiled cats instead of a dog. In addition to writing, any spare time is devoted to reading, mastering new computer programs, and socializing with friends.

Contact Information
E-mail: aj@ajadaire.com
Website: http://www.ajadaire.com
Facebook: http://www.facebook.com/ajadaire
Desert Palm Press: www.desertpalmpress.com

Awaiting My Assignment

Chapter 1

Amanda raised both hands to her head and although tempted to use them to cover her ears, she ran her fingers through her dark auburn hair instead. Exhaling a long sigh, she drew herself up to her full height of just over five feet then crossed her arms in front of her chest, her hazel eyes unsympathetic. Bernie was still pleading her case but, this time, Amanda ignored the excuses and explanations, all of which were achingly familiar.

"Look," Amanda said, her tone measured, her voice more calm than her wrath would indicate, "I told you the last time I caught you cheating that there would never be a next time or I'd leave you. As you can see, I meant it. There will be no more chances."

"But honey…"

"Don't 'but honey' me." Amanda could feel her anger creeping into her voice. It was time to end this debate.

"Okay sweetie, you're right," Bernie said, trying a new tactic. "It was just a one night stand. You know she doesn't mean anything to me. I love you. With her it was just sex. With you, I make love."

"You're pathetic. Love? You don't even know the meaning of the word. I'm done here." Amanda shook her head in disgust.

It was clear that this pronouncement had no impact because when she turned to head for the bedroom Bernie followed, close on her heels. She strode from the room hoping that would be the end of their discussion. She felt her shoulders slump when she heard Bernie following her down the hallway. Amanda grabbed her matched set of luggage from the hall closet before she entered the bedroom to begin packing. Without making an effort to sort things properly, she grabbed stacks of items she thought she might need for the next few days and jammed them into her suitcase with little care for how wrinkled they would be.

"Where do you think you're going?"

"Away from you. I told you, I'm done here." Amanda repeated her intent as much to convince herself as to convince Bernie she was serious.

As Amanda began packing her belongings, a realization of how little there was in the house reflective of her taste compounded her sadness. Their custom built home, not a size or style she particularly liked, was paid for mostly with Bernie's money. Amanda had been so enamored with the magnetic woman at the time that she would have done anything to make her happy. When Amanda couldn't afford the lavish home Bernie desired, they agreed she'd contribute what she could afford and Bernie would provide the rest. For that reason, Amanda had acquiesced on nearly every decorating decision in their three bedroom home from, in her opinion, the tacky, ornate, and overdone bedroom furniture to the sleek white modern, extremely uncomfortable living room set. None of the artwork was her taste, nor had she picked any of the paint colors which ranged in shades from eggshell to pale almond. It distressed her to admit how much of herself she had surrendered to be Bernie's partner. She always felt that living in their house was like living in a snowstorm.

Amanda's haven was her office. She decorated it with dark green walls, crisp white trim, comfortable leather chairs, a roll top desk, shutter covered windows, and ceiling to floor bookshelves. Books had surrounded her all her adult life. How was it possible that she'd become involved with someone who didn't enjoy the printed word? It was ironic. She was an author, for God's sake, involved with a woman who hated to read.

The house was uncharacteristically quiet. Left to her own devices, Bernie would have the television on twenty-four seven. Not in the beginning of their relationship, but for the past few months, Bernie even hated to turn it off when they had sex. *What possessed me? What was I thinking? How could I have been so stupid to have not seen what she was up to?*

"Okay, I'm sorry. Is that what you need to hear?"

Amanda recognized Bernie's statement for what it was, another attempt to deter her and responded, her voice tight. "No. You remain completely clueless about what I need to hear."

"Well, then that makes us even, since you're clueless about what I need, too. I need a little excitement in the bedroom, not that bland huggy-kissy, touchy-feely pablum-like, lukewarm sex you like. You bore me to death sexually. If you'd spiced things up a little, maybe I wouldn't have strayed."

The education in various sexual techniques and positions that Bernie had provided over their years together gave Amanda confidence and left her with no doubts about her sexual prowess. Amanda knew that Bernie was simply trying to be hurtful. Amanda wanted to say, 'Yeah, maybe being the operative word in that sentence.' Or, 'So now it's my fault that you cheat?' But Amanda's resolve to maintain control steeled her. She managed to clamp her mouth closed and refrain from spitting out either retort. It was important to her that she not allow herself to be pulled into exchanging hurtful barbs with the woman she at one time thought she loved and who she thought loved her in return. But their definition of love turned out to be too disparate. Although she had to bite her tongue to keep from tossing a final insult that burned to be released, she managed to remain silent. Instead, Amanda picked up the overnight bag, slipped the strap over her head, and adjusted its weight on her shoulder.

Bernie grasped Amanda's upper arm with enough pressure to cause her to wince. She pulled Amanda around to face her, gesturing expansively with her free hand. "Are you just going to throw all this away? Aren't you even going to fight for our relationship?"

"What for...so you can cheat again? How truly stupid do you think I am?" Amanda shrugged her arm free from Bernie's painful grasp, slid the large suitcase from the bed, and extended the handle. "I'll come back to get the rest of my stuff after you leave on your trip."

"Coward," Bernie uttered. The word was just barely audible as she changed strategy again.

Amanda glanced back at her, noting Bernie's sad expression she didn't for a minute think was genuine. "I can't believe you. You have the balls of life!" In a momentary lapse of control, Amanda allowed herself to be hooked in. "Cheater!" She snapped the word back, her voice strident.

Bernie's eyes flashed. "If you walk out that door, don't think I'll let you come crawling back. I can have that empty spot you'll leave in the bed filled three times over before it's even cold."

Despite the angry and bitter feelings she had yet to express, she replied in a calm and measured tone, "I don't doubt for a minute the veracity of that statement." Amanda was too exhausted to argue.

Although slamming the door might have been more dramatic, Amanda opted to close it quietly behind her, refusing to allow her tears to come until she was alone in the car and a block away from the house. She pulled to the side of the road when she no longer could see well enough to drive. Okay, that was certainly a dramatic exit, but what the hell are you going to do now?

She had no friends on this coast that were exclusively her own and didn't want to put their mutual friends in the uncomfortable position of having to take sides. Her emotions once again in control, Amanda decided to get a motel room. As she drove, thoughts swirled in her head. She realized she was thankful that, except for the house, they had maintained separate financial accounts, opting not to co-mingle their money. At least she wouldn't have that hassle to deal with on top of everything else.

Amanda settled into her motel room, after a cursory look around the simple but functional room decorated in a combination of green and orange stripes and flowers. Idly, she wondered when designers had begun believing that the different contrasting patterns like stripes, plaids, and floral prints went together. "Well, at least it's clean." After spying the pot on the dresser, she added as an afterthought, "And it has coffee."

Because her profession as a writer was a solitary endeavor, other than the friends she and Bernie had met together at social gatherings, Amanda had made no new friends of her own since she relocated from her apartment about fifty minutes south of their current home in San Francisco, to move in with Bernie. It wasn't as if she didn't like people or was unlikeable herself, she had simply gotten out of the habit of doing things and placing herself in environments where she might meet people. Bernie's job in hotel management required frequent travel. When Bernie came home for a week off before her next trip to Brazil or across the country somewhere, they would rarely socialize. Sometimes, they might get together with another couple, but more often, they would simply fall into bed or work. Bernie always brought work home with her to do, even on what was considered her down time.

They had been together for twelve years...but when had their relationship really ended? Certainly it had changed at least a couple of years ago when she had called Bernie's hotel room early one morning and another woman sleepily answered the phone. She thought back to the confrontation they had upon Bernie's return home. She swore that would be the last time but, of course, it wasn't. Amanda had her suspicions before, but this time there had been proof Bernie couldn't explain away.

Alone, thinking over her earlier dialogue with Bernie, self-doubts began to clamor in her brain. Were all those cruel things Bernie had said about me true? Am I boring in life and in bed? It was true that Bernie did most of the talking when she came home, but it seemed that she enjoyed the sound of her own voice, so Amanda just let her talk. She was never interested in any project Amanda was working on and had shown absolutely no interest at all in the novel she was writing.

Their sex life had changed too, from loving and exciting to something darker and more edgy. Although Bernie had never hurt her, she had become sexually more aggressive, dominating her physically and verbally. At the outset of their relationship, Amanda would miss Bernie when she was gone, but recently she dreaded Bernie's return home from a trip.

Examining her feelings, it took a few minutes to realize that while it was sad that their relationship was over, she was not sorry she had ended it. As she exhaled a long sigh she felt some of her tension release. Truth was, in all honesty, the primary emotion she was feeling was relief.

Desiring support and needing to unburden herself, Amanda called Dana in New York.

Dana had obviously checked her caller ID, because she answered with, "Hey girlfriend! What's happening?"

Amanda grinned at her always-upbeat best friend's greeting. Her petite frame, rusty-hair, blue-eyes, and freckle-faced appearance combined with her unflaggingly cheerful and good-natured personality made Dana someone that everyone liked. Born two days later in the month than her own January fifteenth birthday, she was Amanda's closest friend.

Amanda had come out to Dana years ago. Fearing rejection, she'd delayed telling Dana that she was gay. The day she finally worked up the courage her palms were sweaty and her stomach queasy from nerves. However, her concerns were unfounded. Dana's response had been to simply pull Amanda into her arms to give her a hug.

"So what," she said. "I still love you."

They became even closer than they were before she'd revealed her secret. Maybe it was because Amanda felt freer to share her thoughts and feelings more openly.

Still smiling at the pleasant memory, she returned her mind to the phone conversation. "You mean what's new other than the fact that I left Bernie."

"I know this will sound unfeeling, but I'm glad."

"I know. I've pretty much come to the same conclusion."

"So, when did you leave?"

Amanda adjusted her pillow under her head and made herself comfortable on the bed. "About two hours ago."

"Where are you now?"

"Motel."

"Are you okay?"

"Yes."

"So what is your next move? Do you plan to stay in California and get an apartment?"

"I don't know." Amanda paused to consider her options. "I haven't really had the chance to process the whole thing yet."

"Are you open to a suggestion?"

"From you, always."

"Okay. Well, less than two weeks from now, I'm leaving for a two and a half to three month assignment in Italy. Why don't you come stay at my place till you figure out what you want to do? Honestly, you'd be doing me a favor." Knowing her diligent and hard working friend all too well, Dana added, "You can work anywhere as long as you have a computer with Internet access and a phone, can't you?"

Amanda smiled as she pictured her friend in her cozy little home. The lovely cape style cabin she owned sat nestled in a small town, bordering a large New York State park, a little over an hour from New York City. A mid-sized international pharmaceutical company employed Dana as a certified translator. She was often required to travel with her boss for her assignments. "Yes, I can work anywhere, but let me think about it. I'll call you in the morning and let you know. It's an extremely attractive offer and I appreciate it very much. The best part is that I'd get to spend a few days with you before you leave."

"Okay, let me know. I'll talk to you tomorrow. Call me if you need me. Good night, sweetie."

Amanda gave about five minutes of serious consideration to her friend's suggestion. There was really no down side to it. She checked flight information, booked her flight, and texted Dana her travel plans along with a thank you for the offer.

***

Amanda knew her partner's schedule as well as Bernie did. In two days, Bernie was set to fly out on her next trip. Amanda organized her plans then waited patiently for time to pass. Two days later, when she returned to the house, Bernie had already left for the airport. It took Amanda less than a day to pack up her office, files, a few personal items, and to have her remaining belongings, that she wanted or cared about, moved into a storage unit or shipped to Dana's place. The rest, mostly clothes, she decided could be collected once she determined where she would settle.

Amanda only took things she had brought to the relationship, leaving everything they'd bought or accumulated while they were together. She left a note on the kitchen counter for Bernie saying that after careful consideration, leaving was for the best and that she would be in touch in a week or two to let her know where she decided to settle. After a final look around, she left for the airport.

***

Dana was waiting for Amanda at the arrival gate in Newark. Dana's parents had died when she was a teenager and her grandparents raised her. Another painful loss struck when her grandfather died just after Dana turned twenty. She had inherited the cabin when her grandmother passed a few years later. Dana had lived there since graduating from college. She loved living so near the park in Harriman, NY. As they pulled up in front of the house, Amanda smiled.

"I'd forgotten how lovely this place is."

While she and Dana grabbed her bags from the trunk, Amanda noticed Dana's neighbor wave in greeting to Dana.

"Mallory, stop over after dinner. I want you to meet my friend," Dana called to the attractive woman with a megawatt smile.

Once inside her house, Dana helped Amanda get settled in the guest bedroom in the loft. Amanda asked, "Do I have time for a quick nap before dinner?"

"Sure. I'll call you when things are ready." From the doorway, Dana gave a quick wave before she closed the door and headed downstairs to prepare dinner.

Chapter 2

When dinner was just about ready, Dana called up the stairs awakening Amanda. Even though she felt more refreshed after her nap, Amanda knew she'd still be able to sleep soundly when she turned in for the night. The emotional strain of the past few days had left her mentally and physically exhausted.

Dinner was delicious and the two long time friends chatted easily throughout the meal. Just as they were finishing up, there was a knock at the door and Mallory let herself in.

"Oh great, I'm glad you're here! You're just in time for coffee and dessert." She wrapped her arm around Mallory's shoulder, leading her to where Amanda sat.

"Mallory, this is my oldest and dearest friend, Amanda. She'll be staying here at the house while I'm away."

Mallory flashed her dazzling smile in greeting. "That's great! I'm glad to have someone next door that I'll know."

Dana's friend is an attractive woman, but when she smiles, she's beautiful. Her hair was an unusual shade of ash blonde, lightened by the sun on top, with a darker layer underneath. Amanda forced herself to drag her eyes away from the woman's sexy mouth so she could meet her eyes.

"Amanda, this is Mallory Barnes. She's the Director of Nursing at the hospital. Her job there requires her to work some strange hours, but she always lets me know her schedule. That way I don't worry when I hear her come home at some odd hour. Also, when I'm traveling, it's useful to have someone I can text or call at odd hours of the day and night, just so someone knows I'm alive and well." Dana gave Mallory's shoulder an affectionate squeeze and offered her a quick wink, for which she received another brilliant smile.

"It's a pleasure to meet you, Mallory. I hope we'll be good friends."

Amanda liked Mallory's warm smile and welcoming demeanor. Mallory was maybe an inch or two taller than Amanda and they had a lean, muscular body type in common. Amanda guessed her age to be a few years older than her own age of thirty-eight. Her birthday would occur four months from now, leaving her only one year until she turned the dreaded forty! Mallory wore just a hint of eyeliner and a light application of mascara, which emphasized her beautiful sparkly greenish blue eyes and hair that was streaked with sun bleached ashy colored highlights.

"So, a Director of Nursing, huh? Do you still do direct care or is your job totally administrative at that level?" Amanda asked.

"For the most part it's administrative, but I'm still able to orient the new nurses, so I get to set standards for my staff. It's true though, that I still have my fair amount of pure paper pushing as well. There are advantages and disadvantages to any supervisory role, but most days, I enjoy my job. What do you do?"

"I'm a writer."

"Have I possibly read any of your work?"

Amanda laughed. "Possibly, I write copy for a direct mail company. So, if you read any of the direct mail fliers, chances are good I've written some of them." She thought for a moment. "I did ghost write a novel that was published last year that you may have heard of."

"Really. Which one?"

"Doctor Jonathan Grant's book on diet and exercise, *Get Fitter Faster*."

"No kidding. I've more than heard of it. Would you believe that I own it? You did a great job of making an extremely boring man sound interesting!" Mallory's engaging grin appeared again and she produced an endearing giggle.

"Oh, you're being too hard on him," Amanda said. "He's a genuinely nice man."

Mallory's smirk and raised eyebrow made Amanda laugh in return. "Okay, I'll agree to nice, if you'll give me boring. Plus, I'll admit that he really knows his subject. I attended a lecture he gave at my college a few years back."

Amanda liked Mallory's conciliatory efforts. She'd bet she was good at her job. Her warmth was conveyed through her quick smile and obvious willingness to compromise. "It's a deal!"

"You know Amanda, like you, Mallory, loves to bike ride. You're welcome to use my bike if you want to ride with her sometime," Dana offered.

Both Amanda and Mallory were enthusiastic at the prospect of having someone to ride with them. During the animated conversations over the remainder of the evening, Amanda and Mallory discovered that they had a lot in common. Besides biking, they both enjoyed reading, hiking, photography, and watching old movies. When the evening ended and Mallory hugged Dana before leaving, it seemed perfectly natural for Amanda and Mallory to hug each other good night as well.

"I really like her," Amanda confided after Mallory had closed the door. "Being able to have someone to do things with will make it much more enjoyable to be here while you're away. What's her story?"

"Story?"

"Yeah, you know. Who does she date, is she involved? The dirt."

"The dirt, huh?" Dana shook her head and rolled her eyes causing them both to laugh. "Honestly, I don't know who or even if she dates. I've never seen her go out with anybody and she's never mentioned anyone she's been serious about since she moved here about a year ago. She seems to work a lot and her hours are extremely irregular. I'd think it would be difficult for her to have a relationship with anyone who follows a regular work schedule. Maybe she just doesn't have time to date."

"Oh, I was just curious."

"Oh, duh!" Dana uttered, just getting it. "If you're asking me about her sexual preference, I honestly don't know. Are you interested?"

"No. Not really. Geez, give me a break here. It's been less than a week since my relationship ended. It's too soon. It's just that she's so darned cute and likable." Amanda refrained from mentioning that Mallory had one of the most kissable mouths she'd ever seen, classifying it as too much information.

"Think about it, Amanda. Your relationship with Bernie has been over since you found out she'd cheated on you the first time, a couple of years ago. You've been drawing back your feelings from her for a long time. Seriously, be honest. How much have you missed your relationship since you ended it?"

"Yes, I guess you're right. I think I've had a more of a sense of relief than anything else. Still, I don't know what I'm going to do, where I'm going to end up, or even where I'm headed." Feeling suddenly fatigued and not wanting to talk about Bernie any more, Amanda stood up and hugged her friend. "I'm bushed. I'm heading up to bed. Thanks again, Dana. You're a lifesaver. I'll see you in the morning."

***

Over the next several days, Dana and Amanda spent their time talking and relaxing together as only old friends can do. Dana had several things to do to prepare for her trip, so they focused on getting together what she needed. Too soon, the time came for Dana's departure. Amanda drove Dana to the airport.

"I'm glad you'll be here to run my car."

"Thanks for letting me use it. I love you, you know. You are the best friend I could ever ask for."

"I know that...and don't you forget it!" Dana grinned and winked at her friend before she pulled her close for a final hug.

"I'll be in touch when I get settled in. If you need me, text me and I'll call you back as soon as I can. Don't forget, I'm about six hours ahead of you in time." After a final good-bye, she gave a jaunty wave and disappeared into the terminal.

***

The day after Dana left for Italy, Amanda spent time reacquainting herself with the area and buying miscellaneous items that didn't get packed when she had hastily left home. She shopped for food for the rest of the week, stocking up on staples and buying some snacks in case Mallory dropped by. A brief stop at the video store yielded two of her favorite old movies to rent, *You've Got Mail* and *Overboard*.

As Amanda pulled into Dana's driveway, she glanced over towards Mallory's house. The car in the driveway indicated that her neighbor was home. Once inside Dana's house Amanda unpacked her purchases, tidied up the kitchen, and gave some thought to dinner. Suddenly feeling very lonely and a bit panicky with nothing to do, she decided that the safest and most productive thing would be to get back to work. Amanda had set up her computer the previous day and knew some extra hours of work would be required to assure she would get caught up, just not today. She couldn't do it today. Instead, she sat down at her computer and pulled up her novel.

The previous year she'd invested in dictation software that allowed her to speak into a microphone and control the computer with her voice. The training period was a bit daunting, but once she'd mastered the program she found it worked very well. Being able to dictate certainly helped alleviate the pain in her neck that radiated downward between her shoulder blades. When she had to sit at the keyboard to type her work, she suffered constantly. Now, instead of perching over her keyboard at a desk, she could just sit on the recliner with the computer on her lap and dictate.

She hadn't written anything for over a week, making it necessary to go back and reread the last few pages to orient herself to where she was in her story. She checked her notes and was just about to begin dictating when the phone rang.

"Hello?"

"It's Mallory, you know, from next door." The hesitancy in her voice conveyed her nervousness.

"Hey! I almost gave you a call when I got back from dropping off Dana, but I was afraid I'd wake you up."

"No, I worked midnight to eight a.m. this week. I slept a few hours when I got home. I have some time off and then I swap to the four p.m. to midnight shift. It'll take me a day or two to get acclimated. This is the last rotation change I'll have to do for a while. Working this shift, the midnight to eight a.m.," she clarified, "I have fewer interruptions. So, I use the late night, quieter hours to work on reports and budgeting, and to meet with the night supervisors. Once that's done, I'll go back to covering day and evening shifts. In a couple of weeks, I have new staff coming on board. I usually stay on schedule with the new folks as much as I can for the first few weeks, just to make sure they get all the training they need. Sometimes, I work part of one shift then part of another. These two I just hired, should be easy, since they're very experienced nurses. I was lucky to get them."

"Our jobs have one thing in common; we both have that unrelenting element. Even though I finish an article or project, there's always another to deal with right away. No breaks from that sense of deadline," said Amanda.

"That's an astute observation. Yes, I do feel that way and sometimes, I wish I could clone myself so that I could be in more than one place at a time. I know the paperwork is an unavoidable evil of the job, but I'd much rather be working with the staff and the patients. The supervisory position pays better, but lately, I've been feeling like there's more to life than just money." She shrugged, a natural gesture indicating some frustration, even though no one was there to see it. After a brief pause, she revealed, "My work schedule leaves very little time for socialization." She chuckled. "Wow! Where did that come from? I hope that wasn't too much information. You're very easy to talk to, you know...and a good listener."

"Thanks. I feel very comfortable with you also." She hoped that Mallory could feel her smiling through the phone.

"Maybe I'd better hang up now, before I disclose where I've hidden my family jewels."

Several quick comments ran through Amanda's head in response to that straight line, but she settled for the most benign. "Well, in keeping with that sentiment, could I interest you in dinner, another opportunity to discover your secrets, and maybe a video? I was thinking of having grilled hotdogs and a salad."

"That sounds delicious. Not healthy, but a great suggestion, regardless. Think there might be enough time before dinner for us to take a walk?"

"Sure, that sounds wonderful. It'll help me wake up. Shall I come collect you or do you want to come here?"

"I'll come to you. See you in a few minutes."

When Amanda realized that her heart was beating a bit faster than usual, she recognized that she was excited by the prospect of spending time alone with Mallory. A few moments later, when they left the house, Amanda gestured for Mallory to lead the way.

"I'm not sure where to go from here, but I'm sure you have a trail you like."

"How much time do we have?"

"Until about a half hour before you reach famished. We just have to grill up the hotdogs. I have potato salad, coleslaw, and some tomatoes to slice. Easy as can be."

"There's about a two mile walk I like a little ways up the road here. Will that be okay with you?"

"Perfect."

The first few minutes were quiet as they adjusted their strides to one that was comfortable for each of them. They were well matched in height, so it wasn't much of an issue. They fell into an easy, ground-consuming pace and before they knew it, they were deep into the shaded woods. They walked for about thirty-five minutes before pausing to rest on a fieldstone wall overlooking a small creek.

"What a beautiful spot," said Amanda. "Just gorgeous."

They sat in companionable silence for a while until Mallory nudged Amanda and gestured with her head upstream. A deer had emerged from the brush and had lowered her head to drink from the water.

"Wish I had my camera with me," Amanda whispered.

The deer looked up, noticed them, and melted back into the undergrowth.

"Isn't it amazing that a large animal like a deer can disappear into the brush like that with hardly a sound?"

"Absolutely," agreed Amanda.

"See that path there?" Mallory pointed. "That's a loop I usually add onto the shorter trail if I take this route with my bike."

"I can't wait to do that. If we walk or bike again tomorrow, I want to bring my camera." We should be getting back. I'm starting to get hungry. How about you?"

***

They retraced their path back to the house. "I'll start the grill while you make the salad," volunteered Mallory.

"Deal. You want onions?"

"Sure, why not. Throw whatever you have in there, I'll eat anything."

"That was great," Mallory said, as she pushed her plate back then wiped her mouth with her napkin. "I'm stuffed."

"In my one concession to good nutrition, I have fruit for dessert."

Mallory laughed. "You might need more than that to make amends for those hotdogs!"

Amanda asked, "Would you like to stay and watch a video with me? I picked up a couple of movies earlier. She retrieved them and slid them across the table.

"The Tom Hanks movie is one of my favorites, but I've never seen *Overboard*, so let's watch that one."

After they cleaned up the dishes and finished dessert, Amanda set up the DVD. The movie was light and funny. They enjoyed laughing together as they watched the show.

"Thank you so much for dinner and the movie. That was wonderful. Any movie that makes me laugh out loud gets five stars in my book," said Mallory.

When Amanda walked her guest to the door to bid her good night, Mallory said, "I mentioned to you that I finally have a couple of days off. Would you be interested in taking a bike ride tomorrow? We could go a bit farther since we'll have more time, see some new scenery, and maybe take a ride around the lake. I'll pack us a lunch and we can make a day of it."

Amanda didn't hesitate at all. She could write at night, or in the morning before they left for their ride. "That sounds great. Would it be okay to leave around ten? If I get up early, I can get some writing done before we take off. What do you think?"

"Sounds like a plan to me. Okay, it's a date then." Mallory gave Amanda a quick hug and left without looking back.

Hm, date. Did she mean 'date' as in a friendly get together or date as in 'date date?' Which did she want it to be? She wasn't even sure if Mallory was gay or straight. Since she'd recognized and accepted her own attraction to women, Amanda had made it a policy to only date other lesbians because she didn't want to bring a straight woman out. She'd seen too many of those relationships end in heartbreak when reality faced them. The pressures of coming out to parents, family, and friends too often sent them running back into the folds of heterosexuality, leaving a wake of pain behind. Amanda's own coming out had been painful enough. She told three of her closest friends about her 'secret' only to have two of them cut her from their lives. Only Dana had stood by her. Telling her family had brought additional heartbreak.

Earlier, while Amanda and Mallory were on their walk, they had talked casually, without divulging too much personal information.

"So, tell me a little about yourself," Amanda asked when they stopped for a rest.

"I finished my degree by attending college in New York City, after which I returned home to Philly. I moved back to New York State a couple of years ago to take the supervisory role at the hospital. I fell in love with this area while I was in school. I liked the rural nature of this area. I wanted to advance in my profession, which was something this supervisory role at the hospital offered me. It didn't take long for me to discover that the grass is not always greener on the other side of the fence."

"What do you mean?"

Mallory shrugged. "Don't get me wrong, although there are numerous aspects of the job that I like, there are just as many that I don't. Once I began working in the supervisory role, I discovered that I missed providing direct care to the patients, and I hate the report writing and the politics of the budgetary process. In the plus column, I do enjoy helping to decide hospital policy and training the new employees. So," she concluded, "there are tradeoffs in everything and since I don't hate the job, I've made myself contented."

"Does the shift work bother you?"

"Not any more. I've adjusted to it I think. It makes socializing difficult sometimes. It's sometimes hard for me to find people to do things with. It's nice that you are able to join me today."

"I'm enjoying our time together too. Ready to push on?"

"Yes, it's starting to get late."

✻✻✻

Amanda locked up the house before she went upstairs. There was ample time to get in a couple of good hours of work before she went to bed. She logged into her email to see if the new assignment from her boss had arrived. There was e-mail from Bernie, which she ignored. She didn't really want to ruin the good mood she was in after her evening with Mallory, by reading what she expected would be a poison pen note from

Bernie. She had closed that door and was happy leaving things as they were.

Before snapping the lid closed on her laptop, Amanda noticed that it was just after one o'clock. She was pleased with her accomplishment of finishing another chapter in her book plus a short article that she'd been putting off writing since she'd gotten there. It was a relief to finish it and e-mail her submission. After setting the alarm to wake her up an hour before Mallory was due to show up the next morning, she slid into bed between the soft sheets and fell asleep almost immediately.

***

Refreshed after a solid night's sleep, Amanda lingered in the shower then ate a breakfast of cereal and fruit. She was just finishing a cup of tea when Mallory knocked at the door.

"Good morning!" Mallory's greeting was as cheerful as she looked. Dressed in a bright red jersey and black body conforming biking shorts, she entered the kitchen and took a seat next to Amanda at the breakfast bar, but not before Amanda got to check out Mallory's tight body in the outfit that fit her like a second skin.

"Want some breakfast or some tea? The water is still hot," Amanda pointed to the kettle on the stove.

"No, thanks, I ate already, but I'm out of juice. Do you have any?"

"There's some OJ in the fridge. Help yourself."

Amanda allowed herself to appreciate the view as Mallory leaned over to get the juice from the fridge. There was no doubt about it; she found Mallory's sporty good looks very attractive. Her eyes, an interesting blue-green mixture, appeared greener in the morning sunlight streaming in the kitchen window. Her lashes were darker than her paler hair color, almost black in fact, giving the appearance that she was wearing mascara although she was not. Mallory was cute, for sure, but when she smiled, her smile lit her face transforming cute into lovely. She had a very kissable mouth, Amanda thought, especially the way her lips turn up at the corners giving the impression that she was always ready to smile.

After finishing their beverages, Amanda rolled Dana's mountain bike out of the garage and they set off following the path they had taken the previous day. They took a trail that headed north at the first intersection and rode for about an hour before they stopped to take a break. Mallory produced some nuts and raisins from her seat bag. She shared them with Amanda who, in her pack, was carrying bottles of water, one of which she shared with Mallory.

"This is a great ride. Not too steep, but it still presents enough of a challenge for someone like me who's out of practice. You're definitely a much better rider than I am."

"You have to be patient with yourself. When was the last time you rode?

"At least a year or more ago. I got focused on working and really didn't pay attention to my health as much as I should have. I'm glad you're here to encourage me to not just sit around and veg out."

Mallory let her eyes travel the length of Amanda's body, boldly assessing and not appearing the least bit self-conscious. "You look to be in good shape. You must have done something, because you're still fit."

"I used to jog or walk, but not often enough. We had a gym in the basement of the house, so I could go there and work out occasionally."

What was that look that flashed across Mallory's face? What had she said? She didn't realize the use of the word 'we' had been a disappointment to Mallory.

"Maybe we should get on with it. Think you can manage another twenty-five minutes or so? There's a wonderful place to stop up the trail a bit further. We can eat lunch and have a rest before we head back."

They rode to the spot Mallory had described and stopped for lunch. Amanda was tired. She hoped she'd be able to make it back and that she wouldn't embarrass herself by having to ask Mallory stop too frequently.

"So, do you ride often, then?" Amanda wondered.

"As often as I can. When I work the day shift, I try to ride to work if my schedule allows and the weather permits it. Other than that, I do try to ride at least five miles two or three times a week. Time is always an issue though, isn't it? Do you find that you generally seem to find time for everyone but yourself?"

Amanda nodded her agreement.

"My mom always told me, 'Pay yourself first.' Of course, she was talking about saving money. She tutored me to think of myself as a bill that I owed and to be sure that I paid myself every pay period just like the telephone, electric and gas bills. I maintain that habit to this day. In the past, I've always been reasonably well disciplined financially, but not always personally, especially as it relates to exercise. When I moved up here, I decided to generalize my mom's rule to include health. So, now I follow my mom's advice, pay myself first by taking time to exercise. Now I'm doing better about putting my health and fitness at the top of my daily list of things to do."

"Sounds like a good policy. Maybe I'll try to emulate your good example! I mean, I always enjoy myself when I'm getting exercise, but left to my own devices, I often just can't muster up the initiative," Amanda said before she finished up her sandwich and took a long swig from her water bottle.

"Well, then, I'm glad you're here. We can motivate each other. Besides its more fun doing it with someone, isn't it?"

"So you're close to your mom?" Amanda asked.

"Yes. I'm especially close to my mother. My dad and I don't always see eye to eye about all things, but we still get along. I think they gave me a good start in life and I love them both. I wish we lived closer sometimes, but I haven't helped that by moving too far away for them to pop over. I was thinking of inviting them up for either Thanksgiving or Christmas, but I haven't decided yet. My family usually tries to get together for at least one of the holidays, but it's getting to be a bit labor intensive for them the older they get."

They sat quietly together enjoying the scenery. Mallory nodded toward the clearing. "Look, a chipmunk."

Amanda followed the progress of the cute little creature as it scurried furtively from the sanctuary of one form of vegetation or shrub to another, darting quickly from beneath a leaf of some plant to another place of safety. Suddenly he slipped into a hole that would have been otherwise virtually invisible had they not been watching so intently.

"Wonder if he has a family in his little burrow?"

"Don't know," Mallory replied. "Maybe we'll see if we watch a little longer. What about you, Amanda? Tell me about your family? You have sisters, brothers?"

"My parents are both deceased. They were smokers and ended up going long before they should have. Dad had lung cancer and mom had breast cancer. I have one brother."

"You must be close, since it's just the two of you now."

Amanda shrugged. "We used to be." She paused. Amanda assumed that Dana would have told Mallory that she was a lesbian. So, after an initial hesitation she revealed, "Um...when I came out, not only did I lose some of my friends, but my parents also disowned me and my older brother stopped speaking to me. The worst part is that he refused to allow me to visit with my nieces and nephew, a punishment that I still can't forgive him for to this day. Despite his refusal to allow me to see the kids, I continued to send the kids cards and gifts on their birthdays and other holidays, but never received any indication from my brother or the kids that they arrived at their proper destination. On the QT, my sister-in-law sends me a picture of the kids each year along with a note and an update on the highlights of their lives. When she sent the first photo, she had begged me not to let him know."

"Thank God for your sister-in-law. At least she has sense in addition to being kind. But never hearing from your brother must be a heartbreaking dismissal, especially since you said you were close before you revealed your sexual orientation.

"Yes. Initially it was devastating. Now, it's just painful." Amanda looked away.

The play of emotions across Amanda's face hinted that, obviously, there was more to the story, but Amanda wasn't ready to share the depth of hurt her brother's dismissal had inflicted. After such a wonderful day, she didn't want to bring down her spirits by digging up how deeply his rejection hurt her. Amanda was grateful that Mallory was willing to allow her to reveal things at her own pace and to not push by asking questions. The silence between them was comfortable.

Referring to the chipmunk, Mallory said, "Well, I suppose the little guy is tucked in for now. You feel rested enough to start back?"

"Ready when you are, I guess." She wanted to ask Mallory more about her family, but Mallory was already packing up the remnants of their lunch and seemed eager to get under way. There's plenty of time, I guess, maybe tonight when we have dinner.

Before she swung her leg over the seat of her bike Mallory said, "You'll probably be glad to hear that the path home is much less strenuous and the ride goes much more quickly than the ride up...I know I sure am!"

Standing together next to their bikes, they took a few minutes to appreciate and comment on the beauty around them. It wouldn't be too many weeks before the leaves began to change. The fall colors of the forest, would only add to the beauty of the mountains in the background. But today, the comfortable, sunny weather contributed to a wonderful day that the new friends were sharing.

The path that Mallory selected for the ride home was exactly as promised, easier than the earlier ride out, because it varied between being flat or, in places, slightly downhill. Mallory instructed Amanda about the most difficult part.

"There's only one steep part that can be difficult. When I signal you to be careful, either get off and walk your bike or take it very carefully. That one curve up ahead can be tricky," cautioned Mallory.

They had ridden a short distance down the trail when Mallory signaled with a downward motion of her hand and they dismounted to survey the difficult part of trail ahead. With Mallory's guidance, they both navigated the trickiest bit of trail. Things were easier after that for both riders. They stopped to rest twice before taking on the final leg of their ride that brought them back home.

"I don't know about you, but I need a shower," Amanda said as she toed the kickstand into place.

"I know what you mean." Mallory stretched out her legs before she turned toward Amanda. "That was a great workout, though. I think I might add a soak in my hot tub to my agenda as well. Want to join me? I bet it would make you less sore tomorrow."

"I definitely can't decline that offer. Let me wash up, get my suit, and I'll meet you at your place as quickly as I can."

Mallory gave a wave as she pedaled towards her garage.

Chapter 3

Amanda washed off, before going in search of her suit. Unable to find it quickly and knowing that Mallory was waiting for her, she gave up searching and settled for a pair of lightweight jogging shorts and an old sleeveless tee shirt that she threw on.

"Well, at least they're clean. Can't wear what I don't have with me. Hopefully, she'll understand," she mumbled.

After she gathered a towel and a comb, Amanda cut across the back yard to Mallory's house. The hot tub was recessed into the deck and Mallory was already in it, submerged to her chin in the furiously bubbling water. The air had already grown cooler since they returned from their ride and the steam was rising from the water.

"I'm sorry I took so long. I couldn't find my suit. Hope what I have on will be okay."

"You don't need anything but your skin! Get out of those clothes and climb in. You'll feel one hundred per cent better."

"You sure?"

"Yes, come on. We're not getting any younger!" Mallory softened the words with a giggle.

Since high school, Amanda couldn't remember a time when she didn't feel shy about being naked in front of anyone who was not her lover. The little voice inside the left side of her head said, *Grow up, she's a nurse, for God's sake. It's not anything she hasn't seen before*" To which the voice on the other side of her head replied, *Yeah, but she hasn't seen mine before!* Amanda looked around for a sheltered spot where she could remove her clothes, and found none, but she saw no neighbors who would have a view of the deck area.

A devilish grin accompanied Mallory's giggle and amused, twinkling eyes. "Come on, nobody can see you but me."

Amanda slipped out of the shorts and took off her T-shirt, leaving the final bastion of modesty for last. Finally, in one quick motion, she bent and stripped off her underwear. As she stepped down into the hot tub, Mallory appreciatively swept her eyes over Amanda's body from head to toe. It was obvious that she didn't miss anything in her quick perusal when she asked Amanda, "So what's the significance of the tattoo?"

Amanda had a bar code tattoo just below her navel done in rainbow colors. Ignoring the rainbow coloration, she replied, "Just my date of birth. The tattoo seemed like a good idea at the time. I've never had any doubts about my sexuality and have always described myself as 'gay from the day I was born.' So in my drunken state one night, I thought the tattoo expressed that sentiment perfectly. It wasn't anything I've ever regretted doing exactly, but I might have considered having it located in a less public place."

Amanda hadn't noticed any change in Mallory's attitude when she mentioned coming out before, but she still waited to see if Mallory's attitude toward her would change.

"What a neat idea. I like it a lot and there's nothing wrong with the location you chose. I don't have any tattoos, too cowardly!"

"Ha! You can dish those needles out, but can't take it, eh?"

"Busted!"

Amanda felt herself respond to Mallory's endearing giggle and warm smile. Once Amanda settled into the water, the two women enjoyed the relaxing heat of the water in shared silence. They soaked in the hot tub together for about ten minutes until the timer chimed.

"I'm cooked. I think I need to get out, but you can probably do another ten minutes or so. I was in for a while before you arrived. How about I go start some dinner? You'll join me, won't you?"

When Amanda nodded her agreement, Mallory reset the timer for another ten minutes, then stood up and walked to the steps providing Amanda an opportunity to appreciate the woman's well-toned body. She felt herself warm in response and was amazed that she could be so attracted to someone so soon after she had ended her relationship with Bernie. After Mallory's departure, as she soaked alone in the tub, she realized that Dana was right about the fact that she'd emotionally left her relationship with Bernie long ago when she found that Bernie had been unfaithful the first time, or at least the first time she had caught her. She suspected there might have been many others she didn't know about.

When the timer turned off the jets in the hot tub, Amanda stepped out, and dried off. She still felt awkward standing outside completely nude, even though she was alone and knew no one was able to see her. From the corner, where the hot tub was tucked in, to the sliding door was nearly the whole length of the house. She didn't feature making the dash naked, so she got out of the tub, hid in the shadows as best she could, quickly threw on her clothes then padded across the length of the deck. Her soft tap at the window drew an invitation to come in from Mallory. Amanda entered the living room of the cozy cottage and appreciatively absorbed the welcoming room. Decorations were in warm earthy colors with splashes of red as the accent color. Two rich reddish brown leather recliners, which faced each other, were placed strategically on either side of the fireplace. A leather sofa in the same shade appeared soft and inviting. It sat opposite the fire, providing a straight on view of the flames through the glass doors that covered the hearth.

"I'm in here, around the corner," Mallory called.

Amanda, moving in the general direction of Mallory's voice, made her way into the modern kitchen. The cherry cabinets and granite countertops with swirls of deep burgundy accents complimented each other and made for a pleasing combination. "Do you want to eat in here at the counter or in the dining room?" Mallory held two plates, napkins, and silverware in her hands.

"Let's eat in here. We don't have to be fancy. What's for dinner?"

Mallory smiled. "Hungry?"

"You bet. It's probably a good idea that we're not going to the dining room. I might gnaw at the table leg and ruin the good table!"

Mallory giggled at the unexpected comment. "Well, then that's good. I defrosted some sauce I made a couple of weeks ago. So, we're having pasta, my special recipe meatballs, and a huge salad. Oh yeah, and some garlic bread." Gesturing toward the sink then at the wine rack, she asked, "Water or wine?

"Wine. Want me to open it?"

Mallory handed the dishes and silverware to Amanda. "How about you set the table and I'll finish up everything else in here." When the meal was ready, the two women sat down to their dinner. Mallory held up her glass and offered a toast. "To a wonderful new friendship."

"Absolutely," replied Amanda. "Cheers!"

"I've really enjoyed the time we've spent together the last two days. I love having company for dinner and having someone to enjoy hiking and biking with has been a gift. There have been many times that I've been lonely since I moved here," Mallory admitted with characteristic candor.

"I can understand that. It must be difficult meeting people when you work such irregular hours. How do you even begin to establish friendships, let alone find anyone to date?"

Mallory shrugged. "Yes, it's tough. Even tougher now that I'm in a supervisory role, which eliminates most of the people I know at the hospital from the friendship pool. It would be too awkward to be friends outside of work with people I supervise and impossible to date anyone from there. I just wouldn't be comfortable. A few months ago, I met a police officer named Jo, who is someone I like a lot. She was on duty at the hospital guarding a prisoner. Because we both work shift work, we've only managed to get together sporadically. I played cards with her and a couple of her friends a few times.

So, honestly, the closest friend I have here is Dana and unfortunately, between her schedule and mine, we don't see each other all that often."

"So how do you go about meeting people, then?"

Mallory paused before she responded, giving thought to her answer. "It seems that I just wait patiently for my neighbor to invite a lovely woman friend of hers to stay at her house—someone with whom I enjoy spending time with immensely. Problem solved!" Mallory winked at Amanda and flashed a wide grin, displaying perfect teeth. "We really have to thank Dana when we talk to her. She's done well by both of us!"

The two women cleaned up the remnants of dinner, storing the leftovers, before they carried their wine into the living room. "Think we need a fire?" Mallory asked.

"Not unless you want one. I'm going to have to be going soon, anyway. I have to check my e-mail to make sure everything was okay with the article I just submitted and I wanted to write a quick e-mail to Dana."

"If you'd like, you can log into your e-mail account from here. You could check your mail and we could write a note to Dana together."

"Great idea! That would be fun, wouldn't it?"

The e-mail to Dana was great fodder for laughter for both women. They commented on Dana's great choice in friends and wrote a breezy, lighthearted account of their day together. Without discussion, neither seemed to feel that it was necessary to describe their soak in the hot tub to their friend, but they mentioned the delicious dinners and how much they both enjoyed eating together the past two days.

Amanda reread the letter aloud one final time to allow for edits and corrections. "Okay?"

"It sounds good to me. Hit the send button!" Mallory stood and stretched. "I think, after our workout today, that we both may be a bit too sore tomorrow for another ride. If that turns out to be true, I wouldn't mind going into town for a leisurely lunch and a movie. I'd love to have some company. Are you up for it?"

"Sure, that sounds great, but I have to do a few hours of work sometime tomorrow. Can we do a later lunch, like around 12:30? Maybe we should check what time the movies start, decide what we want to see first, and then let the movie time dictate when we eat."

Mallory nodded her agreement. "Works for me. I'm going to use the facilities. Do you mind looking up the movies for us?"

"Sure. Not a problem."

"I'll be right back."

Amanda reached for the laptop and turned the screen to face her. The screensaver was rotating through several pictures. Each picture showed Mallory with a very attractive blonde woman. They were touching in each picture, either clowning for the camera or standing with their arms linked or one behind the other with their hands on the other's shoulders. The next photo was a picture of the two women close, face-to-face, looking into each other's eyes. Mallory was kissing the other woman on the nose. The lovely, fun photo revealed a deep intimacy between the pair. The meaning left little, if any, doubt in Amanda's mind that Mallory and this woman had a romantic relationship with each other.

When she heard the toilet flush she quickly looked up the local movie theater. By the time Mallory returned, she had the current show times up on the screen. She didn't know if she should address the information that she had just learned about Mallory or wait for Malory to tell her about the relationship on her own. She decided not to mention anything right away, but before she allowed herself to become too attached to Mallory, she needed to know something about the status of her relationship with the attractive blonde. Perhaps they still had a long distance relationship.

"So, did you pick out a movie?" Mallory asked as she returned to the living room.

"No," Amanda smiled. "Thought I'd wait for you so we can pick it together."

They selected a movie that began at two-fifteen, and agreed to hold lunch till one o'clock.

"Do you have a favorite place for lunch?" Amanda asked.

"Yes, I do, and I think you'll like it too." Mallory quickly pulled up the restaurant's website and clicked on their lunch menu.

"Umm, I'm sure I can find about ten things I'd love to eat on this menu." Amanda exclaimed. "Okay, I'd better get back home so I can get up and do what I have to do tomorrow before we meet. Thank you, Mallory, for a very enjoyable day and an amazing dinner. Shall I pick you up tomorrow at, what...twelve-thirty or so?"

"That would be wonderful. I'll see you tomorrow then." Mallory walked Amanda to the door. "I had a great time today and am really looking forward to another day with you tomorrow." She gave Amanda's hand a quick squeeze before Amanda slipped out the door and headed home.

Before she stepped off the deck, Amanda glanced back to find Mallory watching her departure, a sad expression on her face. Amanda gave a quick wave, which was rewarded by a sweet smile from Mallory.

Awaiting My Assignment Friends Book 2 is out now in ebook. Available at Amazon and Smashwords.

Look for AJ Adaire's third book in the Friends Series, Anything Your Heart Desires, coming in 2014 from Desert Palm Press.

Other books from Desert Palm Press

The Guardian Series by Stein Willard
A Guardian's Touch – Book 1
A Guardian's Love – Book 2
A Guardian's Passion – Book 3

Scarred for Life by SL Kassidy

Awaiting My Assignment – Friends Book 2 by AJ Adaire

Books available from Smashwords and Amazon

Coming soon

Anything Your Heart Desires – Friends Book 3 by AJ Adaire
A Guardian's Salvation – Book 4 by Stein Willard
The Unbroken Warrior by Stein Willard

Desert Palm Press

www.desertpalmpress.com